My NOT-SO-SECRET Santa

THE HOT UNDER THE MISTLETOE SERIES

AUTHOR OF TEMPTING TASTE

SARA WHITNEY

I've got a secret.

The new girl at work? The one I've got a crush on?

She's got a crush too—on the stripper who's dressing like Santa every weekend in December.

And that's my secret. I'm him. The Saturday night Santa stripper.

Liv has no idea it's her new work buddy under the fake white beard and tiny red hot pants, and every time she blushes when she talks about him, I burn with jealousy over myself.

But Liv's also starting to get close to me—the real me—and seems interested in Christmas Eve activities that'll put us both on the so-naughty-it's-nice list. I just hope she'll still want to sit on Santa's lap after I tell her the truth.

Keep in touch!

Scan to
follow
Sara

Newsletter,
free books,
social media,
and more!

To the flirty waiter with the knowing smirk who started it all. And to Dana, Holly, and Missy, who had joined me for tacos and tequila and agreed he'd make a great hero.

ONE

Jonesy

I clock her the instant she walks through the door.

Headed to the four-top in my section. Tall boots, sleek ponytail, tight ass.

Once she and her friend are seated, she sweeps her coolly assessing gaze around the dining room in a slow pass, skimming over the tables packed with execs cramming in a fifty-minute lunch and the riot of offbeat murals decorating the walls.

She's picked a seat directly under one of the upcycled light fixtures, and it acts like a spotlight for her reddish-brown ponytail, bright-green sweater, and lush pink lips. Forget the murals. She's the only artwork this restaurant needs.

"Is that for us?"

The annoyed voice of the banker-lawyer-accountant from table six makes me realize I've been staring at the woman who's glowing like an angel in my section instead of dropping off the extra butter the trio of suits had requested.

I swing into action, handing the dish off to one of the titans of industry with an apology and an *aw-shucks* smile—dudes like that always love a waiter scrambling to beg their pardon—before moving to her table.

"I'm still *furious*," her cardigan-wearing friend announces as I approach.

My ponytail angel unwinds a scarf from around her neck, her mouth as tight as the folds she's making in the red material. "Don't be. It's fine." She tucks the folded scarf into her purse, her ponytail sliding over her shoulder as she does.

"It's not fine! It's inexcusable," Cardigan says. "I vote murder. We can dissolve him in quicklime. They'll never find the body."

Ponytail just shakes her head, and I take the opportunity to clear my throat.

"Hi, ladies. Welcome to Verdant. I'm Jonesy, and I'll be the third party to your criminal conspiracy today."

Ponytail's flat expression doesn't change, but her cardigan-wearing friend bleats out a laugh.

"Trust me. We'd be doing the world a favor." Cardigan's interested eyes take in my face and travel down to my arms, and I oblige her by flexing just a little under my white button-down. Hey, I work hard for the tips those arms bring me.

"Can I start you with some drinks?" I lean a little closer to ask. "Something to help you plot?"

Cardigan glances at me through her lashes as she points to the menu in front of her.

"A Gingerbread White Russian, please." She's in leggings and running shoes, and she's clearly not worried about Kahlúa over lunch on a Wednesday in the middle of November.

"Excellent choice," I tell her, then turn to Ponytail,

who's finally noticed the mural on the wall to her left, the one the waitstaff privately refer to as *The Lion Fucks Tonight*. I wouldn't have chosen to decorate a brunch/lunch restaurant with a pair of lions who look like they're doing something a little more intimate than fighting, but it's a great way to tell which customers are going to be cool and which are going to be uptight pains in my ass.

Let's find out which one Ponytail is.

"And for you?" I ask her. "Naughty or nice?"

That pulls her attention away from the questionable art, and she blinks as if she's truly noticing me for the first time. "Sorry, what?"

"Your drink order." I clasp my hands behind my back and curve my lips into my most winning smile, the one that reliably turns ones into tens. "Are you feeling naughty or nice?"

She flushes and drops her gaze to the menu, where the seasonal drinks are divided into two lists, alcoholic Naughty and non-alcoholic Nice.

"Oh, um, a c-cranberry bourbon sour?"

Well, well. I do believe I just made this uptight lady stammer. I like that feeling so much that I wink at her as I say, "Naughty it is." As I hoped, she pinks up again and tucks a nonexistent strand of hair behind her ear.

I'm burning with impatience as I wait at the bar for their drinks. Sure, I'm curious about whose murder the two of them are planning, but I'm more interested in what else might make Ponytail blush. My rule is to never hit on people while I'm on the clock here, but that doesn't mean I can't enjoy teasing my tightly wound guest just a little.

On my return to the table, I learn a lot more.

"—the fucking nerve!" Cardigan's practically hollering

as I set the White Russian in front of her. "I cannot believe the audacity of that man."

Ponytail lifts her shoulders and lets them drop. "For all the good it did him." Her fingers brush mine as she accepts the bourbon, her skin warm next to the cool glass.

"I can't believe you're so calm about this." Cardigan turns to me. "What would *you* do if you packed up your whole life and moved to Canada for a great job, then three weeks later your boss framed you for embezzlement and got you deported?"

All I can do is blink. "For real?" Not even in my wildest speculations would I have pictured Ponytail as an international fugitive.

"For real," Ponytail says. Although her voice is level, anger burns in her eyes. It's the first real emotion I've seen from her, and it's spectacular. "To be clear," she adds, "I didn't do it."

"But Canada kicked her out anyway!" her friend says.

"That is totally fuc—" I rock back on my heels, struggling to bite back a word that isn't on the approved list for the waitstaff. "Uh, messed up. Totally messed up."

"On the bright side, I'm now extremely familiar with the Canadian legal system," Ponytail says, tapping her nails against the side of the glass in a *tic, tic, tic* of agitation. "The investigators figured out pretty quickly that it was my boss and not me, but not before he made sure I got perp-walked out of the building in front of the whole office."

Her jaw tenses in a way that makes me want to find that Tim Hortons-loving motherfucker and moose-stomp him.

My expression must show my bloody thoughts because Cardigan gestures to me. "See? Jonesy gets it. *Murder.*"

"Got a truck out back you can borrow if you need to move a body," I offer cheerfully, jerking my thumb over my shoulder to the staff parking lot. "She'll get you over the border and back."

Ponytail shakes her head as she lifts the glass. "That might be tough since my former boss is locked up pending trial." She lets her brown eyes drift shut as the bourbon hits her lips and she savors and swallows. "It's tempting though," she murmurs with her eyes still closed.

I steal the opportunity to study her. Christ, she's elegant. Great body, strict posture. Not a strand of hair out of place and not a speck on her expensive-looking sweater. In my experience, getting a woman like her into bed could go one of two ways, full starfish or full porn star. My body tightens with the sudden need to find out which one she'd be.

The scrape of silverware against plates at a nearby table pulls me away from my racing thoughts, and I give myself a mental shake. It's been forever since anybody got under my skin this quickly at either of my jobs, and naturally, she's at the one where I'd never act on it. Ain't that a fucking shame?

I clear my throat, purge any thoughts that aren't about providing good service, and ask, "Are you two ready to order?"

"Yes, but only if you forget this conversation." Ponytail's back to the cool control from earlier, and she turns it on her friend next. "That means you too. This is the last time I talk about it with anybody. I'm putting it behind me."

Cardigan raises her hands in mock surrender, and I take the hint and go about my business as if they were any other table. I keep their glasses full, deliver their tacos, and check in on them with my usual just-this-side-of-flirty banter that guarantees a thirty percent tip at the end of the meal. As much as I'd like to see what she's like outside of these four walls, the holiday hopes and dreams of five little kids depend on me socking away as much cash as I can, as fast as I can, and I'm not willing to risk that for a shot with this gingerbread-haired angel.

I'm congratulating myself on only wondering three or four times about the color of Ponytail's nipples—brown, right? I bet they're lightish brown like her hair—as I swing by with their bill. The two are speaking more quietly now, their conversation barely audible over the Christmas music that's been pumping through the dining room since the beginning of the month.

"Did you want to hit that boutique tomorrow?" Cardigan asks.

"Sure," Ponytail replies as I pick up one of their empty dishes.

"Just a heads-up," Cardigan says as she reaches for her purse, "it's in a tiny town an hour from here that doesn't have zoning per se, so it's next to a strip club."

The unexpected reference to the Crimson Lounge surprises me so much that I drop the plate back onto the table with a thunk. Thankfully, they're both too busy reaching for their bill folders to notice.

"I wonder if they ever do a ladies' night." Cardigan slips her credit card into the folder and holds it out for me to take.

"Would you believe I didn't study up on central Illinois' male stripper population before I fled the Great White North?" Ponytail says dryly.

I can't help it. The tiniest smirk crosses my face. It's there and gone, but she notices. I can see it in the slight narrowing of her eyes, the flash of curiosity prompted by my amusement.

Our gazes lock, and the crowded dining room falls away

as her lips part. She's about to form a question, and everything in me whispers, *Yes, ask. Let me tell you what you want to know.* The things I'd fill her ears with would put a blush on way more than her cheeks.

But after a beat, she blinks and breaks the spell, the spark in her eyes cooling to politeness yet again. She holds her folder out for me to take, then turns to continue the conversation with her friend, putting me out of her mind.

And that's for the best. I keep my familiarity with the schedule at the Crimson Lounge as far from this family-friendly place as possible. I've learned my lesson about mixing my night job and my day job. Hell, I'm constantly exhausted just from *doing* my night job and my day job. I already know something has to give, and adding sex to the mix would only make it worse.

Still, I'm disappointed that Ponytail paid with cash. Unlike Cardigan—Charlotte West, according to her Visa—the gorgeous non-embezzler is destined to remain nameless.

Too bad. Before she stuffed it back down, I saw that anger simmering hot and wild under her skin, and I felt her sharp interest in the secrets I was keeping. I bet I could pull those big, messy emotions to the surface and set them loose. I bet she'd like it. I know *I* would.

Well, the *other* me could. And both he and I think that's a great idea.

The thought of it fires my reckless side, and I scrawl a note on my order pad that I tuck into the folder with her receipt. Fuck it. What have I got to lose, right? Other than my dignity and my job, that is.

When I breeze back to her table, Ponytail's looking at those lions again. This time, though, her expression's different. Harder. Her lip curls with disgust, and it vibrates through the taut lines of her neck, the stiff set of her shoulders.

I pull up short at the judgment pouring off of her. It upends what I thought I'd seen beneath that calm facade. I've read people wrong in the past, and even with as few shits as I give about what people think about someone who takes their clothes off for money, it still fucking stings to watch them jump from surprise to disapproval to good old-fashioned slut-shaming in front of my eyes.

Their loss, of course. But I don't need to set myself up for that today just because a strange woman looked good under the restaurant lights.

Cursing my own stupidly soft underbelly, I flip open her bill folder, grab my note, and stuff it into my pocket. I might be curious about whether I could undo the woman who jokes about strip clubs after getting booted from our very polite neighbor to the north, but I'm not interested in exploring that with someone who gets all pinch-mouthed about two hot-pink lions rocking combat-boners in front of a sickly green sky.

I set their bill folders on the table and remind myself that it's ridiculous to be disappointed by a woman I don't even know. Still, I hover nearby as Ponytail takes her time sliding into her coat and winding the scarf back around her neck.

"Thanks again." Her eyes flick to my chest, and my blood heats at the thought that she's ogling me just as blatantly as her friend did earlier. That she saw something in me too, and that it might be worth breaking my rules after all.

I'm sliding my hand into my pocket to pull out that damn note again when she straightens and offers me a bland smile. "Have a nice rest of your day, Jonesy." Then she turns and walks out, leaving me staring down at the name tag on my shirt.

Of course that's what she was looking at. She didn't even remember my name.

I yank the note out of my pocket, disgusted with myself, and toss it into the watery remains of her drink. The thin paper immediately dissolves into pulp.

Her loss.

Except for some reason, this one feels like my loss too.

TWO

Liv

"Absolutely not."

My voice is soft but firm, resolute in its opposition. And as she's done since we met on day one of college orientation, CJ completely ignores it.

"Absolutely yes." She waves a handful of lingerie like she's taunting me with silk and lace and buckles and bows. "At least try something on."

"We're here so *you* can buy new bras," I say, but even as I object, I let her herd me toward the dressing room.

"We're also here to make sure you're recovering from your trauma."

"It wasn't that traumatic," I mutter as she shoves me through the door.

"Strip," she orders. "And if it wasn't that traumatic, why are you hiding here with me instead of staying with your folks and obsessively job hunting or, I don't know, starting your own firm like you should've done years ago?"

I pop my head around the door. "I'm not hiding." I choose to ignore the rest.

"Okay, vacationing. Just casually taking a six-week vacay with your best friend," she says. "*Strip*."

I know better than to argue with Charlotte Jane West when she gets like this, so I slowly unbutton my shirt. We made good on our plans over lunch yesterday and headed to the tiny town of North Village, which appears to be made up of four streets, a dozen houses, two churches, an antique store, and a lingerie shop situated next to a strip club, as promised. The town's almost exactly between Beaucoeur and Chicago, and according to CJ, people flock here from both directions because the owner of Fantasia is famous for her ability to match boobs to bras.

I have no reason to doubt her. It's the Friday before Thanksgiving, not even peak holiday shopping yet, and the place is packed with people crowding the colorful displays and popping in and out of dressing rooms while the employees scurry around providing measurements and restocking.

I don't know how CJ manages to wrangle the owner herself for my fitting, but it's the snowy-haired Jessica who knocks on the door of my dressing room moments later to ask if I'm ready.

"Let's do it," I say, bowing to the inevitable. I undo the last of my buttons as she slips inside and briskly transfers the measuring tape from around her neck to underneath my rib cage.

"Mmm." She studies the tape, then wraps it around the fullest part of my breasts. She frowns when she peeks at the tag on the perfectly serviceable beige underwire I'd worn into the shop. "Two inches smaller and one cup size bigger," she says, writing the correct size on a slip of paper. She hands it to one of her employees who zips off to consult with CJ on what I'm about to try on.

While we wait, Jessica gestures for me to unhook my bra. I do, although I clutch it to my chest rather than let it slide down my arms in an attempt to maintain my dignity. There may be no mysteries between you and your fitter, but I don't need to be tits out while we wait.

"New to the area?" asks Jessica, who's presumably used to having conversations with naked-from-the-waist-up clients.

"Um. Yes." I glance at the goosebumps covering my forearms. What was I thinking moving to Canada when I can barely handle a global-warming winter fifteen hundred miles south of that? Maybe it's for the best that I fled the country in shame and outrage. "I'm staying in Beaucoeur while I look for a new job."

"Well, welcome. I hope you love it here." Jessica's cheeks plump as she smiles, creating gentle creases in her round face. I've obviously got Christmas on the brain because all it would take is a frilly red hat to turn her into the perfect Mrs. Claus, especially with the tiny glasses perched on the end of her nose. Then again, I can't imagine Mrs. Claus reaching into a stranger's bra to reposition a wayward breast, which is exactly what happened to CJ a few minutes ago.

My overeager best friend chooses that moment to fling the door open with something small and red clutched in her hand. "I feel good about this," she declares as she hands it over.

Jessica helps tug the straps into place, which I'm grateful for. I'm less grateful two seconds later when she's feeling me up.

"Scoop from the side," she says, settling my left breast

and half the skin from my back more firmly in the red lace cup. She repeats the action for righty, then steps back and gestures to the mirror. "See?"

"Okay. Wow." I blink at my reflection, where my extremely average breasts sit high on my chest, looking plumper than I've ever seen them. And the band is... comfortable? Is that even possible? I twist and turn, bend and snap, putting the bra through its paces. Through some sort of gravity-defying magic, it stays put and doesn't even pinch. It has strategically transparent lace in front, with thin red satin straps that curve up and away from my sternum in the center to skim the tops of my breasts before joining the sturdier elastic straps above the cups.

"This isn't me." I almost whisper it, my eyes fixed on the woman in the mirror. It's easily the sexiest thing I've ever had on my body.

"That's exactly why you buy it." Jessica adjusts the bottom of the band in the back. "It's part of our Christmas collection."

"What, like a gift for the man in your life?"

The waiter from yesterday pops into my mind unbidden. If I'd been wearing something this bold, maybe I'd have smiled at him more. I definitely would've socked Richie in the jaw on my way out of SparkNexus instead of walking out without a fight. What, like Canada was going to deport me twice?

Jessica peers at me over her half-moon glasses, blissfully unaware of my sex-and-violence fantasies. "A man? Honey, it's a gift to yourself." She pats my shoulder and steps out of the dressing room, leaving me alone with the woman in the mirror, who looks about four hundred percent more daring than I actually am.

With a cursory knock, CJ barges into the dressing room and squeals, "Holy shit!"

"Yeah?"

"Girl." CJ stands behind me and wraps her arms around my midsection, resting her chin on my shoulder. "Just imagine our waiter stripping off your shirt to find you in this."

Her mouth falls open in a playfully shocked expression, clearly anticipating my surprise that she noticed me noticing the way-too-hot, way-too-charming Jonesy.

You know, the guy I was thinking about not fifteen seconds ago.

"He wouldn't—I mean, I'm not..."

My bright-red cheeks give me away, and CJ laughs. "You weren't subtle when you stopped to check him out as we were leaving."

"I wasn't checking him out," I say primly. "I was curious what it said on his name tag. It really was just 'Jonesy.'"

True, I was curious about the name thing, but I mostly wanted an excuse to spend a few more seconds absorbing him in all his dark-haired, dark-eyed, sexy-scruffy glory before he moved on to his next table and forgot all about us.

Oh god what am I even doing? Like I need to hand CJ any more ammunition to tease me about my momentary infatuation with a pretty boy.

"Anyway, this isn't how I should be spending money," I say, deflecting like mad. "Did you forget the part where I don't have a job?"

CJ takes the bait and rolls her eyes. "Like you'd let me forget."

I glance back up at the mirror. My cheeks are still a little pink at the memory of Jonesy's grin, all full of dirty thoughts and kept promises. "A new bra isn't necessary."

"But it makes you feel good."

The insane confidence of having my boobs look this good is starting to burn away my critical thinking skills, so I shove CJ out of the dressing room and reach behind me to unclasp the hooks. Her sigh slips through the door. "You're not buying it, are you?"

"Nope," I say in my best nonnegotiable voice. "I'm full up on unwise decisions at the moment." Actually, I may have reached my lifetime quota of unwise decisions by going to work for SparkNexus Marketing.

I had a plan. I was on a path. Take my double major in fine art and graphic design and become an art director at a top marketing agency. But instead of being patient and working my way up the ladder in Phoenix, where I'd been for six years, I took a leap and joined Richie Mulligan's flashy new Canadian marketing firm. My old college classmate had been after me for months to join his wildly successful start-up, and every time I said no, he'd come back with a bigger offer. More money, more responsibility, autonomy to create my own campaigns, a company car, and a signing bonus. He made the unrestrained creativity happening at SparkNexus' ad incubator sound too good to be true.

It was, of course, and three weeks and two days after my big international move, the Canadian Revenue Agency was hard at work calculating Richie's many financial crimes and I was numbly boarding a plane back home because my work permit barred me from earning money at any Canadian company other than the now incredibly out-of-business SparkNexus.

The first time I was able to take a deep breath without the risk of a panic attack was when CJ met me at the airport yesterday and whisked me to lunch, then to her place, where I slept for eighteen hours. I'm now giving myself until the end of the year to figure out my life. There are no open doors for me in Phoenix, which means I'm hustling to find a new job literally anywhere in the United States so I can start my corporate climb all over again.

The moral of the story is simple. No more risks. Only practical decisions moving forward. And this bra is the opposite of practical.

"Liv! If you're not wearing that bra out of the store, get changed and let's go!" my delicate flower of a best friend hollers through the door.

By the time I'm fully clothed, beige bra back on my body, Jessica has CJ's purchases rung up, and the two of them are animatedly discussing a flier in CJ's hands.

"Look! Can you believe it?" She's practically dancing with excitement as she shoves the paper under my nose. "We were just joking about this!"

She stabs the words on the page with a shiny red nail, and I blink as she reads the text out loud.

"The area's hottest men are ready to be unwrapped like a present every Saturday through Christmas at the Crimson Lounge." She glances up at Jessica. "Level with us. Exactly how hot are we talking?"

The shop owner's lips twitch. "You'll have no complaints."

CJ dramatically bites her fist, then says, "Come on, we haven't done anything wild in years. It's time to Liv, laugh, love!"

"Well..." I glance uncomfortably at Jessica. Even though the woman's seen more of my naked breasts than the last three guys I dated, I don't know how I feel about discussing the objectification of local men in front of her. "Isn't it kind of early for holiday shows?" It's a weak objection, but it's the only one I can come up with.

Jessica smiles as if she senses my embarrassment. "My husband runs the club, and he only hires the best," she says. "People come from all over the state for my fittings, but they also come for the Saturday night performances. And the Christmas show is pure fun. They'll have costumes, choreography—"

"And cocks!" CJ finishes for her.

Jessica laughs as she reaches under the counter and pulls a few slips of paper from a small booklet. "Here. Drink vouchers. Make it a night out and enjoy yourselves."

CJ's hand shoots out to accept the coupons. "Thank you so much! You're our holiday angel." She nudges my side. "Isn't she?"

"You are," I say faintly. This is why I came here, after all. CJ's always been the wild child to my practical panda. If anybody can make me forget the Richie debacle, it's her. And I guess watching men take it all off onstage is the NSFW version of our old college hijinks, although those were usually limited to late-night donut runs and hitting frat parties even though I had a big exam the next morning.

"Thank you," I murmur to Jessica, who smiles so broadly that her eyes almost disappear into her pillowy cheeks.

"Have fun!" she calls after us as we leave.

By the time we reach the car, CJ's already making plans.

"I was hoping to introduce you to my friends, so this is perfect. I'm sure Rachel will be in, and Em should be able to leave her kids with her husband. Oh my god, I can't wait!"

I glance at the thoroughly unexciting exterior of the

club attached to Jessica's shop. The walls are white cinderblock, and the neon sign bearing the words CRIMSON LOUNGE might be spectacular when it's lit up, but at four in the afternoon, it's all a little underwhelming.

"How hot can these guys be?" I ask dubiously as we drive past the grain elevator at the edge of town to start the fifty-minute drive back to Beaucoeur. "North Village isn't exactly a booming metropolis."

CJ gives my arm a light pinch. "You came here so I could cheer you up."

"And that requires men in thongs?"

"Absolutely, it does."

"Awesome." I arrange myself more comfortably in my seat. "This is *exactly* the American homecoming I was hoping for."

CJ throws her head back in a cackle. "Oh shut up, you're gonna love it. Next stop, the bank. We'll need lots of cash."

THREE

Liv

I'm calling it. Operation Cheer Up Liv has officially spiraled out of control.

"You know I was being sarcastic about this being the welcome home I wanted, right?" I have to raise my voice over the music pumping through the club, but CJ just rattles the ice in her already empty drink.

"And you know I'm never sarcastic about hot men in tiny pants, right?" Her hair glows pink, then green, then blue under the colorful lights swirling above our stage-side table. I insisted we didn't need to sit this close to the action but was shouted down by the rest of our group. They're so enthusiastic, in fact, that I feel the need to remind everyone of the ground rules.

"No special treatment." I hit CJ with a stern look, then turn it on her friends. "No pushing me up onstage or anything."

"You got it," Em says immediately, and Rachel nods in agreement, the diamond stud in her nose winking under the lights. CJ, though, tucks her tiny drink straw in her mouth and makes a show of sucking up the last of her G&T rather than agreeing.

"I'm serious," I tell her. "I'm sure I'll enjoy all the hot, oiled-up dancing men, but I'd prefer to enjoy them from a respectful distance."

CJ rolls her eyes but huffs her agreement. "Fine. A respectful distance it is."

With that settled, I'm able to be marginally more relaxed. As long as Operation Cheer Up Liv doesn't turn into Operation Let's Force Liv Onstage, tonight will be fine. Assuming I can stay awake, of course. I already find myself stifling a yawn. Em catches me and laughs.

"Same, sister. It's an hour past bedtime for me." She's a high school math teacher and a mom of three, and I'm trusting her to help me keep CJ in check tonight.

"You know what'll wake you up?" CJ throws an arm in the air, signaling our server. "More alcohol."

"Alcohol's actually a depressant," I remind her, but she just gives my ear a playful flick. I bat her hand away, although I'm not actually annoyed. The energy in the room is contagious as excited groups pack the tables surrounding the stage.

Tonight's all-male show is happening on the second floor of the Crimson Lounge. It's a smaller space than the main floor stage, where women dance six nights a week, and it's packed for this once-a-week show. I count three bachelorette parties, a table of college-aged guys, and at least one birthday girl in the house tonight, along with smaller groups like ours. The women at the next table drove down from the Chicago suburbs for the night and are already screaming and stamping their feet in time to the thumping, pulsing music.

The shirtless blond hunk who brought us our first round heads over to our table, smoldering as he deposits fresh drinks. Then the lights dim and the music lowers, and cheers rip through the room.

"Here!" CJ shoves an envelope into my hands, then gives another one to Rachel and one to Em. Shouting to be heard over the din, she calls, "Spend it wisely!"

I gulp when I open the envelope to discover a wad of ones, tens, and twenties. There's no way CJ's letting us out of here until it's all gone.

"Lllllladies and gentlemennnnnn," a voice booms over the loudspeaker, "welcome to the Crimson Lounge! Tonight's the debut of this year's holiday spectacular, featuring the sexiest elves this side of the Arctic."

Elves? I mouth to CJ, who shrugs and lifts her arms in a joyful scream.

"Now put your hands together for Rocket Ray!" the announcer tells us, and we do. Oh, we do, myself included, as a sandy-haired man strides onto the stage in tight white pants and a red hoodie to start his performance. It's... muscular. Lots of one-armed push-ups to a driving beat. Plenty of hip thrusts and lunges. All that cardio reminds me that I need to find a gym while I'm in town.

"Show us your candy cane!" a woman on the opposite side of the stage shrieks, and Rocket flips to his feet and stalks over to her, ever so slowly unzipping his sweatshirt to uncover a rock-hard chest. Her table cheers as he rips off his pants and exposes the red-and-white striped G-string underneath.

Now that he's unencumbered by clothes, he thrusts his way around the stage, stopping in front of each table as the women scream their approval and shove bills at him. Our table's no exception, and we shower him with cash. It's only polite after all, and he's definitely working up a sweat for us. We do the same when a Mack truck of a guy named Diesel comes storming onto the stage dressed like a polar bear. Weirdly, it works, from the little white ears tucked in his dark hair to the round black nose attached to the front of his thong. And he lives up to his name, pumping his hips like an engine as he gyrates to a disco-y version of "Sleigh Ride." He's beefier than Rocket, and it's... yeah, it's nice. Tree trunk legs. Biceps the size of my head. He's objectively attractive.

Yet my loins remain unbothered. The vibe is pure campy fun. The bachelorette party behind us is worked into a frenzy, and CJ and Rachel lose their damn minds when three men take the stage dressed as elves who seem to have misplaced most of their wardrobe in what I can only assume was a tragic accident at Santa's workshop. They're hot as hell, executing their choreography with military precision and stage-flirting with the audience to a degree I didn't know was possible. They stop to bump and grind in unison directly in front of our table, and my mouth falls open when one of them hops off the stage and straddles Em's lap.

"Hey, Mrs. Salazar!" he happily shouts.

"Hello, Benjamin," she primly replies. "I see you finally stopped cutting gym class."

Her eyes drop to his extraordinarily built chest, and he belts out a laugh.

"That I did," he says as she tucks a bill into his thong. "Thank you kindly. May I be excused?"

Now she's the one laughing. "Go," she says. "Dance up on my friend Liv. She needs cheering up."

"Oh, no, I—"

Hot elf Benjamin ignores my objections and smashes

his pecs against the back of my head for a bit before he moves on.

Once he's gone, Em notices all three of us staring at her and flips a breezy hand in our direction. "Benjamin was in my Algebra I class, oh, four or five years ago?"

Rachel blinks. "And that wasn't weird for you?"

Em shrugs the shrug of a veteran teacher. "I see my former students all over. One of them's my OB-GYN."

The rest of us reach for our drinks as we process this revelation, and when yet another team of dancers takes the stage, CJ asks, "Just so we're prepared, did you teach any of them long division?"

Our table melts into laughter both at the joke and at the sight of grown men in reindeer antlers peeling off their brown onesies. As they form a line to shimmy their way across the stage, I start to fully relax. There are no wild risks here. The vibe is sexy-silly, and while I'm perfectly happy to hand over my cash to the hot dudes dancing their asses off, in no way am I tempted to throw my unmentionables onto the stage like the maid of honor behind us just threatened to do.

It's gotten easier to enthusiastically cheer along with everyone else when the deejay announces the next dancer and a blond guy appears onstage in a blocky blue costume. All four of us squint and tilt our heads as a violin- and clarinet-heavy song kicks on.

"Is he..." Em starts.

"Oh my god, he's a *dreidel!*" Rachel shrieks. Then the dancer who goes by Kelvin starts to spin. And spin. And spin. One by one, he pulls off the panels covering his torso, each of which has a Hebrew letter on it, and by the end of his act, he's simply a man in a blue thong with no fear of dizziness.

"This," Rachel says in quiet awe as Kelvin finishes his act in a frenzy of ass-shaking. "This is the inclusivity my people have been dreaming of. If this turns out to be the highlight of my holiday, dayenu."

We're laughing so hard at her gobsmacked expression that we almost miss the next dancer's introduction.

"Did he say Luke Lawless?" I shout at CJ, who turns her grin my way.

"He's *lawless*, Liv!" she screams in delight, wiggling her fingers in a *gimme* motion that has us all laughing. But when Luke takes the stage, there's not an outlaw accessory in sight.

He's Santa. We can tell by his red vest and pants, along with the velvet Santa hat and the short white beard covering most of his face. He's also wearing aviator sunglasses for some reason, and it's so goofy and weird that I slap my hands to my cheeks *Home Alone* style, bracing myself for the secondhand embarrassment, particularly when the opening strains of "Back Door Santa" crackle over the sound system.

Then he starts to move, and everything in me locks up and melts down at the same time.

"Oh. Oh my god." I whisper the words, but thankfully nobody at my table seems to notice. They're all equally transfixed by the man in the spotlight.

Luke flows like liquid across the stage, moving his body to the music in a way that's seductive where the other dancers had been over the top. Controlled and powerful where they'd been strong and energetic.

His Santa pants cling to his thighs as he drops to his knees and spins, pulling the vest off as he does to reveal a tight white tank top and red suspenders.

"He can come down my chimney right now," a woman

at the next table breathes, and all I can do is nod helplessly. Luke's hips roll as he struts around the stage, stopping to drop one suspender and then another to the deafening cheers of the crowd. Then he pivots to the center of the stage, plants his feet, and rips the thin tank top off his body —literally rips it from the neckline on down—and the place dissolves into mayhem.

His chest is perfect. He's not as bulky as most of the guys who came before him, although every one of the muscles on his lean body is tight and defined, from the swell of his arms to his flat pecs and sharp abs. Even his clavicles are attractive, for goodness' sake.

"This is verrrrrry good local talent," CJ says, and all I can do is give a helpless little grunt of agreement.

With a smooth kick, Luke flips to face downward, undulating across the floor like gravity can't quite touch him. It's equal parts sex and muscle control, and I can't decide which part is working for me more. Another kick and he's back on his feet, lifting his chin in a cocky head tilt.

I thought his clavicles were hot? They've got nothing on the tendons running down the side of his neck. *His neck tendons.* And he's still wearing the Santa beard! What is *wrong* with me?

The slice of mouth that's visible through the fake white curls curves into a lopsided smile as his gaze sweeps the crowd. Although his eyes are hidden behind his sunglasses, he pauses when he hits our table, tilting his head again before pivoting to give the other side of the room the same treatment.

"Another former student?" Rachel asks, and Em dazedly replies, "God, I hope not."

As I've been squeezing my knees together and willing myself to keep it under control, Santa Luke has taken off his pants to reveal the rest of his body. His lovely long thigh muscles and defined calves flex as he flows into a body roll that the crowd deeply, deeply appreciates. The only thing he's wearing now is a red thong that shows off his gorgeous round ass, and when he turns around to face our side of the room, I gasp. Because there it is. The exact shape of his cock, outlined in the stretchy red material. Like the rest of him, it's perfect. And why wouldn't it be? Everything about Luke Lawless is carved from marble, like a sculptor got ahold of the proportions of my dream man from the blueprints in my head and gifted them to the person flowing bonelessly in our direction. In *my* direction.

The song changes then, something less campy and far sexier involving mistletoe and a woman sitting on the singer's lap. Luke's mouth curves into another of those smiles, and before I can suck in a breath, he plants his right hand on the stage and lifts his body up in a one-armed handstand that he holds for a long moment, every muscle in his body tensed and hard. We all hold our breath until he lets himself drop to the floor with a twist, spinning to land lightly on his feet. Then he's walking toward me, his hips swiveling in time to the song. That smile is back, barely visible behind his fake beard.

Every eye in the room is pinned on him, all those bright, avid gazes, but he's only looking at me. I flush, and it travels from the roots of my hair to the backs of my knees. In something close to a panic, I try to turn so I'm facing the table and not the stage, but he just laughs. Then the room is in motion as he grabs the back of my chair and swivels it to face him, and me along with it. My knees brush his shins, and there's nowhere to hide as he places one hand on the table behind me and leans forward. This unreal creature is standing so close that I can smell coconut oil and clean sweat on his skin.

"Naughty or nice?" His husky voice is for my ears only.

Every word of the English language deserts me as he brushes a finger along my jaw to lift my chin, then trails it down my neck. He comes to a stop at the hollow of my throat, which jumps as I open my mouth and desperately suck in a breath.

"Mmmm," he growls, deepening his voice even more. "Naughty. Definitely naughty." It's too dark in here to see behind the lenses of his sunglasses, and I have to clench my hands into fists to keep from reaching up and yanking them off; that's how badly I want to see what color his eyes are.

Before I can give in to temptation, he pushes himself off my chair to perform a body roll that has every one of those muscles flexing mere inches from my nose. His shoulders move to the left while his hips rotate to the right, and every-thing—absolutely *everything*—ripples. Heat pours off his body, and I have no idea what to do with my hands, but touching him all over seems like a great idea.

I start to reach for him, and my greedy fingers are a whisper away from landing on his damp chest when I realize what I'm doing. I'm about to become the woman at the strip club who loses her mind and mauls a dancer.

Sweet baby Jesus, I want to. I'm actually a little unnerved at how badly I want to touch the compact, glis-tening abs of this person who's just trying to do his job. Which is why I force myself to pull it together. Forcing myself to ignore the fact that I'm about to go up in flames from being so close to him, I grab the fraying ends of my self-control, reach for my envelope, and fish out a couple of twenties. With a small, amused smile, I fold up the cash and tuck it into the red elastic riding low on his hips.

"*I'm* not the naughty one," I say, giving the bills a brisk pat. "Here you go. For the reindeer."

His body reacts to that, the tiniest of flinches that I only notice because my fingers are still resting on his overheated skin, and I'm not quite sure what happened, but it makes me want to rewind ten seconds. It's like me shoving cash at him violated some agreement between us. But the tiny moment is over fast, and he's grinning again. He's done with me. He spins to dance on CJ, then Rachel and Em, then the bachelorette and her crew at the next table.

When his song ends, the crowd hoots and cheers, and he vanishes behind the curtain, leaving me feeling hot and cold, a little ashamed, and a lot turned on.

FOUR

Jonesy

"**H**ey, man, everything okay?"

Deke's peering at me with concern on his face, and I give one more vicious scrub of the towel across my chest before tossing it down.

"I'm great." I'm aiming for affable but it comes out like a bark, and Deke's whole body droops. He's the beefiest dancer in the club, but he has the most delicate temperament.

"Sorry," he says, clearly wounded by my sharpness. "It's just that you were a little slow on the group number, and you kept playing to the left side of the stage."

Christ almighty, those eagle eyes of his don't miss a thing. And now I feel bad for making him feel bad.

"Seriously, I'm good." I sell it better this time, forcing a smile and stroking my chin. "Just different dancing in the Santa beard."

Fuck, I'm not up to chatting about my feelings tonight. I

just need to get through the rest of this shift and crawl home to sleep off the sour feeling in my stomach.

It's Little Miss Ponytail's fault.

I was fucking thrilled when the girl from the restaurant magically turned up at the club. It was the unexpected do-over I'd been wishing for, and that's why I'd felt it like a slap when her eyes had shifted from turned-on to transactional. But this time she didn't have to glance down at my name tag to remind me that I'm just the help. She did it by stuffing cash a few inches away from my dick.

My big-brain brother would probably tell me my inferiority complex is making me overly sensitive. Wyatt's an asshole like that. He's also usually right. The woman hadn't technically done anything wrong. I dance for cash. She gave me cash. That should be the end of it. But I just can't let it go.

And hell, I need to because it's time for my inferiority complex and me to mingle with the audience before the final number where we pull a handful of audience members onstage for the full-contact experience. It'd serve Ponytail right if I picked her to dry hump while her friends screamed their encouragement. Something tells me she'd hate that. Which means I'd hate it too, and normally it's one of my favorite parts of the job.

The strict diet, the never-ending workouts, the shaving and waxing, the joint pain and pulled muscles, those are the worst. But actually dancing for someone? Making her—or him, depending on the crowd—blush and laugh and breathe a little harder because I'm making DEFCON 1-level eye contact while I move my body? It's the best.

Not tonight though. I still feel Ponytail's money burning against my hip even though I stashed it with the rest of the cash I'd earned. I work for tips, but for some reason I don't want them from her.

Christ, I'm being an idiot. Her money'll spend as well as everyone else's here tonight. And I have at least eight million Christmas gifts to shop for, so I can't let her prissy little smile fuck up the rest of my night or the stash of holiday money I'm stockpiling.

I consider sliding on my jeans but leaving them unbuttoned and hanging off my hips for a slightly more dressed shirtless-guy-next-door approach to go one-on-one with the crowd, but fuck that. I drop my jeans back into my bag and pull on my red booty shorts instead. They ride low on my hips and cut off just below the curve of my ass. It's the modesty version of a thong, if your definition of modesty includes how much of your dick will poke out over the top of your waistband when you get hard. Little Miss Tight Ass wants body and nothing more? I'll give it to her, and I'll give it to her without the hat and beard.

I'm not usually this casual about mixing my two identities, but the stupidest, most impulsive part of me wants her to see my face and know exactly why I smirked when she brought this place up at the restaurant. To know that the man she wanted to touch earlier tonight was the waiter whose name she couldn't even remember.

"You ready?" Deke asks. When I nod, he claps one of his big paws on my shoulder, fluffs up his shoulder-length black curls, and shakes his ass all the way out of the dressing room in full Diesel mode. I slide on my sunglasses and push through the door right after him, setting my smile to stun.

The seating area's packed, buzzing with laughter and conversation over the *thump-thump-thump* of the music our deejay-slash-emcee Eugenio's spinning. I try not to look at her table right away, but I last about five seconds. When I give in and glance in her direction, she's not there.

She left. She got what she paid for, so she and her friends took off.

I haven't shared more than a few words with this woman. I don't even know her fucking name. There's no reason to let her throw me off my game, but I find myself scowling at the bachelorette in a light-up penis necklace who's now sitting in Ponytail's chair.

Deke stares me down from across the room, concern in his puppy dog eyes, so I pull it the fuck together and flash him a thumbs-up. Then I slap on my best *you know you want me* grin and set out to charm the women who did stay.

It's what I'm here to do after all. And I'm very, very good at it.

"Hi, can I hel…"

My voice trails off in what I hope isn't a strangled choke as I take in the last person I expected to ever lay eyes on again.

It's Ponytail, smiling politely from the opposite side of the hostess stand in a black dress and heels, as gorgeous and composed as I remember from her first visit to the restaurant last week.

My shock morphs into delight at seeing her in the flesh, but that only lasts for a few seconds before I realize that I am well and truly fucked. After three years of working both jobs, someone I danced for figured out my dual life and followed me to Verdant, where my very nice, very religious boss is within earshot.

It's actually happening. This is how I lose my job.

Maybe both jobs. Darryl's never going to put up with a stripper on his payroll, and most other serving gigs are going to clash with my dancing schedule. Shit, shit, *shit.*

"Are you okay?" Ponytail's looking at me with concern, and I give her a weak grin as I try to suck enough air into my lungs.

"Sure, yeah. Yeah. What are you umm..."

I eyeball her nervously with no idea what comes next in the gorgeous stalker handbook. Is she going to call me Luke? Demand I strip off my pants to give her a lap dance in nothing but my service apron? Most of the Saturday night crowd at the Crimson Lounge comes from the Chicago area, but there's always been a chance that someone from Beaucoeur would turn up and then connect the dots back to their friendly hometown brunch waiter. After a nervous few months working both jobs, though, I started to relax. What are the odds, right?

Fuck, I should've been more careful. I always dance in sunglasses, but maybe that's not enough. I should've used hair-darkening gel onstage or done more to disguise my voice. And I definitely shouldn't have given Ponytail any clues that I recognized her on Saturday, but my fucking cock overruled my already shaky common sense. And look where that got me.

I'm about two seconds away from a full-blown panic attack when she says, "I'm here about the job."

An "ungggh" sound spills from my mouth as my sputtering brain lurches to a halt. Does this mean she didn't track down Luke Lawless like some kind of well-dressed Terminator? In my confusion, I blurt out the first thing I think of. "The dishwashing job?"

Her gingerbread brows arch. "I suppose I can wash dishes if that's what you need."

She's waiting with such calm patience that I start to realize she actually has no idea it was me under the Santa outfit on Saturday, which is ninety-eight percent great. My secret appears to be safe. Of course, there's also the two percent that wants her to know I was the one who made her gasp and press her knees together—fuck yeah, I noticed—before she hauled herself back under control and made me feel about three feet tall. And right now, I need that two percent to shut the hell up so I can get out of this without losing any paychecks.

Ponytail clears her throat and shifts her weight from foot to foot, and I realize I've been staring at her like I'm the potential stalker and not the other way around.

I manage a jerky nod and say, "Right. Of course, right. Let me go grab Darryl."

I hope it doesn't look like I turn and sprint to the manager's office even though I definitely turn and sprint to the manager's office. So she's not here for Luke, but that doesn't mean she isn't going to recognize me eventually. I'd been close enough to her on Saturday that I felt her breath catch as I dragged my fingers down her throat. Then again, I was in a hat, beard, and glasses, and it's not like she had any reason to remember the details about her waiter from a few days before.

Get a grip, Jonesy. She's in the restaurant foyer acting perfectly normal. I'm the one making it weird. So what if I spent huge chunks of my weekend obsessing about her while she clearly wasn't giving me a second thought? That doesn't mean I can make it her problem. I'm not going to make it her problem because it's not going to *be* a problem. Everything's fine. So far nobody figured out who Luke Lawless really is, and that isn't changing today.

I take a second to catch my breath outside of Darryl's

office so everything seems normal before I knock on the door.

"Hey, boss." Shit, my voice is an octave higher than it should be. I try again. "A woman's here about a job?"

Darryl's been hunched over his desk, frowning at the computer, and he brightens and hits save on his spreadsheet. "Great! That'll be Olivia Fielding. She's here for the hostessing position."

"Olivia," I murmur. Then I blurt, "Hostessing position?"

He looks at me like I'm speaking Martian. I've never been quite this scattered at Verdant before. Even when we're in the weeds with a post-church mob here to order everything and tip nothing and I'm so sleep-deprived that I can feel the individual blood vessels pulsing in my brain, I'm unruffled and smiling on the outside. But Olivia's sudden appearance—*Olivia, fuck, I know her name now, it's Olivia*—has me wild-eyed and sweaty.

Darryl groans as he hauls his puffy sixty-something body out of his chair and stretches the muscles in his back. "Brita landed a spot in some kind of holiday chorale in Chicago and raced out of town Friday like her butt was on fire," he says. "She'll be back after Christmas, so we just need somebody for the next few weeks."

"Oh." I'm always a zombie on Mondays after performing all weekend or else I might've been curious about why one of the newer waitresses had been half-assedly working the hostess stand today. I sag against the wall as the rest of it clicks into place.

Ponytail—Olivia—wants a job here. Here, where I work and occasionally have dirty thoughts about her that I'm hoping will go away, like any day now. I let my head fall against the bulletin board pressing into my back, knocking an OSHA poster loose as I consider whether to laugh or cry or fall to my knees in gratitude.

"Well? Are you coming?"

I lift my head to find Darryl straightening his tie, his broad pink face a perfect match for the ugly paisley pattern.

"Coming where?"

"I want you to sit in on the interview. Get June to cover your tables."

He's gone before I can object or even ask why. And to be honest, I don't want to fight it. I'm dying to sit across the table from Olivia as she talks about herself. God, please let her be so boring that I get over this weird obsession.

I push myself off the wall and give June instructions about covering my current tables, although I sneak constant glances at the four-top where Olivia and Darryl are seated. At least we're in the lull between breakfast and lunch when the flow of guests has mostly slowed to a trickle, so I probably won't lose too much in tips. Then again, I stand to lose a lot more than a few tables' worth of tips if Olivia suddenly realizes she saw a hell of a lot of me on Saturday night and blurts it out to Darryl.

My heart starts to race again—*don't get fired, can't get fired, not this close to Christmas*—and I take slow, deep breaths until I'm calm enough to claim the chair next to Darryl. I even sound like a mostly normal human adult when I say, "Hi, Olivia."

"Call me Liv." A smile lights her face, and goddammit, I can't help but smile back. "What should I call you?"

She cocks her head, clearly waiting for me to offer up my first name. Ha. The only person here who knows that is Darryl, and that's only because he took the info on my Social Security card for my hiring paperwork and promptly forgot it.

"Jonesy." The pathetic hurt feelings from our last two interactions bob to the surface, and I pointedly add, "Which you know from my name tag."

Her face pulls into a frown as if she senses I'm annoyed but doesn't know why, and now I want to smooth my thumb along that confused line where her brows meet to see if I can make her catch her breath again. Fuck, this woman makes me feel every feeling under the sun, and I'm not sure what to be most worried about. My wild attraction to her? Her general indifference to me except when I'm in a thong? Or the fact that she could blow my cover about wearing said thong for money?

Yeah, that last one seems especially worth worrying about.

"Jeez, Jonesy, rough weekend?" Darryl elbows me, and I realize I've been staring at Liv in silence.

"Little bit, yeah." Saturday night was as long as usual, and then Derek, Landon, and I did a private party last night in Rockford. I made it back to Beaucoeur a couple of hours before my shift, so I'm definitely not my sharpest this morning.

"Anyway," I say after clearing my throat. "I'm the one who brought you Gochujang shrimp tacos last week."

Her eyes flash. "Yes, I remember."

And that's when I realize that I know something about her too. She's seen the inside of a Canadian jail. And what does it say that I perk right up when I remember that I can drop this into the conversation when she least expects it? She doesn't know that she knows my secret, but she knows that I know hers.

She must notice the shift in my whole aura because her gaze locks on me and her mouth presses into a flat line. It's a clear warning not to bring up the tiny bit of dirt that I have on her.

"Like I was telling Darryl, I worked as a hostess all the way through college, and since I'm between jobs"—her gaze flicks over to mine—"this situation is perfect."

"And where was your last job?" I ask, all innocent smiles now that the shoe's on the other foot.

Her eyes narrow. "Canada." The word emerges slowly, as if she's not sure what I'll say next. I have no idea why she's so worried. It's not like she actually did anything wrong. But it clearly bothers her, and after the accidental scare she just gave me, I can't help but let her twist just a little.

"Canada, huh?" I drawl, leaning forward so I can prop my chin on my fist. "I hear the Mounties are really good at protecting their borders."

I grin at her, all easy charm, and she tilts her head down until her hair forms a curtain around her face. I don't usually pay much attention to women's hairstyles, but everything about Liv grabs me by the throat and forces me to notice her, which is why I know for a fact that her hair this morning's as stick-straight as it was when she first came into Verdant, while on Saturday at the club, it fell around her shoulders in a fluffy, curly cloud that I wanted to grip and pull until she gasped my name.

Good thing I resisted the urge. Because that would've made this awkward.

Oh shit, I already made it awkward by pushing the joke too far because her head's still tilted down to hide her expression. I'm opening my mouth for a hasty subject change when she turns her head the slightest bit toward me and I can see that her cheeks are curved as if she's holding back a laugh. When she finally straightens, her expression is composed but her eyes are bright with amusement.

"Yeah, those Mounties mean business." She slides me a look that says she's trusting me to be cool about this. Then she's back to Darryl.

"More relevant for you," she says smoothly, like she didn't just semi-threaten me with a look, "I've got almost five years of experience managing waitlists and seating charts and keeping guests happy. Plus, I can roll silverware faster than anybody on your staff, guaranteed."

"Ooooh," I singsong. "You think so, do you?"

"Bring it on." There isn't a trace of modesty in her voice, and I love it.

"You do understand this isn't a permanent position," Darryl says, completely oblivious to the conversational undercurrents happening around him. "Once Brita's back, she'll slide into her spot again."

Liv nods. "I'm in the process of setting up interviews with marketing firms all over the country after the first of the year. I just wanted something to keep me busy while I'm in Beaucoeur."

Darryl slaps his hands on the table, rattling the rustic metal pail in the center that holds napkins and condiments. "You're hired. You're a lifesaver, frankly. Tomorrow okay to start?" At her nod, he stands. "Perfect. Jonesy'll be the one showing you the ropes."

"I will?" I blurt at the same time Liv says, "He will?" Our gazes clash. Hers is unreadable, and I don't want to picture what she sees in mine.

Good old thick-as-a-brick Darryl beams at both of us. "He's our best server. You'll be in good hands."

I want to laugh at the thought of being anybody's best

anything, particularly when Liv looks at me expectantly once Darryl's off to his hidey-hole.

"So," she says brightly, "you're going to teach me every-thing you know."

"Appears so." I sling my arm over the back of my chair, slouching to hide the mix of lust and nerves and tiny bit of resentment this girl makes me feel.

"Mmm." She tips her head to the side. "And after those ten minutes are up, what'll we do with the rest of the day?"

After a startled beat, I give a roar of laughter that has every guest in the section looking our way.

"Oh, Livvie-Liv," I say as she gives me the first real grin I've seen from her and lust takes the lead. "I think we're gonna get along just fine."

FIVE

Liv

"**W**ell? Did you get the job?"

CJ's sprawled on the couch, her voice muffled by the pillow over her face.

"The Boston job? Not yet." I hang my coat on one of the hooks by the door, kick off my heels, and sink onto the cushion next to her, flexing my toes with a sigh. "But the restaurant job's a yes." I should probably rethink my choice of shoes for hostessing. I'm not nineteen anymore, and I've been working a desk job for way too long. "I'll have Mondays and Tuesdays off and work Wednesdays through Sundays until their regular hostess is back in January."

"What a grind. I told you, you don't have to go out and earn money," CJ says into the pillow. "I'm delighted to have you freeload for a while. Freeload for as long as you want."

She's being serious. When CJ's corporate consulting job went fully remote, she moved to Beaucoeur, where housing is still affordable. But her work is solitary and her hours are whatever she wants them to be, and as a result she's gone a little feral. Even if we didn't love each other like sisters, she'd be thrilled to have me as a roommate if only to stay in better contact with the outside world. Still, there was no way I could sit around her house for weeks feeling sorry for myself. It felt like serendipity when I caught the SEASONAL HELP WANTED sign in Verdant's front window.

"I'll need the money to relocate to Boston once they realize I'm the creative director they're looking for," I say. "And I can't just watch TV in your house all day while you're running the Singapore Exchange or whatever it is you do."

CJ yanks the pillow off her face and squints at me. "Plus, there's the hot waiter."

"There is the hot waiter," I calmly agree, praying that CJ can't tell how much I was looking forward to potentially seeing Jonesy today. And then I did, and he was clearly weirded out by me being there. I went from foolishly hoping he'd remember me to being horrified that he remembered me for some terrible reason. I almost turned and walked out.

"He sat in on my interview and basically threatened to tell my new boss about my legal issues."

"Seriously?" CJ blinks. "He seemed way cooler than that when he was waiting on us."

"No, no, he's super cool," I say, recalling the glint in his eye once he started acting like the wildly appealing guy I remembered from the week before. "He was just messing with me."

"You've already got inside jokes!" CJ claps in excitement. "I'm thinking a spring wedding."

"I don't think he's the marrying type." I was only at Verdant for an hour today, and I saw Jonesy turn his teasing charm on pretty much every server, busboy, and customer he interacted with.

CJ smirks. "A fling would be good for you."

"Oh no," I say with a laugh. "I locked eyes with him during my interview. Those eyes have seen things. Things I'm not ready for." Things I've only fumbled toward in the dark with my last couple of perfectly polite boyfriends.

I suppress a quiver at the thought of being alone in the dark with Jonesy, the man with no first name.

"So if the hot waiter's out of the question, I guess that means you're *really* not ready for a fling with the Santa stripper instead." CJ's hair slipped out of its ponytail during her nap, and she's too busy yanking out the elastic and rebundling it on top of her head to see my whole body go slack at the thought. First Jonesy, then the Santa from the Crimson Lounge? It's too much for someone in the middle of a sex drought.

"I wouldn't even know where to *start* with him," I say faintly.

"Start by getting him to take off the beard so you can see if the face matches the body."

"Perfect, you mean?" Santa Luke's aerodynamic V-shaped torso drifts through my mind, and at the memory of his husky "naughty or nice?" in my ear, I swear my Fallopian tube drops an egg.

It also shakes a memory loose. Funny, that's what Jonesy asked when he took our drinks order at Verdant last week. But his question wasn't an invitation to have sex with him for hours at the North Pole.

"So you've got snake-hips Santa in your spank bank and Jonesy in your workplace, you lucky girl," CJ says.

"Amazing body, meet amazing face." Kind of great

personality too. Not many people can pull me out of my own head when I'm anxious about impressing a potential boss, but somehow Jonesy managed it.

"Combine the two, and you've got the perfect man," CJ says.

"And just think, without Richie trying to get me locked up for a decade on international fraud charges, I'd never have met either of them."

"Fucking Richie!" CJ seethes. "I never liked him."

"You dated him for three months."

She gasps in outrage. "When I was a *sophomore* and in my pretty boy phase. I knew nothing about life back then."

"Fair," I acknowledge. "And hey, let it be a lesson. You can't trust handsome men."

"I vote you make an exception for Jonesy," she says, hopping up. "Welp. Objectification break's over. Back to work for me." She rolls her shoulders like she's about to step into a boxing ring. "Cool that Jonsey's as adorable as you remember. Lemme know if you want to head back to the club this weekend to see if Santa's as sexy on a second viewing too."

"I'm not in Beaucoeur to become a VIP at the Crimson Lounge!" I call as she disappears down the hall toward her office. Her answering laugh is audible as the door clicks shut behind her.

I'm frowning at a government form the next morning when the smell of coffee wafts toward my nose.

"Here."

I glance up to see Jonesy standing in front of me with half-lidded eyes and a mug he thrusts into my hand.

"Ohhhh, thank you," I croon as I take it and drain half in one long, scalding gulp. "I forgot how early six a.m. actually is. You just saved my life."

"That's what I do." He leans against the wall, and his eyes drift shut.

We have an hour before Verdant opens for my first shift as hostess, and I'm filling out employment paperwork in Darryl's office, which seems to double as a storage room for excess dry goods, from what I can tell. "Are you here to offload the sum total of your knowledge onto me?"

"Yep," he says through a yawn. "Verdant doesn't take reservations, no matter how much people beg. We close at three every afternoon, and we stop seating people ten minutes before that. Umm... everyone avoids Rob the busboy because he's an absolute creep, and you should stretch before attempting a backflip."

When he stops talking, I cock my head. "That's it?"

"Wait, always double down on eleven in blackjack." He rolls his eyes toward the ceiling like he's searching his brain for any hidden facts. "Yep, that's it. The sum total of my knowledge."

I scrawl my signature on the bottom of the final page in front of me and toss the pen back on the desk. "That actually took more time than I expected."

He laughs at my shit-giving. "It's humbling to meet somebody who gets me immediately." He yawns again and gives his cheeks a quick series of slaps, clearly still trying to wake himself up. "C'mon. I'll introduce you to the head chef. He's also a co-owner, and he's chipper until the first guest walks through the door. Then it's downhill from there."

Head chef and co-owner Samson turns out to be a lot of

things. Intense. High energy. Covered in tattoos. But chipper?

"What, Jonesy?" he snaps when my tour guide escorts me through the swinging doors into the kitchen.

"Meet Liv. She's filling in for Brita this month."

Samson grunts but doesn't look up from where he's dicing onions.

"You're gonna want to watch out for this one," Jonesy continues cheerfully. "She's wanted in Canada for reasons she hasn't fully disclosed to me."

"Um no," I say. "I'm *not* wanted in Canada, remember?"

It's unbelievable that I'm in a joking place about the whole arrest and deportation situation, but for some reason, Jonesy teasing me about it makes the whole thing less humiliating. A side effect of that sparkling, charming, *you know you want to kiss me all over* grin, maybe.

My disclosure gets Samson to flick his gaze up to me. "Does this mean you know people who can smuggle out the good stuff for me?"

"Oh, definitely. I've got a guy," I say. "But only if you're talking about maple syrup."

The scary-ass head chef snorts. "Sure." He glances at Jonesy. "She's allowed to help with inventory. Now leave."

Once we're out of earshot, I whisper, "That was chipper?"

"That was him at his most sunshiney." Jonesy steers me toward the hostess stand at the front of house. "So the good news is that he likes you. Samson doesn't trust just anybody with inventory."

I feel like I've won some sort of booby-trapped prize. "What's the bad news?"

"You're going to join me in PTSD-land when we miscount the forks and he reprimands us."

"Reprimands?"

"Screams at." He gives a comical wince, but all I can think is how fun it'll be to count silverware with him even if it ends in shouting.

"Put me in, coach." I give a little salute and immediately regret making such a dumb gesture. But Jonesy smiles as his eyes drift to the neckline of my wrap dress.

"Great coordination," he says.

"Um." The conversational hop is confusing until he jerks his head toward the entrance and I realize my forest-green dress is, in fact, a close match to the walls. Good to know that when he looks at me, he thinks about paint colors.

"Oh. Thanks."

Jonesy shakes his head. "Darryl's never gonna want to let you go."

"Well, he's going to have to." I use my most crisp delivery, pivoting to an all-business tone since that's clearly where Jonesy's head is too. "I'm gone in a couple of weeks. My dream job in Boston's calling my name."

"Boston, huh?" He grimaces, but before I can ask if it's an East Coast thing or a Paul Revere thing or what, a cute, curly-haired brunette swings by the hostess station.

"Hey, big guy," she says. "Wanna talk about who gets what tables today?"

"Yes, ma'am," he replies, then turns to me. "You good here? It's always a fight over which of us has to do the haunted section."

Before I can follow up with six million questions about which section is haunted and more importantly, haunted with *what*, he ambles off to chat with the brunette and the other three servers on staff this morning. It gives me a chance to explore my new workstation, and by the time the doors open for the seven a.m. breakfast crowd, I'm forced to admit something horribly embarrassing. I'm *beyond* fascinated by my flirty new coworker.

"**E**njoy your lunch," I say to the middle-aged couple I've just seated in Jonesy's section. As I move back to my home base, I come close to accidentally clipping his shoulder, but he just sidesteps me with a deft spin and a wink.

"I need a little more warning if you want me to do the *Dirty Dancing* lift with you," he says as he doles out sodas to his waiting guests.

I retreat to the safety of my little wooden sanctuary, where I shuffle the menus into a tidier stack in order to have something to do with my eyes other than ogle my coworker. I'm halfway through my second week at Verdant, and it's a battle I've been consistently fighting and consistently losing.

"You have the best view in the house."

I glance over my shoulder to see Marcus, a gangly twenty-year-old, doing the exact ogling I was trying to avoid. We watch in silent appreciation as Jonesy makes a tired-looking man and his three little kids laugh with his attempts to fold one of their napkins into an origami bird.

We're joined by Ariel, the curly brunette who ended up with the haunted section today, just as Jonesy throws his head back in a boisterous laugh at something the littlest girl at his table says.

"God, he's just so..." Ariel breaks off and waves her hands in vague helplessness. She and Marcus are dating, but I think they both also kind of want to date Jonesy too.

"Yeah," Marcus says. "He really is just... *so*."

I don't chime in even though I agree. The Verdant staff absorbs new people into their friendly, gossipy group immediately, and because of that, I know that Jonesy's the primary object of fascination for pretty much everyone here. Of course he is, with his laid-back, lazy smiles and his scruffy jaw and his goddamn pheromones. He's the class clown and the homecoming king and the bad boy all rolled into one, and he has great hair to boot.

"What did he mean about the *Dirty Dancing* lift?"

At my question, Ariel's eyes flutter shut.

"Exactly what it sounds like. He does the lift," she says. "Like if you ask him after we close, he'll let you run at him, and he'll catch you and..."

She doesn't finish the thought, but I get the gist. "Like Ryan Gosling in *Crazy, Stupid, Love*?"

"Exactly like that," Marcus says. "He even did me once."

"Really?" I eyeball my tall, skinny coworker.

"He's got all kinds of muscles under that shirt," Ariel says as Jonesy breezes by balancing a tray loaded with dirty dishes on one hand. He and Marcus exchange a fist-bump, hand-shake explosion, and I have to work not to swallow my own tongue at how effortlessly he multitasks with a heavy tray.

"Dude, I'm so sorry," he says to Marcus, "I forgot to write down my workout routine for you. Hit me up before you leave today?"

"Sweet!" Marcus' face lights up. "I will."

Maybe I should ask Jonesy for his workout routine. It seems to spark joy. Then I look more closely at Jonesy's chest and arms, curious what kind of workouts he does. The Verdant button-downs aren't tight, but they fit well enough to give the impression of muscles. And now I'm thinking about Jonesy setting down that tray so he can put his hands on my hips to hoist me over his head, smiling up at me as his fingers grip tighter and—

Ariel smirks. "Swear to god, he'll *Dirty Dance* lift you in a heartbeat if you show the slightest bit of interest."

I shake off my Jonesy/Patrick Swayze/Ryan Gosling fantasy. Thank god Jonesy disappeared into the kitchen with the tray so he doesn't overhear us gossiping about him.

"You think?"

Marcus scoffs good-naturedly. "Come on, he loves women, and he loves flirting. Maybe you've noticed?"

"He is awfully devoted to 'training' you," Ariel adds.

"I guess so." For the past two weeks at Verdant, Jonesy's been a constant presence at my side, chatting when he has downtime, helping me roll silverware and restock the take-out supplies, and making the day go faster with his jokes and observations and running commentary. Part of me hoped it was because he enjoyed my company, but maybe that's just what he does when a fresh face joins this little band of Verdant employees.

"*Hello?* Can we please get a table for three?"

I snap out of my pity party to see three salon-blond women scowling at me with identically crossed arms. Their leader throws a glance at the other two and mutters, "Is it so hard to hire people who actually want to work these days?"

Marcus and Ariel melt away as I make a show of studying the seating map. "Oh gosh," I say, oozing faux sympathy. "It's a forty-minute wait for a table." Just as they start to fuss and fidget, I say, "Maybe you'd be willing to eat at the bar? There's no wait."

After a great deal of huffing, they agree to my proposal, and I grab three menus and lead the trio to the bar, going the long way to avoid Rob. Jonesy was spot-on in his assessment during my short orientation. The perpetually greasy busboy keeps trying to smell my hair, and while I want these three sourpusses to have to talk over the margarita machine all through their lunch, I'm not cruel enough to intentionally throw them into Rob's orbit.

Two hours later, my feet hurt from standing, my cheeks hurt from pretend smiling, and I'm cursing myself for not just living my life on CJ's couch this month.

"Figured a white-collar criminal like yourself would've forgotten how tough these shifts can be."

Jonesy caught me pushing up on my toes to stretch my tired calf muscles, and I settle back onto my heels with a groan. "I've gotten soft."

His lower lip catches in his teeth as he studies me. "Nothing wrong with soft."

It's not personal. He just likes to flirt. Even knowing that I understand why everybody here loses their minds when he tosses them a compliment. That sincere voice and those meltingly dark eyes? Nobody stands a chance.

"Oh hey, I looked up those ads you said you worked on," he says, leaning against the stand so his shoulder brushes mine.

I can't help but grin. "Really?" He seriously tracked down the campaign I oversaw for a tiny mail-order ice cream company in Phoenix that went viral on social media? Like, he thought about me in his off hours and Googled until he found the poppy, upbeat videos of ice cream melting away to reveal dreamy watercolors of the pre-melted version in the background?

"It was cool as hell, Fielding," he says. "The music, the art sneak attack... I was ready to pay twelve bucks for a tiny carton."

"That was the goal," I say, unable to keep the satisfaction out of my voice. "I was actually the one who suggested on the day of the shoot that we needed something more interesting in the background than the pink backdrop. The rest is history."

"Legend!" he says. "So where'd you get the drawings so fast?"

"I did them."

His mouth widens in delight. "Get out. Really? *You* drew them? Like on set? Triple legend!"

"Thanks, Jonesy." He's looking at me like I just admitted to walking on water, and I'm way too thrilled by the admiration on his face. I desperately grope for safer conversational ground and land on the first thing that pops into my head. "Listen, I cannot keep calling you that. What's your real name?"

He immediately snaps into teasing flirt mode. "Wouldn't you like to know?"

"I would," I reply tartly. "That's why I asked." Not knowing has been killing me, and getting him to share it would feel like a major victory. Like I'm not just the latest in a series of new people he sets out to charm. But he holds the smirk, pressing his lips even more tightly together.

"Fine. Keep your secrets." I wave my hands in exasperation. "Here's something you might be able to answer. Darryl's got the holiday soundtrack from hell playing, but there are zero Christmas decorations up. *Why?*"

He looks around at the undecorated walls in surprise.

"Huh. I never thought about it one way or another."

"Ohhhhh." I drag the word out. "You're one of *those* guys."

"Probably," he says cheerfully. "Which guys?"

"You know." I mimic his position and lean an elbow on

the hostess stand. "Apartment with bare walls, or if not bare, then some kind of framed sports memorabilia. I'm thinking a Bears jersey, or maybe the Blackhawks. Other than that, one big, ugly couch and a huge TV are the only decor you need, and you've definitely never considered bringing any kind of Christmas decorations into your home."

"Joke's on you. I own zero sports things." Even though I've insulted his home sight unseen, his eyes dance with laughter. "I do own movie posters though."

"Let me guess." I squint in thought. "*The Godfather*, right? Or *Fight Club*? *John Wick* if you go modern classics, or *A Clockwork Orange* if you prefer classic classics. You know, the go-to woman-repellants."

His smile vanishes. "How the hell did you—"

I wave a dismissive hand. "Please. I dated you all through my twenties. No *Fight Club* poster guy in the history of time has ever thought twice about holiday decorations."

"Guilty." He's smiling again and his tone is light, but something about it feels forced. "Guys like me don't decorate for Christmas, and our hideous homes drive away quality women who should really know better."

The ending of that sentence veered into truth-telling territory, and I immediately regret teasing him. "Hey, I was just kiddi—"

"Pssht," he says. "I know I'm awesome. But don't blame my decor for the lack of quality women in my life. I drive them away all on my own."

"You do?" I ask skeptically.

He gives a mock bow. "Unreliable and irresponsible, at your service."

The words fall from his lips like a warning, but they don't sit quite right.

"Really."

"Really," he says. "Ask me how many restaurants I left before I landed here."

My raised brows are the only encouragement he needs.

"Eleven," he says. "That's a fairly major percentage of Beaucoeur restaurants."

My brows are definitely still up. "Quit or fired?"

"Both." He shrugs in faux modesty. "I have a gift for fighting with my managers. And unwisely dating coworkers. And just not showing up."

I glance around the restaurant at the employees I've seen flocking to him all day, clamoring for his attention or hoping to make him laugh. Verdant also has customers who are obvious Jonesy regulars too.

"And how many years have you worked here?"

His smile slowly fades. "Almost four."

"No fights with your managers? And you were somehow able to show up for your shifts?"

He shrugs, his expression almost pained. "Mostly, yeah."

I don't have the heart to ask about dating coworkers because I don't want to risk the potential jealousy. "And you were how old at those other restaurants?"

"I see what you're doing." He scowls, but he answers. "Late teens, early twenties mostly."

I pat his hand and try not to linger too long. "That's actually pretty good evidence of developing maturity, my friend. Because everyone here seems to count on you now."

His jaw bunches like he's about to argue when June, a server of indeterminate age with weather-beaten skin and a long blond-fading-to-gray braid rushes up to us.

"Hey, Jonesy, can you help me split the bill for that table of ten? I always screw it up."

He straightens immediately. "Three seconds and I'm all yours."

"Okay!"

Once she's gone, I wave my hands in a magician's flourish. "Look at that! Someone relying on you!"

He rolls his eyes. "Being a good server isn't the same as being a good brother or a good son or a good boyfriend."

Before I can ask about those extremely specific examples, he saunters away, whistling.

SIX

Jonesy

I'm tackling my end-of-shift tasks on Saturday when June flags me down.

"I found two vagrants hanging around outside and put them in your section."

I swipe my cleaning cloth over table fourteen one last time and break into a grin when I see the pair in the booth.

"Looks like trouble to me. Did you ask Samson if he could spare some leftover risotto?"

"I did, which means you owe me." She pats my shoulder. "See you tomorrow, cutie."

"See you tomorrow."

June shoulders her massive mom bag and hustles toward the exit, leaving me free to saunter over to the table where my best friend is making out with his wife. Gabe and Darby have only been married for a couple of months, so they're still very much in the honeymoon phase. It's why I haven't seen much of them recently, and it's why they both leap to their feet to hug me.

"Jonesy!" Darby exclaims. "You're looking good!" Then she steps back to peer at me more closely. "Wait, you're looking tired. Are you working too hard?"

"Great to see you too." I glance over at Gabe. "Is she this good at bedroom talk?"

He pulls me into a hug and claps me on the back. "Don't be an ass."

"You guys are late," I say, slipping into the opposite side of the booth from the newlyweds. They promised to swing by during my shift, but here it is, twenty minutes after close. Hanging with them after hours means I won't be able to fit in a workout before the show tonight, but I can skip this once. I'm thrilled they stopped by even if seeing Gabe triggers a pulse of guilt.

"My fault," Darby says. "We were putting lights on the trees in our front yard, and it took forever."

"Well, it sounds like June took care of you," I say. "Let me finish up and grab the food."

I hop up, intending to speed through the last of my wipe-down work, and find Liv wiping down the table I left half-cleaned.

"I can finish up if you want to hang with your friends."

She wiggles a clean rag and a spray bottle at me.

"No way. You didn't eat on your break, right?" I steer her toward Gabe and Darby's booth. "Sit with my friends, and I'll join you in a sec. Unless you've got someplace else to be?"

"Me? The visitor to Beaucoeur who knows three people outside of this restaurant?"

I herd her toward the booth.

"Liv Fielding, meet Gabe Dickinson and Darby St. Claire. There, now you know two more people in town," I tell her as I press her down onto the bench seat. "Darby's the coolest librarian you'll ever meet, and Gabe's a land-scaper with terrible taste in best friends. Gabe and Darby, Liv's an unrepentant criminal on the run from the Canadian authorities."

"I am not," she says haughtily as I spin to wipe down the final tables. Then I head to the kitchen to face down Samson.

"I'm not here to cook for your friends." He bangs a stack of plates down on the sparkling stainless-steel counter in front of him.

"Not even the ones who planted those incredible Japanese maple trees in your yard last year?" My grin bounces off his scowling exterior, but he stops complaining and hands over a family-style bowl of steaming mushroom risotto.

"Tell him Ansel wants flowering bushes next year."

"Noted. I'll clean up when we're done."

"You're goddamn right you will." He sets the final pot in the sink and unties his apron. "Set the security code when you leave."

I nod my acknowledgment as I stack the plates and food onto a tray and slide out of the kitchen, grateful to escape with my life.

"Samson says the payment for feeding you after hours is planting fancy bushes for his husband this spring," I say as I unload the tray onto the table and slide in next to Liv.

"Sure." Gabe grabs a spoon and scoops a huge serving of the rice dish onto his plate. "As long as you're the one doing it."

I stiffen but don't respond. Darby does though.

"Seriously, when are you going to quit your jobs and join Hot Guy Landscaping?"

This is what I get for bringing up the business. I clench my jaw as I serve myself a small helping of risotto.

"What are we talking about?" Liv looks between the three of us, and my jaw tightens even more.

"My extremely talented man opened HG Landscaping last year with the understanding that his very best friend in the world would come on board as the design expert," Darby says.

"But has he devoted his eye for color and his many muscles toward making the business grow?" Gabe asks. "He has not."

The smothering weight of their hopeful, encouraging eyes falls on me.

"You guys know it's not a good time," I mumble.

"It hasn't been a good time for a year and a half now," Gabe points out. "It's never going to be a good time, so just make now the time."

His voice has an edge of frustration, which is rare for him. And he's not wrong. First it was my fear of being deadweight on the payroll of a fledgling business. Then it was Mom's surgery throwing the family into financial and emotional crisis mode. Now it's the pressure to make sure everybody has the Christmas they deserve after such a hard, shitty year.

"Seriously, Jonesy, don't you want to quit your jobs and just play in the dirt?" Darby wheedles.

"Jobs plural?" Liv's trying to keep up with the conversation, and alarm crackles down my spine.

I'm saved by the buzz of her phone. "Oh, CJ's here to pick me up." She glances at the remaining risotto in the bowl. "Do you think we have enough for one more?"

"More, merrier, etcetera," I say. Anything to steal a few more minutes with her after work hours.

I stand to let her out of the booth, and while we wait for her to let CJ in, Gabe asks, "Still on for Golfmas?"

"Like I'd miss it."

"Wyatt too?"

I grimace. "If we're lucky, no." Gabe just sends me a long look, and I sigh. "I'll check."

Before he can lecture me about what a good but misunderstood guy my brother is, Liv's back with CJ, who's all smiles as she introduces herself. Liv ends up smushed in the middle of the booth between her friend and me, and now I have the sweet torture of her body pressing tightly against mine in this two-person booth. How on earth does she smell so good after a full day in a restaurant?

"You work at the library, right?" CJ's dressed as casually today as the last time I saw her, and she doesn't hesitate before launching into conversation with two strangers. But the stranger vibe doesn't last, and before I know it, Gabe and I are raising our brows as the three women make plans for a mani-pedi-wine bar-Christmas shopping excursion.

"Jeez, is it that easy for women to make new friends as adults?" Gabe asks.

"It is when the women are as delightful as we are," Darby tells him.

Liv nudges me. "Men too. We're buddies, right?"

"Buddies," I say faintly. Can you be buddies with a woman when you've lost sleep imagining how her hair would feel against your cheek and chest and cock?

"So you're best buds with the hot waiter. That's one down," CJ says. "Next up, make friends with snake-hips Santa."

One thing I know for sure about Liv. She isn't usually over-the-top dramatic. But here she is covering her face with her hands and slumping forward with a wail. "Oh my god, CJ!"

"Snake-hips Santa?" Gabe asks.

CJ nods enthusiastically. "I dragged my darling friend to the strip club in North Village last weekend, and since then, she's been obsessed with the guy who was dressed like Santa."

The guy who...

"Like can't stop thinking about him," CJ says. "Totally gone for a guy whose name she doesn't know."

The guy who was dressed...

"I know his name." Liv's voice is muffled by her hands. "It's Luke."

Luke. The guy who was dressed like Santa.

Me. Liv's obsessed with *me.*

"Wait, what?" Darby asks at the same time Gabe says, "Dude, aren't you—*ouch!* What was that for?"

He contorts himself to rub his shin under the table where I've just kicked him.

"Sorry," I grind out. "Leg cramp. Needed to stretch."

Zero subtlety there, but what I really need is for both of them to shut the fuck up while I figure out how to handle eighteen different emotions at once. Elation. Horror. *Fuck-yeah* smugness. More horror. Oh god.

Gabe and Darby are staring at me in confusion and amusement, but all I can feel is my heartbeat throbbing in my ears as I turn to Liv with no idea what to say or how to say it.

"Liv, I... I, uh—"

"We are not. Talking. About. This," she grinds out. Her face is still buried in her hands, so she's missing the circus act happening around her.

"You sure about that? Tell us more about Luke," Gabe

says with a grin, swiveling his legs to the side so they're out of kicking range. I'm forced to settle on a silent, wide-eyed message for him to *shutttttt the fuckkkkkk uuppppp.*

When Liv finally lifts her head, her face is so red I can feel the heat radiating off her soft skin. I know it's soft because I brushed my fingers over it when I was snake-hips Santa and was allowed to touch her.

Snake-hips Santa. Fuck, that's a good nickname.

I have to tell her. I can't be her buddy Jonesy while I keep her in the dark about this. And I have no idea how she's gonna take it.

Oh my god, this is bad. This is incredible. This is *so bad.*

"Okay!" Liv claps her hands to get the table's attention. "To those of you who don't know me, I'm not usually like this. I don't get wild crushes on strangers! Yes, Luke Lawless has the most perfect body I've ever seen, and he moved it in ways that didn't seem human and that I thought about for days afterward, but it was a one-time thing, and I'm done."

"No more visits to the Crimson Lounge, huh?" Gabe's lips twitch as his eyes flick to me.

"*No,*" she says. "It's never happening again, and I'm going to change the passwords to all of CJ's streaming services as punishment for bringing this up in front of new people."

CJ shrugs unapologetically. "Sorry, love."

"So that's that!" Liv declares, holding her hands out in front of her like a crossing guard stopping traffic. "In a few weeks, I'll have my dream job at ThinkOutLoud Marketing in Boston, and I'll never think about snake-hips Santa again. Putting it behind me! Now, can somebody please change the subject?"

I run shaky fingers over my jaw. Change the subject? I want to hear more about the effects my perfect body has on

Liv. I want to hear *everything*. Does this mean she's touched herself while thinking about me? Did she end up tossing and turning in bed after watching me dance, and did she slide her fingers into her panties to find herself drenched? If so, did she draw it out, teasing herself to make the pleasure last as long as possible? Or did she work herself so hard and fast that she had to press her face into the pillow to keep her roommate from hearing her come? All because of me.

Well. Because of *him*. I've never felt more split between my two selves than I do right now, when the girl I'm crazy about has me friend-zoned but thinks Luke's her perfect guy.

Luke. Me. Him. Us.

Fuck, this is confusing.

"Ummmm..." Darby's sympathetic gaze lands on me briefly before she looks past me in search of a new topic. "Why is there zero Christmas in here?"

Liv laughs softly, gratefully. "Right? That's what I asked Jonesy." She nudges me with her shoulder, all buddy-buddy, and I force a smile.

"Since I've been here, nobody's bothered to decorate."

Liv shakes her head. "What a missed opportunity."

"Speaking of missing things." CJ checks her phone. "We should get out of here if you want to get changed before we see that movie and grab dinner." But instead of standing, she leans forward and peeks around Liv to give me a hard look. "Liv was right," she finally declares. "You're as cute as I remember."

"Oh my god." Liv snaps into her all-business mode and shoves her friend until they're both out of the booth. "Gabe, a pleasure. Darby, can I get your number from Jonesy so we can make plans for next week? And Jonesy, I'll see you tomorrow."

"Bye!" CJ calls as Liv tows her away. Then they're gone, and I'm left with two pairs of eyes boring into me.

"Well," Gabe says, "*that* was interesting."

"Fuck off," I mutter, watching enviously as he goes for a second helping of risotto. It's delicious, but I'm dancing tonight, so I can't indulge. "I'm the guy she complains about Christmas decorations with. He's the guy she gets off to."

"That's also you, sweetie," Darby says gently. "How does she not know that?"

"I didn't..." I jam my fingers in my hair in bewilderment. "I didn't know! I waited on them two weeks ago and thought Liv was completely..." I sigh, uncomfortable with talking about feelings quite this openly. "I wanted to follow her to her car and beg to drink her bathwater if she'd let me, okay? But I figured I'd never see her again, and then she turned up at the club that Saturday."

"How did she not recognize you?" Gabe asks around a mouthful of risotto. Lucky fucker.

"Santa hat and beard. Sunglasses. Dark lighting." I shrug. "And then she turned up here looking for a job without mentioning anything about Luke, and I figured she forgot all about him. Me. Whatever."

"So you're going to tell her now." Darby's telling, not asking.

"Hell. I guess so? I didn't mean to keep anything from her. I just figured she forgot all about him—uh, me—two seconds after she left the club. If I'd known she hadn't, I would've kept you two far away from her." I gesture to the spot next to me as if she were still sitting there. "She did say she was never going back, so maybe that's the last time she'll think about him. Um, me."

When Darby slants me a stern librarian look, Gabe steps in.

"He's kind of got a point. Wouldn't Jonesy's telling her just to clear his conscience actually make it weirder for her?"

And weirder for me. "Thing is," I say, "women who know me as a dancer first have all these... *ideas*. They want the crazy, no-inhibitions sex guy, and that's fun for a while, but it makes having an actual relationship impossible." I shrug uncomfortably. "A year ago, that wouldn't have bothered me as much. But if Liv finds out I'm Luke and she treats me like some kind of plaything..." I scrub my hand over my eyes, unwilling to look at them for this last bit. "I don't know if I can take it."

I realize Gabe and Darby have both frozen as I've been talking. Gabe recovers first. "An actual relationship?" he asks, his eyebrows practically touching his hairline.

Darby beams at me. "Oh honey, you like her!"

"Well, you've met her. How can I not?"

I've lived for every one of the slow smiles I've earned from her as I buzz by the hostess stand, saving up my best conversational nuggets just for her. Working with Liv is the most fun I've ever had at Verdant, and I don't want to risk all that by coming clean. But I also can't *not* tell her.

"Maybe it's moot," I say slowly. "She's leaving town in a few weeks, so it's not like we can actually be anything serious." If she was even interested in dating the funny-guy waiter she just met, which I'm sure she's not. "If she's really putting it behind her like she said, why tell her the truth and make her uncomfortable around me?"

It's a cop-out, but it's a cop-out that spares Liv from harm, so I'm going to embrace it.

Gabe wolfs down his final bite and pushes the plate away from him. "You know, if you were working with me, you wouldn't have any of these problems." He links his hands over his stomach and looks at me expectantly.

He wants me to quit dancing and quit my job here so I can work with him at the landscaping company. Hell, even though Darby likes to joke that HG stands for "hot guy," I know Gabe named it after the two of us.

Temptation rises hard and fast until I remember how easy it is for new businesses to fail in their first five years. So I tap into my most Jonesy self and shoot them a *no fucks given* smile, even though it hurts me to do it.

"Only one job, and I never have to lie about it? Where's the fun in that?"

Better they think I'm not willing to stop chasing thrills than the actual truth. I'm terrified about Gabe putting his trust in me. That I'll fuck it up and cost him and Darby their future. That my family's just started to rely on me, and I could let them down too. All my chatter at Liv the other day about being unreliable? I wasn't actually kidding. Ask anybody and they'll tell you. Wyatt's the good one, and Jonesy's the fuckup.

Well. My mom wouldn't say "fuckup," but we all know that Wyatt has the MBA and the Beamer and the boring fiancée. Me? I have the high school diploma and the job I won't talk about in front of my siblings and the string of two-week hookups who get off on screaming matches and tend to steal my shit when they finally leave.

"Seriously, you're doing great without me," I tell the man who foolishly wants to go into business with the guy who opened his first savings account last year. "Give it another planting season and see if you still need me on board."

His mouth tightens. "I'm not going to give up and hire somebody else."

"We'll see." I stand and grab our dishes, dumping them all on the tray. "Let me put this away so Samson has one less thing to yell about tomorrow."

I disappear into the kitchen to clean up all traces of our after-hours meal. When I emerge, Gabe's helping Darby into her coat, and as I walk them to the exit, Darby says, "Tomorrow? I thought you didn't work Sundays."

"Yeahhhhh, uhhh." Fuck it. Might as well pull off the Band-Aid. "Liv works Wednesday through Sunday, so I shifted my schedule to be on when she is." Before either of them can comment, I say, "Darryl asked me to train her, so I'm just following orders."

"Sure. Darryl." Gabe laughs as he escorts his wife through the door. "You've got it bad, buddy."

"You have no idea," I mutter as I wave at them through the glass and snap the lock shut. At least I've only got fourteen hours and one night of raunchy performances to get through until I can see her again.

SEVEN

Liv

The Crimson Lounge looks different at night.

The red neon sign promises sex and titillation and an escape from your boring, non-sexy life. It paints the brick around it with a lurid glow that spreads into the parking lot, and when I hesitate outside the entrance, it lights up CJ's hair like a candle.

"Well? This was your idea," she says impatiently, rubbing her hands over her arms since she refused to wear a coat over her cute pink dress. "Are we spending the rest of the night standing on asphalt?"

"Maybe." I fidget as I fight with myself one more time. Does being here make me a liar? I'd like to think it doesn't. I'd meant what I said this afternoon when I was about to go up in embarrassed flames in front of Jonesy and his friends. I had zero intention of coming back to the Crimson Lounge, ever. I thought snake-hips Santa could live in my memory as an impossibly perfect person I encountered in a rare moment when I ventured outside of my comfort zone, never to be tarnished by a second meeting.

Then CJ brought him up over risotto, and I haven't been able to stop thinking about him. His razor-sharp abs, the glistening sweat on his chest, that hint of a cocky smirk peeking through the fake beard covering most of his face. He lurked in my mind all the way through dinner and then the rom-com CJ and I caught. What would've happened if I'd wrapped my hand around the back of his neck or tugged on those white curls until I could see his lips? If I'd been braver, I'd know what his skin felt like under my hand. How hot? How hard? I missed my chance to find out.

Maybe that's why I blurted, "What if we popped by the strip club?" on the drive home. And my best friend being my best friend, CJ just grinned and swung her car into a wide U-turn at the next intersection. Now an hour later, here we are, and my stomach's a mess of excitement and butterflies and second thoughts.

"I'm not losing my mind, right?"

I didn't mean to say it out loud, but CJ just laughs and slides her arm through mine. "Lady, we're all mad here."

She flashes me her best Cheshire Cat grin, her teeth gleaming red under the neon, and it's so surreal that I give myself permission to descend into the madness with her.

"Okay. Let's do it."

CJ and I clear the mountainous bouncer, pay our cover fee, and venture into the lobby. True to the club's name, the carpeting, walls, and curtains are all shades of crimson. Like last time, a closed set of doors separates us from the main floor stage, and when they swing open to let a group of men swagger out, we're hit by a thunderclap of electronica and swirling lights and crowd sounds and alcohol fumes. But that's where the women dance, and the reason we're here is performing one floor up.

"Good evening," says a voice to our left. We turn to see a tall, stout man with a tidy white beard and a big smile. "Can I help you ladies find your way?"

"You bet!" CJ chirps. "Show us to the men."

A laugh booms out of him. "Right this way," he says, leading us toward the stairs to the second floor. "Is this your first visit?"

"We were here two weeks ago," I say with a sigh.

He looks over his shoulder, a quizzical expression on his ruddy face. "And why does that sound like a tragedy?"

"She's got the hots for your Santa," CJ says.

My groan's almost as loud as the man's laugh.

"Oh yes, Luke is very popular. The real Santa wishes he had moves like that."

"He's got snake hips." I swear I didn't mean to say that out loud, but that seems to be what happens when I set foot in this place.

Our guide shakes his head with a chuckle. "Snake hips. I like that." He pivots at the foot of the stairs and extends a big hand for me to shake. "I'm Nick, the owner."

"Oh, you're Jessica's husband!"

His smile brightens even more. "That I am. She's the very best part of me." He looks so besotted that my insides go all gooey, and judging by CJ's little sigh, my brash bestie feels the same.

"I'm wearing one of her fits right now," she confides, giving a little shimmy. Nick nods in approval, although his gaze doesn't stray below her chin.

"I'm so proud of what she's built," he says.

When I reply, "She sounded equally proud of you and

the club," he slaps his hand over his red-flannel-covered heart.

"Ah, my Jess."

His cheeks redden even more, and for some reason, Jonesy pops into my mind. When the waitstaff were discussing their weekend plans during the downtime between breakfast and lunch today, Jonesy was tight-lipped about his, saying only that he had "a thing" tonight. Everybody else shrugged it off like that was par for the course, but it left me curious. Was his "thing" a date? He'd made a point of telling me that he doesn't do girlfriends, but now I'm wondering what kind of woman would make him smile the way Nick does when he talks about Jessica. Who would he choose to be the recipient of all that effortless charm? For all I know, he actually *is* on a date tonight. Whoever she is, I think I hate her a little, this imaginary woman I've built up in my head.

I blink back to the present to see Nick waiting patiently for me to head up the stairs after CJ.

"Oh, um, thank you," I gather myself enough to say. "And I swear I know it's all fantasy and Luke is a professional, and I'm not going to make it weird or anything."

He bends close and taps the side of his nose. "We're all about making fantasies real here. Don't apologize for enjoying it." Then he straightens and gestures up the stairs. With a murmured thanks, I start to ascend, almost giddy with anticipation for my next run-in with Luke.

Jonesy

The jingle of dog collars is the only warning I get before Donnie and Vix burst into the dressing room. I immediately drop to my knees, grateful I'm still in jeans as dogs the size of small ponies dig their claws into my thighs and jockey for position on my lap.

"Hey, boy! Hey, girl!" I squeeze my eyes shut as they lick sloppy kisses all over my face. "Where's your dad?"

Nick and his wife own a half dozen enormous brown mutts, and he generally brings at least one with him to the club on Saturdays.

"Here!" my boss calls, wheezing a little as he fills the doorway. The club owner's always slow on the stairs up to the third-floor room where the male dancers get ready for their performances.

"Gotta lay off the sweet stuff, old man," I joke. All of us like to tease him about his fondness for any type of baked good, and like always, Nick just slaps his ample belly with a laugh.

"Never. Not even for your snake hips."

"What?" I snap my head up from where I've been nuzzling Vix's broad brown head. "What did you say?"

"Snake hips. It's how one of our guests tonight described you when she asked for you by name."

Frustrated at being ignored, Donnie headbutts me, and I'm so distracted by what Nick's just said that it knocks me flat on my ass.

"Did she... was she..." I'm sprawled on the floor, looking up at the big man helplessly, not sure what to ask first. "What name did she use?"

"Luke," he quickly reassures me. "She's a particular fan of Luke's, it seems."

"Does she have"—my lungs compress at the thought—"long reddish-brown hair?"

Not to mention the sweetest smile and the prettiest eyes and the quickest brain. But Nick doesn't need the full list of Liv's best qualities.

"She does," he confirms. At his words, my muscles give out entirely, and I end up flat on my back, staring at the water-stained tile ceiling while two horse-dogs climb all over me.

"That's Liv," I say. "I think I love her."

Nick chuckles, and I shove Donnie's big ol' paw off my chest so I can sit up.

"No, seriously, she's classy and smart and funny, and she works with me at the restaurant, but she doesn't know what I do here, and I..." I shake my head. "I haven't figured out how to tell her yet. And she's *here* tonight?"

Nick nods, and I curse, glancing wildly around the dressing room.

"She can't find out like this." I plunge my fingers into my hair, which is stiff with the darkening gel I borrowed from Ben to try out. But that and my sunglasses aren't enough to hide who I am from her.

"Do the whole night as Santa," Nick says immediately. "Wear the hat and beard."

"You don't mind?" The holiday part's only supposed to take up the first half of the show, and then it'd be me and my sunglasses onstage for the rest of the night. The thought has me curling in on myself in horror at Liv finding out this way.

"'Tis the season," Nick says. "I'll give Eugenio a heads-up for music cues, and then I'll see if Miss Liv might prefer a VIP table that's a little farther from the stage just to be safe."

"Thank you." I clamber to my feet. "And I swear, I'm

going to tell her. I didn't think she'd come back, but now that she has..."

"I know you'll do the right thing," Nick says. "You're a good man."

He disappears before I can correct him, leaving me frantic to cover as much of my face as I possibly can before setting foot onstage.

How can I describe the exquisite torture of dancing for Liv without actually dancing for Liv?

From the moment I step in front of the crowd, I'm hyperaware of the fact that she's out there somewhere, her eyes following the lines of my body as I move. I'm not sure what exactly Nick did, but the stage lights are lower tonight and dominated by blues and greens and reds instead of bright white, which illuminate our bodies while keeping our faces slightly more obscured.

It makes me brave enough to perform like I usually do, full out, holding nothing back, moving without concern for my muscles and ligaments and joints. I know for a fact that my audience loves those fluid motions, that they're wild with curiosity about whether my moves are equally smooth in bed. They are, of course. And as eager as I used to be to show them off to a chosen woman after a show, it's been ages since I had that urge.

Tonight, though, I'm nothing but *want*, and it's all for Liv. My face may be hidden, but with every slide of my hips and undulation of my torso, I'm telling her how good I'd make it for her. How I'd use my body to worship hers. How I'd ruin her for any other men.

But the crowd doesn't know that. Each person

squirming in their seat thinks I'm dancing for *them*, and I'm glad of it. I may be thinking about one person, but I'm here for all of them, teasing and grinning, focusing on the tables ringing the stage. Judging by the screams and the bills being tossed my way, it's working.

I do eventually spot her and CJ at a table that's dead center and halfway back in the crowd. CJ's waving her arms over her head, screaming her approval, but Liv... she's lost in me. Even through the dark lenses of my sunglasses, I can see the haziness in her eyes, the way her tongue darts out to moisten her lower lip. It makes my movements even more sexual as I picture that tongue exploring my mouth, my chest, my cock. I almost groan onstage at the thought of my gingerbread angel falling under my spell.

I'm practically in a fugue state when I stumble offstage after my first set, but Deke snaps me out of it by dramatically fanning himself.

"Dude, I think you got *me* pregnant with that."

"Ha." I snatch the towel he holds out and yank off the hat, beard, and sunglasses to mop myself off.

"You got a girl out there or something?" He chuckles at the thought of it, then breaks off when he notices my stricken expression. "Oh shit, *do* you? You got a girl, Jonesy?"

"No." I chuck the towel into the hamper that sits backstage for that exact purpose. "I mean, there's a girl, but she's not..." I gesture helplessly, not sure what to say or how to describe this woman who has me twisted into knots at both of my jobs.

"Ah." Deke nods. He gets it, how fucking hard it can be to balance what we do with maintaining a new relationship. "Lemme know if I can help."

I grimace. "Just be cool with me wearing this shitty

beard all night. And for god's sake, don't call me Jonesy around her."

"I would never." He drops his Diesel grin to cross his thick index finger over his heart in a *hope-to-die* promise. "You ready to get back out there?"

I know I can't have Liv tonight, which means I'm going to need so much brown liquor to calm down after the show. But until then, I have a performance to give, even if the thought leaves me feeling exhausted and a little empty.

I push the weird mood aside and tug my sweat-damp Santa hat back on.

"Hell yeah, I am." I readjust the itchy monstrosity around my ears and over my chin and head back onstage. I may not get to take Liv home, but I'll make goddamn sure she thinks about me when she's finally alone tonight.

EIGHT

Liv

The only person less awake than me this morning is Jonesy.

"Are you gonna make it?" I ask the lump of humanity that is everyone's favorite coworker. He's on the break room floor, propped against the wall of lockers with his limbs sprawled out like they aren't functioning yet.

All he manages in response is a grunt.

"Should we be worried?" I ask June when she bustles in to hang her coat and bag in her locker. Last Sunday Jonesy was a little sluggish for the first hour of service, but today is something else entirely. Heck, CJ and I were at the Crimson Lounge until super late last night, yet compared to Jonesy, I look ready to win the Boston Marathon.

"Nah." She spares Jonesy a glance. "He doesn't usually work Sundays, but when he does, it takes a while before he's fully human."

The husk of a person who used to be Jonesy grumbles, "My ears still work, y'know."

"Then make better weekend choices," June says with no trace of sympathy.

I squat next to him, careful to tuck my skirt under my knees so I don't accidentally give him a show.

"I think you need this more than I do." I press my ginormous, mostly full cup of gas station coffee into his hands, and he accepts it with another grunt. Then he lifts it to his lips and drains it in a series of greedy swallows that June and I watch in both horror and amazement. When it's empty, he drops the cup on the linoleum next to him and sucks in a long, ragged breath.

"Feel better?" June asks.

"I think," he says, lifting his head for the first time, "I'll survive the day." His eyes are slits against the harsh overhead lights, and his jaw is stubbled. I tell myself I don't actually want to run my fingers over it to feel the bristles against my skin.

"Well, thank god for that," June says. "Haunted section's yours."

She bustles out, ignoring Jonesy's cry of "Hey, no fair!"

When he looks up at me helplessly, I stand and hold out my hand to haul him to his feet. He rises in a surprisingly graceful motion for someone so clearly hungover, but he groans and clutches his head once he's fully upright, leaning against me for support. It's all I can do not to wrap my arm around his waist and pepper him with a million questions about what—or let's be honest, *who*—he did last night. Instead of doing either of those things though, I say, "Someday, one of you has *got* to tell me what makes that section haunted."

"Cold spots. Silverware that rolls off the table when nobody's touching it." His voice is a croak, but his gaze is slightly more alert. "A pervasive sense of doom."

"I thought the pervasive sense of doom was the whole restaurant," I say lightly.

"Right, right. My mistake."

I watch as the rest of his brain starts to come online, and as the animation returns to his face, so does a flicker of wariness.

"Everything okay?" I ask.

He blinks, then nods jerkily. "Yeah. Uh, yeah." As he turns to his locker to grab his service apron, he says, "Everything good with you?"

He tilts his head to watch me out of the corner of his eye, and I glance away so he won't see the color creeping into my cheeks.

"Of course!" Just a relaxing evening watching my new sexual fantasy bring a roomful of women to their knees and then a restless night dreaming about him doing the same thing to me in my bedroom.

Jonesy looks up after securing the strings around his waist and offers me a tired smile. "Okay." His gaze moves over my face, and he apparently sees what he wanted to see because the tension in his shoulders falls away. "Okay," he says again. "Let's do it."

He holds up his fist for a knuckle bump, which I deliver even though it's a bro-y, buddy-buddy gesture that makes me die a little inside. I need the reminder that he's like this with everybody, not just me. But at least being around Jonesy makes snake-hips Santa recede into the background, which I'm grateful for.

When the doors open for the day, I watch with interest as a subdued Jonesy works his tables. He's so... normal. There's no joking, no wild flirting with the old ladies, no origami napkin art.

"It's spooky, right?" Marcus says as he pauses at the

hostess stand, nodding toward Jonesy. He's frowning as he writes down an order for the family of five fueling up before a Christmas tree-buying expedition.

"Right? What on earth was he doing last night?"

Marcus laughs. "With Jonesy, who knows. An orgy? All-night video games? A midnight yacht cruise on Lake Michigan where he was the one driving the yacht?" He wiggles his bushy black brows at me. "The world may never know."

Three hours later, I can tell things are getting back to normal when I lead a group of teenagers in church clothes to the three tables we've pushed together in Ariel's section, and I find Jonesy juggling spoons for a quartet of forty-something women on their third mimosas.

I drift closer to watch, as enraptured by the sight of a hot guy tossing and catching cutlery as the guests are.

"You ladies didn't know you'd be getting dinner with a show, did you?" I say over Jonesy's shoulder. He glances back at me with a glint in his eyes.

"It's like you're new here," he says, effortlessly switching from the smooth toss pattern to a two-up, one-down rhythm. After a beat he catches the first and second spoons in his right hand and launches the third one into the air in a tall arc. With a wink to the table, he thrusts his left hip forward and pulls his apron pocket open, neatly catching it as it tumbles back to earth. The women loudly applaud the perfect catch, and he gives a little bow.

"I'll be right back with your mimosas," he says, and the two of us walk off to the sound of flustered, girlish giggles.

I shake my head when we reach the hostess stand. "Is all of that on purpose?"

"All of what?"

"The flirting. The nonstop charm. The... the juggling!"

I wave my arms. "The whole making-people-blush-and-stammer thing."

His brow creases. "I guess I don't really think about it. That's just how I am, and it's good for tips." Then one side of his mouth quirks up. "But when I waited on you, I was making an effort."

This stops me cold. "An effort to what?"

He leans close. "To make you blush." His voice drops to a whisper. "And it worked."

"It... why would... oh," I say faintly. Dammit. Now I'm the one blushing and stammering and confused about what he thinks about me.

"What'd I tell you? Unpredictable. Can't be trusted." This time I'm the object of that cocky wink. "That's me."

At the end of the day, I'm pulling on my coat and preparing to head out when Jonesy catches me.

"Is CJ picking you up?"

"Nope. She let me take her car this morning."

He nods, looking unusually serious. "Mind if I walk out with you?"

"Sure." Weird that he'd be so formal about it, but I'm happy to wait while he tosses his apron into his locker and pulls on his puffer coat. It's the first day of December, and central Illinois decided to remind us that it can, in fact, get cold here. Not Canada cold, but I'm glad I grabbed a hat and mittens this morning.

We call goodbye to the last of the waitstaff and head out the back to the staff parking lot. The late afternoon air cuts right through my coat, and I edge closer to Jonesy, not-so-subtly using him as a windbreak.

"So what's CJ up to today that she loaned you her car?"

"Probably still in bed," I say. "We, uh, had a late night last night."

His eyes cut to mine. "Oh yeah?"

Hell. I'm about to be stupidly honest. "Yeah. We kiiiind of ended up at the Crimson Lounge last night."

We've reached CJ's car, and I unlock the door and fling my purse inside, grabbing my phone as I do and opening the email app to have an excuse not to meet his eye. But all he says is a mild, "Hmm."

"Snake-hips Santa was as spectacular as I remembered," I confess, keeping my gaze pinned to the new emails popping into my inbox. It feels right to confess since he was there yesterday for the start of it, but I'm still a little embarrassed that my crush knows about my other crush.

"Actually," he says, "I wanted to talk to you about—"

"Shit," I gasp. Tears rush to my eyes, making it hard to see the screen. But I don't need to see the email again to confirm what I just read. "Shit!"

"What's wrong?" Jonesy sounds alarmed as he steps close and rests his hands on my shoulders, his gaze wildly sweeping the parking area behind me for threats. "Who do I need to fight?" Then his hands fall away, and he takes a step back. "Unless this is about last night?"

"What?" I press the top of my right mitten underneath one eye and then the other, trying to keep the tears from falling and ruining my mascara. "No."

I blink away the last of the moisture in my eyes and see a stricken expression on his face, so I thrust my phone at him where the words are still visible on the screen. *We regret to inform you that the position you applied for has been filled. Thank you for your interest and...* Blah, blah.

"So much for my dream job," I say dully.

A breath rushes out of him, and this time he wraps his arms around me, pulling me into a hug. "Boston?"

I nod against this chest, too upset about the news to fully appreciate the fact that *Jonesy is hugging me.*

"Fucking Boston," he seethes. "They're idiots for not choosing you."

I give a watery laugh. "You have no idea whether I'm good at my job."

"Of course you're good at your job." He pulls me tight to rest his chin on top of my head. "You're great at your job. Any job you want, you'd crush it."

I relax against his chest, marveling at how good it feels to just rest there for a second while he rubs soothing circles on my back. I even let my hands wrap around his waist so he can squeeze me tighter. We stand like that for a few minutes even though it's cold and my feet ache—and if mine ache, I'm sure his ache twice as much. He hums a mindless little tune and rocks me back and forth like I'm a little kid.

Eventually he breaks our hug, but he only pulls back far enough to rub his thumb along the edge of my cheek. He's not wearing gloves, and his skin is cold and a little rough. I want to turn my head and catch the tip of that finger between my teeth, to pull it into my mouth and suck it. But I don't, and eventually he lets his hand fall away.

"Gonna be okay?"

I nod. "Yes. Thank you. I just can't believe all of this is happening because I trusted a friend from college."

Jonesy tilts his head in the universal gesture of *please explain*, and I say, "The guy in Canada who set me up for all the crimes? We were tight in college, and he aggressively recruited me to come work for him. And then he destroyed my life. As if I didn't have enough trust issues with men."

I laugh like it's funny when it's really not, and judging

by Jonesy's wince, he doesn't think so either. It also reminds me that I completely cut him off earlier. "Sorry, you were going to tell me something before, and I interrupted you. What's up?"

He steps all the way away, leaving me cold.

"You know what, it doesn't matter." He shoves his hands in his pockets and hunches his shoulders. "I'm sorry about the Boston job. And Canada. And your former friend."

"Already forgotten." Even though I give a toss-away flick of my hand like I'm throwing out the bad news, my stomach still churns from the rejection. "I mean, who wants to live in Massachusetts anyway? Not me." And as the words come out of my mouth, I realize it's actually kind of true. I enjoyed my time in Phoenix, and I sure as hell didn't want to be rejected for the Boston job, but I'm a Midwest-erner at heart. My parents still live in the Indianapolis suburb where I grew up, and finding a job near cows and cornfields might soothe my soul in a way I didn't know I needed until I spent time in Beaucoeur.

"So, what now?"

The parking lot lights cast a yellow glow over both of us, and while I'm scared to consider how sallow and haggard it likely makes me look, it's somehow flattering to the man standing just out of arm's reach. Good bone structure is its own reward, I guess.

But we're focused on my struggling career. "I'm talking to a couple other agencies and have a great lead in Portland."

"Maine or Oregon?"

"Oregon. They loved the stop-motion recycling PSA I did with actual scrap metal from a junkyard last year. Plus, a couple of former clients have reached out about freelance work." I shrug, putting on a brave face. "I'll find something by the time Brita's back."

Because I'm leaving and the real Verdant hostess is coming back and none of this really matters. Not this confusing interlude or the questions I'm now asking about whether Jonesy and I are buddies or something a little more.

"No girl fights over the hostess stand, no matter how much Rob would enjoy it," he says with a carefree Jonesy smile that tips the balance back toward friend territory.

"No girl fights," I repeat. Then my stupid mouth opens up and says, "Hey, we've both got the next two days off." *Ask me to hang out with you outside of work.*

"Two whole days. Can't wait." His gaze holds mine for a beat before he blinks away. "See you Wednesday, Livvie-Liv."

It's an obvious blow-off, and it stings more than the rejection from the Boston job, which says everything about my messed-up priorities right now.

"See you Wednesday," I mutter, but he's already striding to his truck.

On the way back to CJ's, I'm thinking about how many marshmallows I can cram into the oversized mug of hot chocolate I'm planning to make as soon as I'm changed into sweats and a hoodie. If I can't have Jonesy and I can't have Santa Luke and I can't have my dream job, at least I can have that.

NINE

Jonesy

I'm still pissed at myself and pissed at those idiots in Boston as I pull up to Deke's place.

"You're late!" he yells from his ancient Range Rover, so I take my sweet time jumping out of my truck, grabbing my bag, and sauntering over to him.

"Oh sorry, are you in a hurry to get somewhere?" I toss my shit in the back and climb into the passenger seat. He responds by grumbling as he guns it down his driveway so we can zip across town to pick up Ben and Landon. We're performing a stripped-down—bad joke—version of our holiday show at one of the Chicago clubs tonight, then sticking around for a private show on Monday. We stand to make decent cash as out-of-towners in the area, especially since we're saving money by crashing with some of the dancers we've gotten to know up there thanks to these occasional talent swaps.

But any excitement I felt at the earning potential over the next few days is dead and gone thanks to the hurt expression on Liv's face when I blew her off. She took me completely by surprise when she hinted at a hangout during our days off, and instead of coming up with literally any semi-plausible excuse for why I couldn't—working a side catering gig, helping a friend move, visiting my nana in the nursing home, robbing a bank—my brain panicked and started playing "Jingle Bell Rock" on a loop. Running away was the worst possible thing I could've done, but it's exactly what happened. She'll probably never ask me to hang out again, which is just fucking great.

That fuckup plus the fact that I haven't figured out a way to tell her about the whole *I'm actually Luke Lawless and had no idea until recently that I should probably tell you* thing means my brain's too busy to let me grab the nap I'd been counting on during the almost three-hour drive. After the show last night and my Verdant shift this morning, I desperately needed one in order to be the best Santa I can be for the good people of Chicago.

I'm still feeling shitty as we're warming up in the dressing room at Wild Nights Chicago when Landon asks, "You really sticking with the hat and beard all night, brother?" He pulls his right knee up to his chest and twists to limber up his hammy, repeating the motion with the left leg. The kid talks like a perma-stoned landlocked surfer, but he's actually a physics major at Rayman College.

"Yep." I squirt another palmful of oil into my hand and smooth it onto my chest. "It's part of the costume now."

"Haven't you heard?" Deke steps in front of the mirror to check his dick placement behind the polar bear nose on his thong. "Jonesy's got a girl who doesn't know he dances."

"No shit?" Ben's head pops up from the suitcase he's crouched behind, the bells on his elf vest jingling.

"She's not my girl," I say irritably.

"But you don't want her to find out that you dance." Deke nods at his reflection and pulls on the white sweats he'll be stripping off momentarily.

"When's the last time Luke Lawless gave a shit what a woman thinks about him?" Ben chortles.

"Actually," Landon says, his brow furrowed in thought, "when's the last time Luke picked a Lady Lawless to entertain after a show?"

"Or *during* a show. He really must have a girl." Ben holds up a hand, and Landon slaps him a high five.

"Jesus Christ, just fuck off about it," I snap, and all three of them fall into shocked silence. I press my thumb to the spot between my eyebrows where a headache's starting to form.

"Sorry," I say in a more normal tone. "I had to blow her off when she asked if I wanted to hang tomorrow, and it killed me that I couldn't tell her why."

"Sucks, dude." Landon pulls me into a bro hug. "Mega sucks."

"Yeah, man, I'm sure she understands," Ben adds, slapping my back.

I'm sure she doesn't, but I appreciate their support. "Thanks, fellas," I manage.

"You wanna hit this?" Landon holds up his vape, and when I shake my head, he and Ben wander off to discuss their plans for tomorrow's bachelorette party.

Deke sidles up to me once they're gone. "Sorry to give you shit. I didn't know all that."

"S'okay. I'll figure out some way to make it up to her." If

she's willing to talk to me again, that is. "Thing is, we've been hanging out at work a lot, and I just found out that she's a really big fan of Luke. And like, I've either got to leave her alone entirely or I've got to tell her that's me. But how am I supposed to do that without making things weird?"

Deke winces. "Tough. But if she takes it bad when you tell her, at least you know she's not worth the trouble."

"Yeah. Maybe."

We fall silent as we watch Ben and Landon drop to the floor in what seems to be a push-up competition.

"Were we ever that young?"

"I don't think so." I turn thirty next month, and I've never felt older than I do right now as I listen to those two not-quite-legal-to-drink boys hold themselves in plank position as they debate how many bridesmaids they can hook up with tomorrow. There was a time when I might've joined them, but not now. Not after the year I've had.

As if he's reading my mind, Deke asks, "How's your mom doing?"

"She's good. Her doctor says her new liver's fully regenerated." I keep my answer short because the whole subject still makes me overly emotional.

"And Wyatt?"

I clench my jaw so hard it creaks. "Saint Wyatt's fine." That answer's even shorter but for a very different reason.

"You're doing your part," Deke says quietly. "And speaking of..."

He gestures toward the stage entrance, and I exhale hard. "Yep. Let's go make some money." We walk out together, and I add, "But I'll leave the bachelorette hookups to you guys."

y phone starts blowing up on the drive back to Beaucoeur on Tuesday morning. It's like Deke asking about my brother summoned him from whatever demon dimension he occupies when he's not making my life hell with his perfection. Of course, he's desperate to talk to me after I've had a particularly exhausting weekend earning money one dollar bill at a time. Since I'm at the wheel while everybody else sleeps it off, I don't feel even a tiny bit bad blowing off his pissy messages demanding that I call him.

Where I go wrong is not texting him back once I'm at home. But all I want to do is collapse and shut off my brain until my Verdant shift tomorrow morning. Last night's bachelorette party was even wilder than I expected, and yeah sure, I came home with bundles of cash, but I don't know if I can keep doing this for much longer. I fucking loved the promise—hell, the *expectation*—of easy sex at these private parties during my first couple of years dancing. But recently, I'm barely tolerating it and have gotten good at saying a polite no to the birthday girl who offers a mid-party blowjob or the partygoer begging for a hookup in the next room. I'll leave the public blowies and anonymous encounters to Ben and Landon and even Deke when he's in the mood. Christ, maybe it's time to leave the whole thing to Ben and Landon and Deke. I still love being onstage. It's the rest of it that's losing its shine.

Rather than dwell on that depressing thought—because who am I if I'm not the wild and crazy guy who shakes his dick for a living?—I stretch out on the couch with my slow-as-shit laptop to read up on a radio story I caught the tail end of as we swung around Joliet. I locate it within a few clicks and give it a read.

"I'll be damned," I murmur when I'm done. Knowing full well that it's going to please him way too much, I shoot Gabe a text.

> dude, did you know we're in climate zone 6a now?

His reply zips back immediately.

> yep, climate change is wild

Of course, he couldn't leave well enough alone and follows up with,

> i'll consider this your application to HG Landscaping. you're hired, start date Jan 2

I snort and toss my phone aside. But instead of rejecting the thought outright, I let myself imagine it. Working with Gabe at the business. He has the plant know-how, and I have the eye for texture and placement. We work great together, and he really was busier than he could handle this past summer. I like physical work, and I like being out in the sun with dirt under my fingernails. Plus, I could ease back on my workouts and clean eating if I wasn't mostly naked onstage every Saturday. I don't hate the thought of that.

Then another one intrudes. Would Liv be happy dating a landscaper? I picture her in one of her classy hostess dresses that skim her curves and hit her just above those fucking hot knee-length boots she loves. She always wears small, expensive-looking gold earrings, and no matter how early in the morning she shows up at Verdant, her hair's sleek and perfect. Even if she was planning to live in Beaucoeur permanently, which she's definitely not, I'd just mess her up in every sense of the word.

"Fucking pathetic," I mutter. "And talking to yourself too. Jesus."

Annoyed at my moping, I roll off the couch, grab the medicine ball I keep in the corner of the living room, and push myself through my most grueling ab workout. Twice. When my brain is nothing but goo and my body is nothing but sweat and screaming muscles, I drag my carcass to the shower, then drag my now-clean carcass into the kitchen to scarf down a chicken breast and some brown rice. Then I head to bed.

The last thought I have before I fall asleep is the question Ben and Landon were debating on Sunday. How long have I been living like a monk? And more importantly, is it really such a bad thing?

The question dogs my steps at Verdant the next morning. Who I was. Who I am. Who I want to be.

Then the person I *never* want to be comes stalking through the door.

"Oh shi—shoot." I shove my order pad into my apron pocket and flash a hasty apology smile at the mother/daughter duo whose order I was halfway through taking. "Excuse me, ladies. I'll be right back with you." Then I hustle to the hostess stand, where my fucking brother's glowering at Liv.

"I'm sorry, but he's in the middle of service at the moment." She's cool and professional, and I love her for not backing down as his expression darkens.

"Like I said"—Wyatt frowns harder—"I just need a quick word with my brother."

"If you'd be willing to—"

"What do you want, Wy?" I ask tiredly, not even concerned that I've interrupted Liv's attempts to shield me.

"I want to know why your Instagram is full of you posing with party girls." He brandishes his phone. "You promised you'd take this seriousl—"

With a hiss, I grab his arm and drag him out of the dining room, through the kitchen, and into the back parking lot. Once we're safely out of earshot of any of my coworkers, most especially Liv, I drop his arm like it burned me.

"What the fuck are you talking about?"

"Check." He sets his jaw and folds his arms over his chest, waiting for me to jump and obey. It's the last thing I want to do, but I have to know what I've been tagged in on Instagram. With dread bubbling in my guts, I pull out my phone and thumb open the app.

"Oh god, this?" Relief trickles through my veins. These pics are from Sunday night when we crashed at Robyn and Pammy's. It's me nursing a beer on a couch sandwiched between the two dancers, and another of me laughing with Pammy and a few of the other women from Wild Nights Chicago who hung out for a bit after the show. "This is nothing."

But it could've been *bad*. For a heart-stopping second, I was convinced I'd open IG to see my personal account tagged with pics of me in the Santa thong, or worse, me in the background looking pained as Ben was getting blown by one of the bridesmaids in the middle of the bachelorette party.

"You told me you were going to stop fucking around and take care of Christmas," Wyatt growls.

"I *am* doing Christmas." I shove my phone back into my

pocket. "This isn't fucking around. It's how I'm paying for it."

Wyatt's lips compress. *This year changed both of us and not for the better.* I wanted nothing more than to be the living donor for Mom's transplant, but Saint Wyatt was the only one whose blood type matched. So not only did my investment banker brother pour his savings into paying down the medical bills that Mom's insurance didn't cover, but he also took a month off work for the procedure, then another month when the incision site developed an infection. Meanwhile, the brother who bounces from job to job was forced to watch as two of the people he loves the most in the world went under the knife. That's why I'm the one who's goddamn making Christmas happen for the family this year, no matter how much Wyatt tries to bully his way in and take over.

"If you'd just text me back, I wouldn't have to track you down." He rubs a hand over his brow, fatigue lines bracketing his mouth.

And there's the guilt again. I was ignoring his texts because I don't like jumping when he summons me or fighting to convince him that he can count on me to do the shopping for everyone. Wy's never been the most easygoing guy, but the slower-than-expected recovery's been frustrating for him. He's thinner than he was before the surgery, and his mood is consistently shitty these days, especially when it comes to me. It's like the doctors took the last of his good moods when they took that chunk of his liver.

He bled on an operating table while you were a glorified babysitter in the waiting room, my brain whispers. *Be a little patient.*

Fucking brain.

"Sorry, Wy. I'll text back next time."

His curt "Thanks" is the most positive exchange we've had in forever. Might as well try to keep it going.

"Do you wanna stay for lunch?" It's the best olive branch I can offer. "My treat." His eyes slide to the door into the restaurant, and I sweeten the deal. "I know you love the burger here."

His nostrils flare, and he shakes his head. "Thanks, but I've got to get back to the bank." Then he narrows his eyes. "Do you swear you've got gifts under control? Because I can—"

"I've got it," I growl, patience gone. He nods in acknowledgment, but at least we walk back into Verdant much more calmly than we left it.

"There is one gift I'm stuck on, though," I say as we hustle through the kitchen, where Samson looks ready to strangle me. "Where can I buy you a whole new personality?"

Wyatt surprises me by tossing his head back in laughter. It's been way too long since I heard that from him. Irresponsible Jonesy acted like a clown until his super-serious brother broke and laughed. The natural order has been restored.

He's still chuckling when we reach Liv's station. She straightens up, clearly curious about what went down outside.

"Please be cool," I mutter to Wyatt. Then I turn to Liv. "Olivia, let me officially introduce you to my brother. Try to be nice. It's not his fault I got all the brains in the family."

That asshole gives her his best broody smolder as they shake hands. "Wyatt Jones. And I apologize for my brother. It was hard for him, growing up knowing I'm the handsome one."

Liv's eyes dart from him to me, and although her lips

twitch, she's all business as she returns his handshake. "Liv Fielding, brains *and* looks."

"You're not wrong," Wyatt says, and I watch in horror as his eyes sweep down her body. "So I haven't seen you around. Are you new—hey!"

"Wyatt's got to go," I call over my shoulder as I haul my brother toward the exit. "Dude. Did you forget about Reese?"

"Broke up," he says tersely.

I stop dead in my tracks, blocking an older couple from the entrance. Now Wyatt's the one pulling me out of the way.

"I'm so sorry, Wy. What happened?" And what the hell kind of person am I that I didn't know my brother broke up with his fiancée?

He shrugs. "It's been a shitty year."

"You said it." We fall silent, and I realize we're both doing the famous Jones stance—hands in pockets, heads down, shoulders hunched like vultures. I straighten. "Still good for Golfmas on the fifteenth?"

"Wouldn't miss it," he says, and I rub my chest where a knot of anxiety just vanished. We've done nothing but snarl at each other recently, but I'm so fucking glad my big brother isn't going to skip our Christmas tradition. "Now about that new hostess—"

"Dude, I'll remove the rest of your liver with my bare hands."

When his mouth flops open like a koi fish, it occurs to me that I may have made a mistake by joking about the thing that threw his whole life in turmoil. Then another laugh bursts out of him and I can breathe again.

"You're getting territorial over a woman? She must be something else."

"She is, not that you're ever going to find out." I give him a not-so-gentle shove away from the restaurant, which earns me another brotherly laugh. By the time he's safely in his car and out of Liv's sight line, I feel better than I have in ages. I love my brother even when I want to strangle him, and if that doesn't sum up family, I don't know what does.

TEN

Liv

I'm turning circles around the living room like a tiger in a tiny cage when CJ emerges from her office.

"Hey." She flops down onto the couch. "I'm finally dunzo with my workweek."

"Yay," I say flatly, not bothering to point out that it's Saturday night. CJ's already aware that she has a weird work/life balance.

"What's up with you?"

I stalk around the room one more time. "Portland hired someone else."

"What? Why am I just finding out about this now?" CJ's outraged. "Always pull me away from work to tell me when we have a new enemy!"

"And interrupt you coordinating your network of international assassins?" Look at me, still able to joke about my best friend's mysterious job in my moment of professional crisis.

She rolls her eyes. "I've told you a million times, corporate consulting involves surprisingly few murders." Then she waves a hand for me to continue.

"I was a great fit. My portfolio's exactly what they said they were looking for. Lots of practical effects and mixed media. And one of the VPs there mentored my boss in Phoenix back in the day, and I know she gave me a good reference."

"So you think the problem was...?"

"Richie!" I'm shouting and waving my arms now. Just a model of calm and collected. "I think they're Googling me and seeing the news stories, or I dunno, he's somehow sending them terrible recommendations from his holding cell." I point a finger at her before she can shoot that idea down. "He's a bad man, Charlotte Jane. He'd figure out a way to do it."

She bobs her head in agreement. "I'm sure he would," she says soothingly.

"It's like my Canadian perp walk is never going to stop," I say in a small voice, sinking to the couch. "I cannot believe Richie did this to me."

I'm not crying—I'm too mad to cry—but CJ pulls me into a hug and strokes my hair like my mom used to when I was a kid overwhelmed with the unfairness of life. Slowly, everything in me starts to unclench.

"We'll figure it out," CJ says once the last of my tension dissolves from my limbs. "You said you had a good lead in Minneapolis, right?"

"A former boss there, yeah. We're talking next week."

"And if that doesn't work out—which it will, obviously —but if it doesn't, then you can reach out to former clients about freelance opportunities. You love those shoestring budget projects."

"True." I sniffle and try to join CJ in seeing the bright

side. "That meal kit company I worked with last year already dropped me a line about creating some Instagram ads for them."

"See?" CJ says. "You got this."

Unfortunately, bringing up Instagram reminds me of my other grievance with today.

I poke at a hole in the cuff of my wallowing sweatshirt and say casually, "Do you think Jonesy's out with that girl tonight?"

After listening to the start of his fight with his brother on Wednesday, I may have done a tiny bit of digging. Turns out, his account was easy to find once I tracked down Darby and scrolled through her feed until I saw him laughing at a grill with Gabe during a cookout this summer. And then I regretted it immediately when I followed his tag and saw the pictures Wyatt was upset about.

Jonesy spends a lot of time surrounded by very hot, very young women. This weekend in particular, he seemed to mostly be in the company of a gorgeous twenty-something blonde with the biggest blue eyes I've ever seen. If that's who he's slinging his arm around during a house party, what use does he have for a thirty-two-year-old unemployed ad exec? No wonder he blew me off when I tried to ask if he wanted to hang out.

CJ doesn't answer because there really isn't a good response to "is my hot coworker out with an equally hot girl tonight?" Instead, she props her feet on the coffee table and rolls her head to face me.

"Know what might make you feel better?"

"Have Richie arrested by the Mexican authorities too? Go for a North American sweep?"

"That's plan B."

"Hmm," I say. "It's Saturday night."

CJ's cheek is squished against the back of the couch, which makes her delighted smile lopsided. "Why, yes, it is!"

"So we're thinking snake-hips Santa, right?" I ask.

"I'm like a proud mama right now." She pretends to wipe away a tear. "Look at this personal growth. From *oh no, no, don't take me to see hot men prance naked onstage* to *I will have my revenge on unworthy men with a very worthy stripper.*"

"Would we call that personal growth?"

"Think about it while you're changing into something cute. I'm taking you to dinner, and then we're going to North Village and I'm buying you a private dance from Luke Lawless."

"Oka—what?"

CJ's still listing the pros of a private dance as we cross the North Village town limits.

"It'll be fun. You deserve fun."

"I do deserve fun." I was convinced before we cleaned up and left the house, but I've been enjoying watching her try to talk me into it with an assist from the margaritas over dinner.

"And you'll be helping Luke pay his way through medical school or support Mrs. Lawless and their brood of little Lawless children or whatever it is he's got going on."

"Also true. And it's not like I'd be up onstage for it."

"Exactly," she says as she turns into the Crimson Lounge parking lot. "I'd never volunteer you for a public grinding session. I don't want you to die of embarrassment."

"I would," I say. "I would die."

When we step out of the car, I notice that the lingerie

shop's all lit up and buzzing with activity. Three cheers for extended holiday hours.

"Hey, Ceej? Can we go on a quick side quest?"

I pivot on my heel without waiting for her to answer and head for Fantasia. After a week of personal and professional disappointment, I'm ready for some unwise decisions. Well, maybe not unwise, but certainly not practical.

I walk straight to the rack with the bra I tried on a month ago. The hangers clink as I search for my size and sail into the dressing room, where I pull off my old one and replace it with the red lace and satin. It's as overtly, gaudily sexy as it was the first time. But unlike that time, I feel ready for it. Ready to be alive and a little dangerous.

With a nod at the vixen in the mirror, I yank the tag off, put my dress back on, and stride to the checkout. "I'm wearing this out," I announce to Jessica as I slap the tag on the counter.

Her soft cheeks plump into a smile. "Nice to see you again, sweetheart! I always love it when someone walks out in my merchandise."

CJ joins us and drops a pair of matching red panties onto the counter. "Go big or go home," she says by way of explanation.

I shrug and let Jessica add them to my total. She insists on wrapping them in candy cane-striped tissue paper and tucking them into a pretty gift bag. "You deserve to unwrap this when you get home," she says with a wink. "Are you headed next door?"

I tap my credit card on the reader and show her all my teeth. "I've got a date with Santa."

Her delighted laugh fills the store. "Give him hell, Liv."

"I will," I say with determination. "I definitely will."

Next door, we pay the cover and settle into a two-person table that sits about halfway back from the stage, like last time. Between getting dressed up and grabbing dinner and then the drive to North Village, we're breezing in with about three seconds to spare before the start of the show.

What a weird interlude this month has been. Like I stepped out of my regular life and reverted to younger Liv. Rooming with CJ, working a restaurant job, going out on the weekends, developing hopeless crushes on people who are way too hot for their own good. Other than the employment setbacks, I've been having so much damn fun. I didn't realize that my life had gotten so *un*-fun recently. All corporate rules and no play. Maybe that's why I gambled on Richie and SparkNexus. I lost, but I'm still standing.

"Hey! It's your guy!" CJ hisses, and I blink back to the present to see Santa Luke strutting onstage.

"Love that for me," I murmur, my eyes fixed on the stage.

Beard, check. Hat, check. Sunglasses, check. Smoking hot body, check, check, check. He pivots, spins, yanks his vest off. Snaps the suspenders, body roll, body roll, rips the tank top, wriggles across the stage, body roll, body roll, body roll. It's sexy as hell, and he's working it hard. When the time comes for Luke to work the crowd one-on-one, he pulls himself into a one-armed handstand on the edge of the stage. Like it always does, the position tightens every one of the muscles in his body, and it's easy to imagine that's how he is during sex, his body tense and coiled as he starts to work himself inside of you. Naturally, the room screams its approval.

Just when I think he can't possibly hold himself up any longer, he launches himself into a twisting spin and lands lightly on his feet.

"Every time I see that, it's impressive."

"Sure as hell is," CJ agrees. "Want to call him over?"

Tempting, but no. I can wait until it's just the two of us. Impatient now, I squirm in my seat as he finishes up the crowd work and leaps back onstage to finish his performance. The rest of the show flies by, and then four women are being chosen from the crowd to join Luke, Diesel, Rocket, and Victor Vice onstage.

CJ starts to wave and point at me as a possible volunteer, then drops her hands with a laugh when I shoot her a death glare. "Just kidding! I do want to stay friends with you."

"Good call," I say, cringing at the thought of being flipped around onstage to the cheers of the crowd.

Like the last time we were here, all four chosen audience members are manhandled by their assigned dancers in an over-the-top display of grinding and cock-in-thong waving and winky allusions to him going down on her or her going down on him, or both. I watch transfixed as Luke flaunts his incredible body, pulling his partner down onto his lap like she has no say in the matter and he gets to decide where she goes and what she feels, which is the impression I left the club with two weeks ago.

Left with. Fantasized about for the next several nights. Potato, potahto. Just thinking about Luke doing that to me in private makes me involuntarily Kegel.

"Okay!" CJ exclaims when the group number is done and the volunteers are stumbling off the stage red-cheeked and grinning. "Let's book some private dances."

"Oh, you're getting one too, are you?"

She shrugs as she waves her hand to get Nick's attention where he's hovering at the edge of the room, watching the crowd. "When in Rome, ya know?"

The white-bearded owner makes his way over with a smile on his face.

"Hello, ladies! Good to see you again," he says in his booming voice. "How'd you enjoy the show?"

"Aces as usual," CJ replies. "We're interested in private dances tonight. How do we go about setting that up?"

Nick chuckles, and it vibrates through his whole barrel-chested body. "I can arrange that. Let me guess," he says, turning to me, "snake-hips Santa?"

"I would like that very much," I say, quashing my nervousness at booking my first private dance from a stripper.

"Excellent." He slaps his belly in approval. "We have a handful of VIP rooms in the back. There's a flat fee, and after that, you and the performer work out your mutual expectations for the performance. Tips are appreciated, and we ask that you abide by all state and local regulations."

"Which are?" CJ asks, every inch the cutthroat corporate consultant-slash-assassin wrangler as she makes sure she understands the operational guidelines.

Nick taps a QR code at the bottom of the drinks menu on the table. "Everything's spelled out here, but you can also check with your dancer for the do's and don'ts. I only ask that everything be consensual and clearly communicated or you'll be asked to leave. That goes for the first floor where the female dancers work as well as the male dancers on the second floor."

CJ and I both murmur our understanding, and Nick taps a headset that's been hidden in his mass of fluffy white curls. "Is Luke still backstage?" He listens briefly. "Okay, tell him to stay put." Then he turns to CJ. "And who would you like to spend time with tonight?"

CJ tilts her head in thought. "You know what I'd like most for Christmas?"

Nick's face lights up. "Tell me."

She leans forward and says conspiratorially, "I would like to see the biggest dick in this place. Like I want to be startled by how big the dick is."

Nick's fluffy brows twitch, but beyond that he has no reaction as he taps the headset again. "Eugenio, tell Diesel he's up." Satisfied that his order's been conveyed, he turns back to us. "I'll head backstage to make sure everything's set up. One of our servers will fetch you when it's ready. In the meantime"—he snaps his fingers toward the bar and gestures to our table—"please enjoy champagne on the house."

He excuses himself, leaving me and CJ grinning at each other like loons.

"What am I feeling?" I ask. "Is this what the kids call being a 'boss bitch'?" I bust out sarcastic air quotes, and CJ snorts as she accepts two flutes of champagne from our shirtless waiter, handing me one and keeping the other.

"What you're feeling," she says, "is the freedom of not giving a fuck what other people think. You're gonna love it."

We clink glasses, and I let the bubbles float across my tongue and sink into my blood, more than ready for whatever comes next.

ELEVEN

Jonesy

I'm not moping in the dressing room while the other guys are working the crowd. I'm dog-sitting Roo so Nick can run the club without distractions.

"Isn't that right, girl?" I croon, scratching behind her floppy ears while she peers up at me with her soulful doggy eyes. "You needed me to hang out with you tonight."

Roo understands me. Roo knows I blundered into this whole set of circumstances completely on accident. Maybe she can tell me how to undo this clusterfuck too. But when Nick's heavy tread hits the stairs, even she puts distance between us, leaping to her feet and trotting to the doorway to greet her human.

"Hey," I say dully from the floor where I'm sitting cross-legged in my tear-away Santa pants.

Lines appear on Nick's forehead as he takes me in. "Everything okay with you?"

"Nope."

"Ah. I'm sorry to hear it."

I lift a shoulder and let it fall. "S'all my fault."

The only sound is the jingle of Roo's collar as she gives herself a frantic head-to-toe shake like she's trying to get the feel of my hands off her. Or maybe I'm just taking everything a little personally right now.

"Is this a bad time to say that a guest has requested a private dance with Santa?" Nick asks carefully.

I slump lower against the wall. "The ladies sure do love Santa."

"This one especially. She's a repeat customer."

That has me straightening. "No fucking way. It's not..."

He nods. "The lovely Liv is back."

At the news, the tips of my fingers go numb and my hearing goes fuzzy. But I'm still painfully aware of the disappointment that crosses Nick's broad, kind face. "You haven't told her yet, have you?"

"I tried," I say tiredly. Then I force myself to be honest. "I didn't try hard enough. I was too scared, and now there's no good way to do it. None. I'm fucked."

Nick shakes his head in that not-mad-but-disappointed way that's been a favorite of my parents and teachers and bosses since I was a kid. Now I can add my surrogate grandpa to the list of people I've let down. Fucking great.

Then another thought hits. Liv wants me to dance for her. Well, Luke. But still. It thrills me and has me burning with jealousy at the same time.

"This could be your chance to make things right." Nick runs a hand down Roo's back, and she wriggles in ecstasy. I swear, that's how I felt last week when I got to run my hand down Liv's back.

"How?" I ask, my eyes searching his face for some kind of answer. "Every option's shit." I hold up my hand and tick off the likely course of action finger by finger. "First, I tell her." One finger down. "Then that makes her pissed as hell that I've been lying to her." Two fingers. "And finally, she hates me forever." Three fingers. "Nobody wins." I spread my hand wide to show that I've ended up with nothing.

Nick's silent for a beat. "Well, if you're not going to tell her, at least try not to make things worse." Then he says, "Five minutes. VIP room two."

He whistles for Roo and leaves me to get ready to be alone with Liv in a dark, private space. On autopilot, I pull on my red booty shorts, the hat and beard, the sunglasses, then leave to face my fate.

Nick did me a solid by putting me in room two at least. It's kitted out with red lighting that turns the small space into a dark, sexy, almost surrealist chamber. It's the room you book for the wildest private shows, the ones where a little anonymity is best for all involved. And maybe that's the answer. Keep it anonymous, keep it short, keep it impersonal. When we see each other again at Verdant, act like normal and she'll never be the wiser. Let her leave town in a few weeks and forget all about this. All about me. I can do that.

With my heartbeat throbbing in my ears, I push open the door to the private room, and the hallway light cuts a slice of white through the deep red enveloping her. She ignored the couch in the corner in favor of the padded stool in the center of the room, and her head snaps up like a startled deer when I step inside. Then the door swings shut and we're alone in a room that glows with the color of my heart every time I look at her.

With this oppressive red lighting, she'll be able to see my body, but as long as I keep the disguise on and limit my conversation, I might be able to get out of this without her realizing who she's paying to keep her company. I'll just keep my hands to myself. If she insists, I'll let her touch my abs, and then I'll thank her and leave.

Let her. Ha. I've imagined Liv touching my body so many times, it'll be a miracle if I don't fall at her feet and beg her to put her hands all over me.

Except that I can't do that. Like Nick said, if I'm not going to tell her, I can at least not make things worse. The next ten minutes aren't about me. They're about her. I can push my feelings for her aside and give her whatever it is she's looking for, then get out.

Nick must've started the music because the dark, sexy beat of my private dance playlist fills the room and, I hope, gives me cover as I lower my voice to a whispery growl.

"Hi there."

"Hi," she says, and I brace myself for the excuses I heard over lunch with Gabe and Darby. She doesn't normally do this. This isn't like her. She's never doing this again. Shit I didn't enjoy hearing from her then and won't enjoy hearing from her now.

"You should know something." She crosses one leg over the other and adjusts the hem of her short ruffled skirt. I've never seen it on her before, and well, let's just say that getting hard and staying hard while I dance for her won't be a problem.

Fuck. No. Focus on *her.*

"What's that?" I ask, rolling my hips as I walk forward. Giving her what she came here for.

She takes a deep breath and lets it out. "I'm a little obsessed with you. You're the Christmas gift I'm giving myself. Well, my friend CJ's giving me." She laughs. "So much for no names."

"Santa-client confidentiality." It's time to be Santa Luke for her. "What's your name, beautiful girl?"

"Liv." She smiles as she says it, her teeth a bright contrast to her face under the dim lighting.

"So, Liv." I prowl around her in a circle, keeping my voice low and my chin tilted down so she's mostly getting hat and sunglasses. "Naughty or nice?"

She laughs shakily. "That's what you asked me last time."

I'm behind her now and lean forward and brush her hair to the side. "I know," I murmur into her ear, inhaling her sweet scent. "I remember."

She gives a little jolt. "You do?"

I move to her other ear, this time letting my lips make contact with the soft lobe. "Of course I do. Now what can Santa bring you for Christmas?"

I'm still standing behind her. It feels safer that way. I can whisper in her ear and pretend it's not me. Or maybe pretend it *is* me. Pretend she knows it's me.

Fuck. That's dangerous thinking. I have to push that all aside so we can both get out of this unscathed.

But ignoring how I feel about her gets more challenging when she relaxes against me and lets her head fall against my chest, making my dick twitch. "The guy I'm crazy about doesn't feel the same way."

White-hot jealousy clouds my vision for a split second. Who is he? Why has she never mentioned him?

"That can't possibly be true," I growl-whisper, curling my fingers around her hip. So much for keeping my hands off her.

"It is though. I asked him out, and he pretended not to get what I was asking." Her laugh is embarrassed. "And then later he posted pictures of himself with some gorgeous blond woman."

That's me. She means me. She's crazy about *me*.

"Then he's an idiot." The truth scrapes over my dry throat. "Is that why you're here with me tonight?"

She shifts on the stool, and I release her immediately, although I stay put at her back.

"Since he doesn't want me, I came here for the fantasy instead."

I stifle a groan. I like her as Jonesy but can't tell her because she doesn't know I'm Luke, and now she's here for Luke because she thinks Jonesy doesn't like her. This is my personal hell.

I should be shutting this down and keeping her from confessing things I have no right to know. Instead, I prowl around so I'm in front of her, angling my face down but keeping my eyes glued on her. "The guy you want isn't your fantasy?"

"Of course he is," she says impatiently. "He's a different kind of fantasy than you. You're the wild weekend, body-glitter-in-my-hair kind."

Don't ask. Don't fucking ask.

"And what kind is he?" Oops. I asked.

"The kind I want in my life for real." Her hands fly to her mouth. "God, I'm sorry. That's incredibly disrespectful to you."

"No, I get it." I don't have to bother hiding my voice, my throat's so tight at learning I'm the person she wants to be with and the person she wants to use at the same time. "That's why people come here."

"I'm sure you've got a lucky Mrs. Claus waiting for you at home." Her fingers twitch toward my chest but she doesn't make contact. She doesn't want to paw at the stripper without permission, and I love her for it.

"No Mrs. Claus." Nope, I'm managing to destroy any hope for that in this very moment.

"So does that mean you're free to..." She scoots to the edge of the stool. It's too dark behind my sunglasses to tell, but I'd bet money that her cheeks are the color of my Santa shorts right now. "Um, how much for me to touch you?"

"H-how much...?" My brain blinks offline.

"And how much for you to touch me?" She fumbles on the stool next to her, her intent unclear until she holds up a stack of cash. "If I wanted to sit on your lap and tell you what I want for Christmas, could I do that?"

"You can have whatever you want."

"I bet you say that to all the girls," she says in a breathy voice.

"I really don't." I step closer to her, hoping she'll hear the honesty in my voice. After-show hookups, sure. But never during private dances. Until Liv. "You can have as much as you want, for as long as you want." Fuck. Too honest.

Her chest lifts as she sucks in a breath.

"Good," she says. Then she yanks down my Santa beard and presses her mouth to mine.

At first I'm too shocked to respond. Too shocked, even, to worry about whether it's dark enough to hide the lower half of my face as her lips slide against mine, soft and warm and searching.

I have to stop this. If I can't kiss her as myself, I sure as fuck can't kiss her as Luke.

Then she moans, and the cash flutters to the floor when she lifts her fingers to bury them in my hair, knocking the hat off. And I've wanted so badly to taste her, to lick into the heat of her mouth and tangle my tongue with hers, that my resolve crumbles. I kiss her back and lose myself in the salt and fire and champagne of her mouth.

When she pulls away with a gasp, I tug the beard back in place with unsteady hands.

"You're the hottest thing I've ever seen," she says on a pant.

My laugh is equally breathless. "You can't see me."

"I know every line of you." She slides the fingers of one hand into the hair at the nape of my neck while the other trails over my stomach, outlining the definition of my abs. "It's not like you'll judge me for this, right? For wanting to feel good?"

"Never." I'd never judge her, although part of me wants to die because she's asking Luke for this, not me.

She lifts her hand and runs it down my neck to the curve of my shoulder. "You're my fantasy. And I want the fantasy tonight." Her voice is almost defiant, like she's ready to fight for the little bit of pleasure she wants. As if I'm gonna give her a hard time for it.

But fuck. I have to give her a hard time for it.

"Beautiful girl," I say, pulling away. "We can't do this."

"Oh," she says. Then, "Oh! Oh god, I'm so sorry." She stands abruptly. "I don't know what I was thinking, asking you to do things you're not comfortable with."

"No! No, that's... that's not the problem." If anything, the problem is wanting it too much. But it's no different than when we're at Verdant. I don't get to have different ethics here.

"Okay. So what is it?" She sounds confused, her confidence wavering.

"I'm using a fake name and wearing a disguise," I say a little desperately, aware that this situation might be spinning out of control. "I could be anybody. I could be somebody you know." I sound like myself. Hell, maybe she'll figure it out herself. Maybe I won't have to be the one to tell her.

I'm such a fucking coward.

My mind starts running through my options.

Leave this room right now without any kind of explanation. She's hurt, and I did the hurting. Lose/lose.

Announce that I'm her new friend Jonesy, and I've been lying to her for weeks. She's betrayed, and I did the betraying. Lose/lose.

Stay here and make her feel good, then keep a respectful distance from her until she leaves town. Win/win/kind-of lose.

Shit. I should've been listening better every time Wyatt got drunk and started talking about game theory.

"Well!" Liv says brightly as she stoops to collect her cash. "I think I'm going to call it a night."

"Why?"

She makes a tiny scoffing noise as she straightens. "I'm extremely uninterested in pestering someone who's not attracted to me."

I laugh, sounding a little unhinged. "You think I'm not attracted to you?" I step forward and pin her between my erection and the stool. "Do you feel how much I want you to pester me?"

"Oh my god." She shifts her hips to rub against mine like she's seeking proof. And my rock-hard dick is nothing *but* proof. I grit my teeth against the white-hot pleasure as she grinds against me.

"Baby, I ache for you," I whisper into her ear.

"So you'd be okay with—"

She squeaks when I swing her into my arms and carry her to the couch, sitting down and positioning her on my lap with her back against my chest. I barely hide a shudder when her ass shifts against my dick. I'm harder than I've ever been, and in this moment, that feels like a win/win/win.

Moving quickly, I pull off the beard and sunglasses. It's a risk, but the couch sits in the darkest corner of the room. She's little more than angles and shadows under the dark red light, and I'm gambling that I'm equally obscured. I'm also gambling that what I'm about to do will lift her up out of her body for long enough that I can get dressed again afterward.

"This is your fantasy," I whisper in her ear, catching the lobe between my teeth and biting. "Say the word and I stop."

"I'm not saying the word," she says immediately, and I huff a laugh.

"You're the boss." I slide my hand over her thigh and under her skirt, pushing aside her panties to find smooth skin. "And fuck, you're bare," I say with a moan.

My cock throbs as I stroke my finger along her seam, and she moans too.

"So wet," I growl. "Is this for me? Or someone else who danced tonight?"

"You," she whimpers. "You, Luke."

That's not my name. I want to shout it and kiss her until she recognizes me. But I can't. And maybe my touch is a little rougher because of it. A little meaner. She likes it, though. She grinds on my lap, her hands clutching my thighs as she rubs against me.

While my left hand is busy playing with her pussy, my right hand slides up to cup her breasts, first over her dress and then underneath, inside her bra. Her nipples are hard, and I pinch them, one and then the other. She cries out, but she lifts an arm behind her and wraps it around my neck, so I know she doesn't want me to stop.

"How many of my fingers do you want?" I slide one into her tight pussy, my breath catching just as loudly as hers does at the intrusion. "Do you want another?"

"Y-y-yessss."

She moves restlessly against my chest, turning and trying to capture my mouth with hers. But we can't have that, can we? I pull my hand out from under her bra and wrap my fingers around her throat, pinning her head to my shoulder.

"You're going to hold still and take it, naughty girl." I've never done Santa kink before, and it shouldn't work, but she groans and pushes herself down on my fingers. "That's right. Fuck my hand. Your pussy's the only thing you're allowed to move, and you only get to do that on my fucking fingers."

And fuck, does she ever, rocking herself against me as I find her clit with my thumb, pressing and circling while she loses her mind. I'm about to lose my mind too. My cock strains upward, desperate to sink into that tight channel, but I force myself to think about her, only her, and not the heat flooding my body as she squirms against me.

"If you... if you keep t-touching me like that," she gasps out, "I'm gonna come."

I loosen my grip on her throat and press a kiss against the pulse fluttering there. "That's the idea, love."

Liv. Love. The two concepts wrap around each other in my mind. My controls snaps, and words spill out of me like water.

"You deserve to feel good." I lay another kiss on her

neck. "You deserve someone who lives and breathes to make you feel good. You deserve someone who's honest with you. You deserve the best man. You deserve someone better than me. Than him. Than us. You deserve this. You deserve everything, Liv. Everything. You're everything."

I'm rambling as my hips drive up against her ass, but she's someplace beyond hearing.

"Oh fuck." She's saying it over and over. "Oh fuck, oh fuck, oh fuck, *ohhhhhhhh fffuuuuu...*"

She chokes on her last words just like her pussy chokes on my fingers as she starts to come. I slide my hand up to her jaw and turn her face to mine, desperate for her mouth so we can form a full circle, my fingers in her cunt, my tongue in her mouth, her orgasm drenching my hand.

My own orgasm takes me by surprise, and I come with a hoarse cry, my cock pulsing against the thin, stretchy material of my shorts.

"Jesus *fuck*, Livvie," I mumble, hauling her against my chest and petting her limbs as she trembles with the aftershocks. She's curled into me, eyes closed as she struggles to catch her breath. The only thing I want in the world is to hold her like this all night, but I have to let her go. Moving as slowly as possible so I don't jostle her, I feel around the bench next to me, locating my beard and sunglasses. I slide them on, but the hat is MIA.

Panic claws at me. After working so hard to keep her from the betrayal of learning who I am, I can't let her find out like *this*. Placing a final kiss on the back of her neck, I gently shift her to the side and stand. There's the hat, on the floor near the stool. I snatch it up and pull it on just as she starts to recover from her post-orgasm stupor.

"I..." I have no idea what to say as she smiles sleepily up at me.

"Thank you." She stretches her arms over her head and dissolves into a shiver. "That was incredible."

"It was." My mouth opens, closes, opens again. Finally, I settle on, "Merry Christmas, Liv."

And I bolt.

TWELVE

Liv

"**C**ome with me."

I say a quick goodbye to the take-out customer I'm finishing up with, then pivot to face Jonesy. "Pardon?"

"Come with me," he repeats. "June'll cover for you."

June steps behind the hostess stand like she and Jonesy planned it, and I let him lead me to the back of the restaurant and through the swinging kitchen door. We scoot past Samson, who's shouting at an unfortunate line cook while the rest of the kitchen staff continue working away, nonchalantly clanking and chopping and stirring. Jonesy gives Samson a jaunty wave, apparently as immune to his moods as the rest of his staff. But I'm sure not, so I pick up the pace until we hit the back hallway.

"He makes me so nervous," I whisper to avoid being overheard by the big, scary chef.

Jonesy whispers back, "All bark, no bite. He'll make you

a cake on your birthday, and it'll be the best thing you've ever tasted."

"Too bad my birthday's in August," I say sadly.

"Right." His lips press together, and then he says, "Come on, short-timer."

He leads me down a rickety set of stairs to a damp brick basement that's twenty percent saggy cardboard boxes, eighty percent cobwebs, and one hundred percent the set of a horror film.

"Umm."

"Trust me," he says with a grin. Then he flips up the top flap of the nearest box and I see a flash of green and red.

"Oh wow!" I gasp theatrically. "Are you going to murder me and hide my body in the Christmas decorations that nobody bothers to put up?"

His smile turns wicked, and he leans in and rests his palm lightly on the base of my throat.

"Before you've had a chance to show me up in silverware rolling?" His fingers curl gently around my neck, and his thumb slides up and down my skin while his dark eyes devour me. I can't help but shudder. Not from fear though. No, this is pure arousal.

He lets go of my neck to start nonchalantly sorting through the boxes, and it's like our sexy fake-murder moment didn't even exist for him. If he's unbothered by the feel of his hand on my neck, then by god, I need to be unbothered too. Just like I've been acting unbothered about what I got up to with Santa Luke at the Crimson Lounge last night. All day, I've been updating waitlists and leading people to their tables as if I didn't have the hottest sexual experience of my life last night with a snake-hipped stranger.

"Darryl gave us the okay to decorate," Jonesy says, "as long as it's after hours."

This banishes all lingering sexy thoughts. "You asked the boss if we could decorate?"

"Seemed important to you, Livvie-Liv," he says as he picks up two of the boxes. Just as my heart's about to expand out of my rib cage because of his thoughtfulness over something only I care about, he adds, "Plus, he's paying us for the overtime. Think you can grab that small one?"

My poor heart roller-coasters right back where it belongs, and I dutifully pick up the box he's pointing at. It takes six more trips to bring all the supplies up to the back hallway, and Jonesy insists on being the one to do it. Apparently, my shoes are too hazardous on the narrow stair treads.

"We could start after work today," I say as we head back to front of house. "No time like the present, right?"

He frowns. "Today?"

"Oh." Now I'm frowning too. "You have plans."

"No, I—"

"That's okay," I say quickly. "I can handle it alone."

He scoffs. "Think you can get rid of me that easily? Of course I'm staying. I don't trust you to execute my vision." Pulling his phone out of his pocket, he shoots off a quick text. "I'm all yours after work."

I smile even though he obviously just canceled plans with someone, and my mind immediately goes to worst-case scenarios. By the time our official workday ends and we're the only two left in the restaurant, I've convinced myself that he broke the news to the cute blonde that he wouldn't be able to watch the Sunday HBO shows with her. In my head, her name is Harley, and she's pierced in places I'm scared to even pinch too hard.

"You ready, Fielding?"

I turn to see that he's moved the decoration boxes into the dining room and is rolling his shoulders, making a show of limbering up for our after-hours work. The action's way more athletic than I'd expect for somebody who laughed off the idea of having framed sports memorabilia decorating his walls.

I don't like to admit it, but the thought improves my mood slightly.

I whirl away to hide my suddenly pink cheeks and start cataloging the supplies. "Let's see... we've got garland here, and some lights that may or may not still work. A bunch of ornaments. Ohhh, bows!" I hold up a red velvet one, pleased to see that its trailing ribbons aren't creased after being stored for lord knows how long.

"This should go on the hostess stand," he says, handing me a huge wreath studded with colorful round ornaments. "Let's make you a centerpiece."

"I would expect nothing less," I say, and from there we jump into action. I assemble the faux tree he found in the back of the basement, coaxing its branches into fluffy fullness. Once it's as majestic as I can make it, I cover it in lights, ornaments, and ribbons. Jonesy, meanwhile, grabs a ladder to hang garland along the entrance perimeter.

We work mostly in silence, and when I glance over at him, he has his tongue poked between his teeth as he weaves a strand of lights through the garland. Without looking up, he says, "Eyes on your own work."

I laugh and put the last of the ornaments on the tree. "There. This place is both merry and bright, at last."

"Not quite." Jonesy points to the boxes of round ornaments each the size of a child's bowling ball. They're too big for the tree, but they're too bold and festive not to do *something* with.

My art director's brain sees the solution immediately. "We should hang these from the ceiling."

"Like in a path from the door into the dining room," Jonesy says, picking up one of the balls.

"Yes! I love it!"

We grin at each other, pleased at our simpatico moment, then start brainstorming how to go about hanging them. While Jonesy threads ribbon through the tops to hang from the metal framework that holds the tin ceiling tiles, I start to lay out the ornaments on the floor in a rough approximation of where they'll hang, mixing the red, green, and gold balls to form a gently curving path from the entrance that explodes outward once it reaches the dining room.

Jonesy steps next to me and cocks his head. "What if…"

When he doesn't finish the thought, I say, "What if…?"

"I dunno, I was thinking…" He rubs the back of his neck. "What if it's all red leading in from the entrance, then mix it a bit until it's all green as it flows into the dining room, with the gold as a border?"

I cock my head at the same angle he's holding his, looking from the door to the seating area, until I see exactly what he means. "All that red in the middle of the green lobby, and then it turns to green in the red dining area. Like one room's being pulled into the other."

"Exactly," he says with an almost shy grin. We shuffle the colors around until we have it nailed down, and I can't help but applaud as we both step back to see how it looks on the floor.

"It's brilliant."

He gets a little pink at my words. "I like this kind of stuff."

"You're good at it," I say, but he waves me off and grabs the ladder to start the ceiling installation.

"Speaking of art," he says from the top of the ladder as I hand up the first ornament for him to hang.

"Were we speaking of art?"

"We are now." When he stretches to place the red ball, his untucked button-down lifts to reveal a line of smooth, taut stomach above his black pants.

I really shouldn't gawk. I really should avert my eyes. Any time now. Looking away aaaaany time now.

"Why do you hate the lions?"

My eyes snap to his face. "What lions?" I ask dumbly, trying to erase the unexpectedly attractive sight of his belly button.

He jerks his head to the right. "*The Lion Fucks Tonight.* When I waited on you that first night, you glared daggers at it. Made me think you might be an uptight bitch."

"Who says I'm not?"

He gives an amused hum. "Trust me, you're not."

"I'm surprised you noticed," I murmur as I work through the fact that Jonesy noticed me noticing that terrible mural and then *remembered* that he'd noticed a couple of weeks later.

"You shouldn't be." He descends the ladder to move it forward a few feet.

I gather more ornaments to hand up to him.

"I'll tell you what I think about the mural if you'll tell me what's up with you and Gabe." I fully expect him to inform me that it's none of my business because it is, in fact, none of my business.

He hangs another two ornaments before speaking.

"Gabe's been my best friend since high school. He lived with me for a while after he dropped out." He positions another ornament, then continues. "We've talked forever about opening a landscape business, and last year he went ahead and did it. He wants me to quit and go full-time with him, but..."

He gives a restless shrug, the one he does where it looks like his joints are attached to his body with rubber bands.

"What's stopping you?" I ask once I'm done writing silent poetry about what a pleasure it is to watch him move his body.

He laughs and ruffles his hair. "Oh God, let's see. It's a new business, and there's no reason for it to support two full-time people right away. Gabe's the plant expert. I just give advice on what might look good in the design. That's not important enough to make me a partner." His face flushes red, like he's embarrassed that his friend would offer him a position like that. "And then there's Darby. He fell in love with her two Christmases ago, and he..."

I hand up another ornament and wait for him to finish. When he doesn't, I list a couple of suggestions. "He changed? Got smug and happy? Unintentionally started cutting you out of his life? I'm speaking from my own experience with my friends here."

He shakes his head. "No, nothing like that. He's actually kind of the best version of himself now. I guess it's just that he's... content." His lips press together, and he works them back and forth like he's thinking about what to say next. "I'm not jealous exactly. Darby's a great girl. Not my type—as if I could handle a smart, pretty, professional, pulled-together woman who doesn't own a single framed movie poster." He grins at me as I hand him another ornament. "I'm happy he's happy. I'm just... I'm very aware that I'm not a part of it all."

He shrugs and reaches for another ornament, which I hand up without comment.

Message received. Gabe's girlfriend isn't his type, which

means I'm not his type. But I'm asking about *him* right now, not obsessing over myself.

"Do you think you'd like it though? Landscape design?" I ask.

His shoulders drop on an exhale. "Yeah. I think I probably would. But am I sure enough to quit my jobs?"

There it is again. "Jobs?"

His eyes fall away from mine. "Ya know. It's a gig economy." Then he smiles that lazy smile, the one that crawls across his face and changes him from handsome to breathtaking. "Now you owe me an explanation about those lions."

Right. The lions.

"Well, I majored in art." I say it like it's enough of an explanation but quickly realize it's not. "And that mural is..."

"Not art?" he asks, wiggling his fingers for the next ornament.

"Oh, it's art, all right." I hand one up to him. "It makes you feel something."

"Yeah?" He has the ornament's ribbon clamped between his teeth. "Howzit make you feel?"

I answer without censoring myself. "Hot and reckless and a little horny."

The green ball hits the ground at my feet, and I look up to see Jonesy's mouth hanging open.

THIRTEEN

Jonesy

"Sorry, could you say that again?" I'm grinning, but I'm also turning my lower half away from her as subtly as I can so she doesn't see that I'm halfway hard because the word "horny" just tumbled from Liv's sophisticated mouth. Then again, that's kind of been my MO since Saturday.

Covertly knowing how your crush sounds when she comes is incredibly distracting when you're trying to remember drink orders for a table of ten.

"I will not," she says primly. "And none of that means the art itself is any good."

She walks over to the mural and studies it with her hands clasped behind her back like she's at a museum.

"The perspective's all off. There's no vanishing point." Her voice turns into a college professor's, and I'm thrilled to be in her personal lecture hall. "See how everything's on the same plane to the viewer? The background should look farther away than the subjects in front, but it's all the same size."

I pivot on the ladder to look where she's pointing.

"Huh. Yeah, I think I see what you mean," I say after a beat. "It's like somebody flattened the scene."

"Exactly! There's not enough depth and dimensionality in the trees. No attempt at shadows or shading." She reaches up to rest her hand on the simplistic leaves on the branches. "The artist needed to either amp up the sense of flatness and sameness to make it intentionally jarring and surreal, or they needed to think carefully about the spatial relationship of the objects they were creating."

"Huh." I say it again but softer this time. "That may be the smartest thing anybody's ever said in here."

I asked Darryl about decorating as a way of making it up to Liv for blowing her off to go to the Chicago thing, making her think I'd be interested in dating anybody but her, and oh yeah, sprinting from the room yesterday to suck the taste of her orgasm off my fingers.

Honestly, it was the least that I could do.

Liv, meanwhile, just shrugs off my compliment. "It's Art 101. This mural shouldn't work at all. But at the same time..." She wanders closer to the lions and runs her fingers over the mane of the bigger one. "I like it. I see the flaws, the clashing colors, the wonky sight lines. But I don't really care. Not when the lions look so—"

"Fierce. Free."

She smiles in agreement. "Exactly. They're standing in for humans who wish they could be that way too."

I have my arm propped on the top of the ladder and my chin resting on my hand, but I'm not looking at the lions. I'm looking at her. Her intelligence and passion and beauty.

Sometimes time stops when I watch her, wishing she'd look at me with the same intensity. The way she looked at fucking *Luke*. Who, again, is me. I cannot emphasize enough how fucked-up this whole situation is.

Santa must've heard my wish because when she turns around, her eyes catch mine, and we both freeze. Her liquid brown eyes devour my face, and I'm pinned in place on the ladder, wishing I could kiss her. Touch her. Knowing that I can't do any of that until I tell her the truth about my alter ego, and that when I do, it's going to shatter what we have now.

"Liv." My whole body tenses with what I need to say, but she's already turning away with a little laugh, breaking the moment and giving me a reprieve.

"Phew. Anyway." She walks back to the ladder and scoops the next ornament off the ground. "Whatever you take from a piece of art is the correct interpretation. It's different for everyone."

Because I'm a coward, I push my confession aside for now. "Could you do better?"

It's not a challenge. It's a genuine question, and she considers it before answering.

"Yes and no," she says. We've moved on to the last of the ornaments now, and our curving path has expanded to cover as much of the dining area as we can cover with the ornaments. "I could do it properly, but I don't know if I could capture the same emotion." She glances at those lions again. "Are they fighting or fucking? Or both? I love that you can't quite tell. But it would be fun to try."

"You should," I say.

She laughs. "I'm rusty. That ice cream ad was a one-off. Not a lot of calls for original art like that in the ad campaigns I design. I'm mostly there to curate the tone of the set decorations and wardrobe."

"Sounds interesting," I say as I climb down to reposition the ladder. Thank god I have thighs of steel or I'd be feeling all the up and down tomorrow.

"Eh," she says. "Someday I'll be the boss, and all my ads'll have original art."

I grab the last ornament's ribbon between my teeth as I figure out the best spot on the metal frame to hang it. "'Zat the kinda thing you could do in a town this size?"

"Depends," she says. "You can do a lot of planning remotely, but I'd have to travel if I wanted to be there for actual shoots. Why? You know a kick-ass Beaucoeur marketing firm that's hiring?"

"Yeah, I've got all kinds of connections to the corporate world around here." With that, I place the final ornament and hop off the ladder. "What do you think?"

She comes to stand next to me. "We need one more string of lights on the garland over the waiting area."

She's right. "I think there's another in one of those boxes. Hang on." I amble over to paw through the unused supplies, and when I turn around, my heart stutters to a halt.

Liv's on the ladder, stretching up to fix an ornament that's gotten tangled around its ribbon. I race over to her, and she gives an undignified squawk when I wrap my arms around her waist and swing her to the ground.

"What do you think you're doing?" I snap.

"Fixing the orna—"

"If anybody's breaking their neck falling off a ladder, it's the server, not the art genius." She doesn't say anything as I adjust the problematic ornament and clamber back down. I try to slide past her, but she grabs my hand.

"Why do you do that?" she asks quietly.

"Do what?" My voice is flat, and I avoid her eyes.

"Put yourself down. I hate it."

I pull my hand out of hers and mutter, "I didn't say anything that isn't true."

"You need a new mirror," she says. "You're clearly not seeing what I'm seeing."

"I know how I look."

I also know she didn't mean my pretty face, but I can't let myself think too hard about her high opinion of me. It makes me want things I shouldn't want and believe things I know aren't true.

I grab the ladder and stalk off to hang the final string of lights. She watches me in silence for a bit, then starts to box up the decorations that we ended up not using. I collect them from her and carry them back down to the basement.

When I come back to the dining room carrying our coats, I find that she's flipped off the overhead lights. The sun set while we were working, and the only illumination is the lights we just hung. They gleam softly off the ornament path we built on the ceiling.

"It's gorgeous." Her voice is barely above a whisper, and I walk over to her.

"It is." We stand side by side and take in the Christmas wonderland we made. "Darryl's gonna be so grateful that he trusted you to do this."

"Trusted us." She nudges me, and when I don't reply, she nudges me harder.

"Trusted us," I dutifully repeat. Then I hold out her coat so she can slide it on, even daring to slip my fingers into her collar to free her hair. It's in a ponytail like that first day at Verdant. I let it go to settle against her back, but I accidentally keep hold of a small section.

"Need a ride home?" I wrap that strand of gingerbread hair around my finger, badly wanting her to say yes even though I'm already late to meet Wyatt.

She turns to face me, and we're standing so close that my eyes have no choice but to drop to her mouth, which means I have a close-up view as she says, "CJ's almost here."

I can't hold back my tiny sigh of disappointment.

"Okay. I'll wait with you until then." I free her hair and we walk together to the back lot, where we lean against the side of my truck. I'm stupid glad she didn't do the "oh no, you don't have to stick around" dance and hope it means she doesn't mind being in my company a little longer.

We don't talk. She just scoots a little closer to me and I scoot a little closer to her, telling myself I'm shielding her from the wind that's picked up now that the sun's gone down. I turn my head to ask if she'd like to wait in my truck while I crank the heat, and I find that she's looking up at me like she's about to say something.

My brain leaps into action and announces that we're standing within kissing distance and she's not pulling away. She wants more from me, and I know this for a fact because she confessed it to someone she thought was a stranger.

Christ, imagine that once upon a time I thought the worst thing that could happen from her knowing was losing my job. At this point, I'd welcome Darryl firing me at high noon during the Sunday brunch rush if it meant I could make this confession to Liv without blowing us up.

Maybe it'll be okay. Her eyes are a warm invitation, her lips parted in a soft smile. Surely, she'll understand. Surely, she won't hate me for keeping Santa Luke a secret for so long, or for giving in and sinking into her heat last night in the VIP room.

I clear my throat. "Can we—"

She blinks away as CJ's headlights sweep across us.

"Unhand my roommate!" her friend rolls down her window to holler.

Liv gives a tiny eye roll and straightens away from me. "Good night, Jonesy. Thanks for waiting with me."

"Night," I say. Then I grope for my usual irreverent cool, which has been MIA for most of the night, and tell CJ, "Keep this one away from lions. They have an *effect* on her."

"Of course you're late." That's my brother's so-very-loving greeting when I pull up outside his house. It's the refrain I've heard my whole life, and my inevitable response comes out like a growl.

"I'm the one doing the favor." For a second, it looks like he's going to lash back, and I brace myself for it, but he just nods instead.

"Right. Thank you."

"So what are we moving exactly?" I ask.

He turns and walks into his house, and I follow. "Reese wants the bedroom set, and I don't want to fight her for it."

I have a million questions about that starting with how long ago they broke up and why they broke up and if he's handing over the furniture because he was a guilty party, but I lock it all away. He'll talk when he's ready to talk.

"Jesus, this is a beast." I preemptively glare at the solid oak set that's gonna be a real bitch to wrestle down the stairs and into my truck. We'll have to manage it piece by piece. My first instinct is to double-check that Wyatt's cleared to lift this much weight, but questions about how he's healing tend to set him off, so I trust that he's not doing anything that's going to cause him any more harm.

Still, he's sweaty and pale by the time I strap down the final nightstand and slam the truck tailgate shut.

"You good?" I ask as I fire up the engine.

"Yep," he says tersely. He gives me Reese's new address, and I point us in that direction. I'm prepared to fill the silence with the radio the whole way there, but Wyatt says, "So. Twice in one week."

"Mom'll be thrilled," I say. "Speaking of, would she like a new embroidery machine, do you think?"

She's always enjoyed sewing and needlework, and in the downtime during her recovery, she's gotten into making elaborate pop-culture designs that she's started selling online.

Wyatt's brows lift. "I think that's a great idea. Do you want me to—"

He bites off his next words, and it makes me feel like shit. He was about to offer to help but is scared I'll be a dick about it. Which, admittedly, I was about to be. Then I think about Liv's earnestness as she tries to convince me I'm something other than what I've been, and it makes me want to be that guy she thinks she sees.

"Would you maybe have time to research models so I know what to buy?" I ask. "You're better at that kind of stuff than I am."

He rolls his eyes, but he's smiling as he does it. "You're perfectly capable of researching shit like that," he says. "But yes, I'd like to help out."

"You already did."

"With something other than my organs and my bank account." He shifts uncomfortably in the passenger seat. "I want to feel normal again."

"Did any of this have to do with your breakup?" I miss the Wyatt who used to tell me things like that.

He's silent for so long that I assume he's chosen to ignore me. But finally, he says, "Yes. And no. It was a fucked-up situation that spiraled, and I don't wanna talk about it yet."

"Okay," I say easily. "I'm here though."

"Thanks."

"And hey, if you can find that damn black cat Cuddle-Puff, that would be amazing. Apparently, it's rarer than Bigfoot."

He pulls out his phone and taps out a note. "I'll see what I can do." But I hear the quiet thread of happiness in his voice that I'm letting him help.

The silence in the car for the rest of the drive isn't nearly as strained, and when we pull up at Reese's new place, she meets us at the door with folded arms and a pinched mouth.

"Upstairs. First door on the right. Don't break anything."

Then she flounces to the kitchen table and ignores us while we move furniture for her like a pair of helper monkeys.

"Dude, what did you *do?*" I mutter as we head out to grab the last of our load. "Cheat on her?"

He stops short, forcing me to slam to a halt too because he's in front of me as we carry the footboard.

"Oh god." I look at him aghast. "You *cheated?*"

"No! We were"—his eyes dart through the open front door, and his voice drops to an urgent whisper—"we were broken up! She'd returned the ring!"

I set the footboard on the ground. "So she was bluffing?"

"Apparently. But she'd already rented this place when she did it, so..."

"Nah. Bullshit." I pick up my end of the heavy oak panel again. "You're in the clear. I absolve you."

"Thanks, buddy."

It's not my imagination that Wyatt's walking a little straighter as we haul in the last piece, like he set down a ninety-pound dumbbell of guilt.

Once everything's in place in Reese's bedroom, we tromp back downstairs, and I hover in the open front door letting in the cold air while Wyatt pauses in front of the woman he'd planned to spend his life with. She's dressed in a prissy, silky shirt and black pants and heels, and it occurs to me that this might be how Liv dresses at her job. But the women are night and day different. Liv's professional and classy and curious and smart and every good thing in this world. Reese is professional and smart and the kind of uptight I might've thought Liv was before I got to know her.

It is, however, the most overlap Wyatt and I have ever had in women.

"Well, thanks, I guess. Have a nice life," Reese says to Wyatt, her voice even colder than the wind at my back. Then that piercing blue-eyed gaze turns on me. "Still dancing, Jonesy? I'll have to catch a show sometime."

"I wouldn't take your money if you paid me to," I say in horror.

Wyatt shoves me out the door with a grunt and slams it behind him. I risk a glance at his face, worried that he's about to turn his mad in my direction, but instead, he's fighting a smile.

"I wouldn't take your money if you paid me to?" he repeats in disbelief.

I shake my head and clap him on the back. "Fuck off. Let's go get a beer."

FOURTEEN

Liv

"Has anyone seen Jonesy?"

Darryl's reedy voice interrupts me, Ariel, and Marcus as we're zipping ourselves into our coats after a particularly gross post-shift Sunday cleanup.

"He left about fifteen minutes ago," I say.

"Well, darn it!" Darryl says. "Mrs. Wickenwarg left these for him earlier, and I forgot to hand them over." He holds up a red-and-green plaid cookie box.

Ariel laughs. "Again? What's this, the second year in a row?"

"Third," Darryl says. "I think it's sweet."

A quick search of my memory confirms that Dorothy Wickenwarg is an eighty-year-old woman with papery, powdery skin and a gap-toothed smile. "It is sweet!" I say. Ask me how I'd feel about it if she were a twenty-something platinum-blond bombshell bringing him cookies though.

Darryl frowns down at the box. "I guess I can hold on to them until tomorrow."

"I can drop them off on my way home," I blurt.

He gives me a gummy smile. "You don't mind?"

"Of course not. Anything for a coworker." I take the box from his hands, ignoring Ariel and Marcus' knowing looks as I grab my phone so Darryl can give me Jonesy's number.

"Mm-hmm. A coworker," Marcus says. Ariel snickers and digs an elbow into his ribs.

"Just a coworker," I repeat, hoping my cheeks aren't turning pink with the lie.

"Speaking of coworkers," Ariel says, "you're coming to the staff holiday party next Saturday, right?"

"I was planning to, yeah. Why?"

"That's how Ariel and I got together," Marcus says with an adoring glance up at his curly-haired girl.

"Cuties!" I say brightly, wondering what this has to do with me.

"Aaaaand Jonesy said he might stick around all night this year. He usually bails early for whatever he does on his Saturday nights." Ariel gives me a shit-eating grin. "Weird that he's choosing this year to hang out with everyone."

"Uh-huh," I say vaguely. It's clear what they're alluding to, but I hate being the focus of coworker gossip, especially when they also made it clear that Jonesy doesn't mess around with his coworkers. I beat a hasty retreat with the cookies, not willing to dream about staff parties that turn friends into lovers while I have an audience. When I get to CJ's car, I set the cookies in the passenger seat, take a deep breath, and send a cheerful text.

Hey, it's Liv! A customer left you some cookies and Darryl asked me to drop them off for you. Is that cool?

It's close enough to the truth, and his reply seems to take forever, especially given how short it ends up being.

> sure, yeah

He sends me his address with zero drama. Also zero excitement, but hell, I'm committed now. I text CJ before putting the car in gear.

> Dropping by Jonesy's with cookies. I couldn't explain it if I wanted to.

Her reply is way too eager.

> Get it!!!!!

His place is only six minutes from Verdant, and I'm drowning in curiosity by the time I pull up to the curb. It's a duplex with blue siding and single-car garages that meet in the middle of the double driveway. Jonesy's is on the right, the one with hedges and the winterized flower bed.

I flip down the mirror on the visor and do a quick check of my reflection. My lipstick's mostly gone, but my lips still have a hint of the dark pink I'd applied that morning. My hair's lying nicely, and my mascara stayed put on my lashes. I'm as cute as can be expected after a day helping feed the citizenry of Beaucoeur. I dig through my bag for the lotion I threw in there to keep my sandpapery winter hands at bay and smooth it on the parts of me visible under my coat.

I'm stalling, so I tuck the lotion away, grab the box, and walk as casually as I can up the sidewalk. My finger doesn't even reach the doorbell when it flies open to reveal Jonesy.

"Missed me already, huh?" He grins and leans against the doorway.

"Yep," I answer honestly, drinking him in. I've only ever seen him in his Verdant service uniform of black pants and a white shirt, so Jonesy in sweats, a T-shirt, and a hoodie is a revelation. He looks invitingly soft.

Well. His clothes look soft. The body underneath looks intriguingly hard, and I curse that everything's a little too baggy to get a better look.

"How are you barefoot? Aren't you freezing?" I ask as I step into his house. If I pretend that this is completely normal, maybe we can make it through this. As it is, I'm about to hyperventilate at this glimpse of Jonesy undone.

He shuts the door behind me and glances at the box in my hands.

"Nice! Dorothy comes through again."

I hand it over, noticing as I do that his hair is damp and curled around his neck. He smells warm and clean, like he just got out of the shower. Good god, I want to lick his neck.

"You've got to try one of the sugar cookies," he calls over his shoulder as he walks through the living room to the open kitchen. "I won't eat that many, and they shouldn't go to waste."

I guess that means I'm invited to stay. After a tiny hesitation, I take off my coat, kick off my heels, and follow him, taking in the surroundings as I do.

"Ha!" I point in triumph at the movie posters flanking the huge TV. Then I look more closely and realize they're not thin paper in cheap plastic frames. Sturdy wood frames and mats surround colorful, artistic takes on famous films. I was right about *John Wick*, but the rest surprise me. *Pitch Perfect* and 28 *Days Later* hang alongside *Amélie* and *Barbarian Time Brigands: Time Flies*.

"Impressive range." I lean closer to study the tiny stylized dragons swooping around the *BTB* art. "These are so cool!"

"If something's wrong with the perspective, I don't want to know about it." Jonesy appears at my side with a napkin-wrapped cookie. I take it and see it's an angel with golden icing wings and hair. I accept it with a murmur of thanks and watch as Jonesy watches me bite into it, my lips closing around the cookie. Sweet, buttery, vanilla-y goodness explodes in my mouth.

"Oh my *god*, Mrs. Wickenwarg!"

"Right?" he says.

A voice I really shouldn't listen to says, *I'd rather be tasting you than this cookie*, so I force my attention back to the art. "These are great. Where'd you get them?"

"Etsy. They're my favorite movies."

"Good taste," I murmur, not bothering to clarify if I'm talking about the cookie or the posters.

He crowds into me and presses his thumb to my lower lip, catching a stray sugar cookie crumb that he licks off. My breath hitches as his tongue swipes along his digit.

"I swear to god," he growls, "if you're thinking about snake-hips Santa right now..."

"I'm horrified that you know about him. I could kill CJ." An embarrassed flush heats my cheeks, and I glance away, afraid he'll be able to see my history with Luke in my expression. "You and Gabe and Darby must've laughed your heads off about it after we left."

"Not in the least," he says. "But you didn't answer my question."

"Oh. N-no." I give a shaky laugh. "Santa Luke never really leaves my mind, if I'm being honest. Does he have the most perfect body I've ever seen? Yes. Do I think he made a deal with the devil to be able to move like that? Absolutely.

Have I imagined what his face looks like under the beard? Only dozens of times."

And do I know how his lips taste and the feel of his cock against my ass and the way he groans when he comes? Extremely yes.

Jonesy exhales softly. "Wow. Okay."

My eyes fly wide when I realize how many of my feverish Luke thoughts I've just unpacked. "Why am I telling you this?" I give a horrified laugh. "I'm sure you really, really, really don't want to hear about my Santa thing."

I thought I was sharing silly little confessions, but Jonesy's face is almost stricken, which makes me rush to overshare in a different, potentially even more embarrassing direction.

"I know he's not real. I mean, *he's* real, but I know it's all a fantasy. A fun, escapist one-time thing that's completely removed from my life." I meet his eyes as I say this next bit. "You, though... you make my days better. Everything that brought me to Beaucoeur was shitty, but somehow it doesn't feel so bad because I got to meet you."

His mouth has slowly fallen open as I rambled, and oh god, what have I done? I try to turn away, but he catches my hand before I can escape.

"I can't tell you how grateful I am that your former boss turned out to be a lowlife jagoff. If not, I'd never have met you." His fingers curl over mine. "I'll still punch him in the face if I ever see him, but I'll thank him while I'm doing it."

I press my lips together, darkly pleased at the protectiveness rolling off him.

"How much longer do I have with you, Liv?" he asks.

He doesn't just mean this afternoon. "I've got an interview in Minneapolis after the first of the year, but it's mostly a formality. The person doing the hiring's a former boss." The thought isn't as gratifying as it might've been a few weeks ago, so I bring up something considerably more fun. "But I hear we get to hang out on Saturday at the staff party."

"Damn straight. You haven't lived 'til you've partied with the crew from Verd—" His head whips toward the front of the house where a loud engine suddenly cuts off. "What the fuck?"

He stalks to the window and pushes the curtain back to reveal a minivan in his driveway.

"Okay, so a couple of things you need to know about me..." he says nervously.

"Oh god, are you married?" I say it mostly as a joke, but when the minivan side door slides open and children come tumbling out like a pack of puppies, I'm suddenly not joking anymore. "Oh god, are you married with a million kids?"

He plunges his fingers into his hair and speaks quickly.

"My mom had me and Wy when she was a teenager. She got married twelve years later and had five more kids."

"So those are..." I gesture at the hoard of small people racing toward his front door.

"My siblings," he says grimly. Then he throws open the door and his whole demeanor changes. It lightens and brightens and generally radiates love and joy and every good thing I've ever seen in him. "My siblings!"

The house explodes with kiddie energy as they scream and throw themselves onto Jonesy, who collapses backward onto the floor and lets them climb all over him. The boys trying to wrestle with him look to be around eight and ten, and the little girl clinging to his ankle must be closer to five.

"Whoa. Are you Hollis' girlfriend?"

I blink away from the gorgeous guy rolling around on

the floor with kids he clearly adores to find two teenage-ish girls studying me. One glowers, and the other grins.

"Um," I say articulately.

"Holly never lets us meet his girlfriends!" The smiling blond one darts forward and hugs me so hard I let out a little wheeze.

"I'm not his—"

The second one's somber as she regards me from a distance, her dark hair falling over one eye.

"So, um. I'm Liv," I tell them with the scant air left in my lungs as the blond girl tries to compress my ribs.

"Becks," she says cheerfully. The other girl narrows the one eye I can see.

"Drea." Her voice drips with suspicion, and I wonder what the hell kind of women Jonesy's brought around before this.

The bellowing of the younger kids and their allegedly adult brother grows in intensity until a voice cracks through the chaos.

"Behave like children, please, and not wild animals."

Everybody freezes, and without a single introduction needed, I know I'm looking at Jonesy's mother.

"Hi, Mom." Jonesy climbs to his feet, hefting one boy under each arm as he does, and leans forward to kiss her cheek. She's tall and thin with hair and eyes the same rich brown as Jonesy's and Wyatt's and the frowning Drea. She wears worry lines on her forehead, next to her eyes, around her mouth, but she's as radiant as a *Madonna and Child* painting from the Renaissance when she looks at her brood.

"Kids, you've gotta give Hollis room to breathe."

Jonesy's eyes flick over to me as he sets the boys back on the ground. "Not that I'm not thrilled to see you guys, but—"

"You didn't answer your phone!" one of the boys shouts. "We wanted to stop by with presents!"

Their mom's eyes cut to me now too, and she does a double-take that would be comical if I weren't so over-whelmed with all the new information flying at me.

She walks over and extends her hand, her eyes flickering from my face to my dress to my bare left-hand ring finger.

"Hi. I'm Kristy Kuhlmann. The mom."

I grip her hand and shake. "Liv Fielding. The coworker."

"Ah," she says, her gaze now drifting to Jonesy. "At...?"

"At Verdant," he says quickly.

Kristy tilts her head a few degrees to the left, clearly not believing that a mere coworker would be hanging out at Jonesy's place like this, but she doesn't press.

"Can I have a cookie?" one of the little ones screeches, and Jonesy looks at his mom with a raised brow.

"One each," she says. "And Tristan, you need to bring in the presents for your brother. This was your idea."

The oldest boy scrambles out to the van and returns with an oversized bag. "Here, Holly! One of them's a sweater," he says proudly as he dumps the bag out onto the couch and four wrapped packages tumble out in a profusion of red and green and silver.

Kristy groans. "Tristan Parker Kuhlmann! What have we talked about?"

"Sorry!" he yells as he charges to the kitchen to choose his cookie. "It's s'posed to be a surprise!"

There's a period of relative silence as the kids descend on the baked goods, which lets Kristy give me a once-over.

"So, Liv, how long have you and Hollis worked together?"

I glance at him and see the tips of his ears turning red,

but I hide my elation at his mom casually spilling all his secrets.

"Not long. Three weeks, maybe? I'm only in town for a little bit before I leave for a new job."

Kristy bends down to swing the littlest girl up onto her hip, not even flinching when a crumby, chocolatey hand tangles in her hair. "And what do you do?"

"She creates ad campaigns," Jonesy says. "She's a crazy talented artist." His smile is warm as he says it.

The kids come tumbling back to surround us.

"Art?" Drea flicks her hair back from her face, interest replacing suspicion in her dark eyes.

"You know those melting ice cream ads?" he asks, and Drea nods. "Liv did those paintings."

The older girls look at me in awe. "Oh my god," Becks squeals. "I always wanted to try the chai spice flavor!"

Drea scoffs. "Like we can afford that ice cream." Then her eyes slip over to me. "But can you, like, give me art pointers?"

"Well." I glance around for help, but Kristy's pulled Jonesy aside for a whispered conversation, so they're no use. "Sure. Let me just get some paper."

I grab my purse where I dropped it near the door, grateful that I always carry a notebook with me. "Let's go to the kitchen."

Before I know it, the four oldest kids have settled around the table. Tristan clearly knows his way around Jonesy's house and fetches pens from a drawer to distribute to everyone as I tear pages out of my notebook.

"Okay, let's draw a... a lion."

I'm obviously not going to show them how to draw the sexy lions that I've been sketching in my free time recently, but I can teach them the friendly Disney version.

"Everybody start with a big circle for the head," I instruct, drawing mine and holding it up to show them. The kids dutifully follow my directions. One of the boys has a tongue poked through his teeth, and Becks glances at Drea's paper before she starts on her own.

A tug on my skirt has me glancing down. It's the youngest girl, standing with her arms raised in the universal "pick me up" position. I comply and lift her onto my lap. She's a warm little weight against my chest as she settles in.

"What's your name?" I ask.

"Sophia." She burrows her head into my solar plexus. "You smell nice."

"Yeah, she does."

Jonesy's there at my back, watching me and his sister with an unreadable expression on his face.

"T-thanks," I say, flustered at being surrounded by Jonesy's big, loud family. I wrap my left arm around Sophia to cuddle her a little closer and return to the drawing lesson. "Okay, let's do a longer oval for the body. Like this."

I draw mine and show it to them to copy, then walk them through the ears, the legs, the tail, and the mane, going over each step in detail as the sketches come to life under their fingers. Jonesy and Kristy circle the table, murmuring encouragement, and ten minutes later, the five of us have sketched an entire pride and they're all sharing the ice cream flavors they'd love to try.

"What about you?" I ask Drea.

She sighs. "The pistachio horchata. The drawing in that video made it look, like, *perfect*." She ducks behind her hair as she says, "Your drawing, I guess."

"Yep," I say, leaning forward to tap on her paper. "And your drawing is fantastic. Look at the detail on this front paw! I want to pet him."

"That's so dumb," she scoffs, but her cheeks turn pink and she can't quite hide her smile.

That's one tough little nut cracked, at least a tiny bit.

"Okay. Last step," I announce, "is to sign your masterpiece." I scrawl a big looping *Olivia Fielding* on the bottom of mine, and the kids all follow suit.

"These are so great!" Kristy exclaims. "Look at how well you did, Kai!"

The younger boy pumps his fist and shoots out of the chair to run a lap around the living room. "Will you hang it on the fridge?" he shouts. Sophia wriggles free and joins him in his victory lap.

"Obviously," Kristy says, collecting the papers into a neat pile. When she passes my chair, she whispers, "Thank you so much. It's the quietest they've been in at least a calendar year."

She reaches for my drawing too, but Jonesy snatches it up. "No way. This stays here." He walks to the fridge and secures my lion front and center with a magnet.

I'm not sure what's happening in my chest as I watch him put my rough, rushed drawing in a place of honor on his fridge, but it's big and hot and threatens to burst through my skin. Without even meaning to, I'm on my feet and drifting over to stand next to him.

"And you said you couldn't do better than the mural artist," he says.

"This is miles worse."

"Too modest." He leans forward to peer at it, resting his hand on my lower back as he does. "It's great. You should keep going. Redo the whole mural so it's right."

"You guys are soooo cute," Becks croons, and I glance up to see her beaming at us. Even Drea's frown is marginally less severe.

"Yuck." Tristan wrinkles his nose without looking up from his paper where he's scribbling a black ink cloud over his lion.

Jonesy straightens away from me, but not before squeezing my shoulder. "Someday you'll understand, kid."

Kristy chuckles, then claps her hands. "Children under the age of eighteen, to the car. We've bugged Hollis enough for one day."

The kids jump to obey, although they each swipe another cookie on their way out.

"Nice to meet you," the oldest girls singsong in almost unison as they vanish with the rest of the kids.

"It was nice," Kristy affirms, giving me a quick hug. "Keep an eye on him for me," she whispers. "Make sure he doesn't work too hard."

"I'll do my best," I say, a little unsure of what exactly just happened here or how Jonesy explained my presence to her during their side chat.

Once the van pulls away, I turn to see him leaning against the wall with his hands in his sweats pockets, watching me warily.

"So," he says.

"So," I reply, deeply unsure what happens next.

FIFTEEN

Jonesy

"**Y**our family is great," Liv says.

"Yeah." I run a hand over my eyes, too tired to keep it all in anymore. The lines I've been trying and failing to draw around my life crumbled this afternoon when the kids invaded and Liv met my mom. Why hold back now? "It's why I'm working so much. Mom had a liver transplant this summer, and money's tight. I told her and my stepdad that I'd take care of Christmas gifts for everyone."

A surprised smile spreads across her face. "That's incredibly kind of you."

I shake my head like that'll chase away the admiration shining in her eyes. "It's nothing. It's the least I can do."

"Is she doing okay?" Liv asks.

"Yeah." Relief still sweeps over me when I think about it. "It was... scary. She had a metabolic liver disease, but the doctors say she should get to live the rest of her life now."

Liv doesn't know about Saint Wyatt covering her

medical bills and giving up a piece of his body, and I don't particularly want to tell her that part of it.

"Now I have to"—I wave a hand toward the driveway—"make sure they've all got something magic under the tree in two weeks. That's the real reason they stopped by. She wanted to check on how it's going."

"And?" Liv's brows lift. "How's it going?"

"I've got a couple of things for the little ones, but mostly it's vague ideas and a pile of cash."

"Do you want help?" she asks cautiously, like she's aware that it's not her business but she can't help it.

"You wouldn't mind?" Disbelief creeps into my voice at the thought of voluntarily signing up to pick gifts for kids she just met. "I'm stumped about the older girls."

"Of course not!" She pulls her phone out of her dress pocket and taps it a couple of times. "Let's see... you're doing your boys-only holiday thing tonight, right?"

"Yep. And you and CJ are getting together with Darby?"

"Yep. But we're both off on Tuesday." She glances up with an inviting smile. "Want to go shopping?"

"Absolutely," I say, aware as I do of the pure delight spreading through me. If I wanted company on my shopping trip, I could just bring Wyatt. No, it's the promise of *Liv's* company that's sending happy chemicals zipping through my brain. It's *Liv* wanting to do that with me.

She's in my house. She met my family. She offered to help with them. And all I can think is how much I want to kiss her until we both run out of oxygen.

I'm staring at the curve of her upper lip as I think these kissing thoughts, which means I'm aware of the precise moment that her mouth curves into a challenging little smile. Then her eyes zip up to mine, and the mischief there sets me on full alert.

"Uhhhh, what's up?" I ask suspiciously.

"Wouldn't you like to know?" Her voice is light and teasing as she adds, "Hollis."

"Fuck," I groan, idiotically surprised that she caught my name the fifty or sixty times my family used it today.

"So your mom really went with Wyatt and Hollis, huh?" she asks as she starts to type. "Was she hoping for a pair of Wild West train bandits?"

She's still typing, and now I'm actually nervous.

"What are you doing?"

"Who, me?" She holds up the phone. "Just letting all of our coworkers know that the mystery of your first name's solved."

"Liv," I say in a warning tone, advancing a step. "Give me the phone."

"No way!" she chirps. I edge closer, but she spins away from my hands when I try to reach for her.

"Liv. Livvie." My voice starts out reasonable, but she dodges to the left, so I move faster, cutting off her access to the living room. "Don't you do it!" I call as she pivots to dart down the hallway and run into the first open door she sees.

It's my bedroom, and I take my time following her, not sure how I'll react to *Liv in my bedroom*.

When I reach the doorway, I find that she's come to a dead stop about three steps in and is looking around at my neatly made bed, the running shoes tossed in the corner, the cluttered nightstand. Thank fucking fuck I don't have any Luke stuff in here.

Nope, no Luke stuff. Just Liv. In my bedroom. In one of those dresses I'm obsessed with.

A predatory pleasure spreads through me, and I reach

up and hook my fingers around the top of the doorframe, boxing her in. When she spins to face me, her eyes widen, her gaze traveling down my body before snapping back to the grin on my face.

"Gotcha," I say lazily. But I don't step into the room. Why would I when I can casually stretch one hand in her direction, wriggling my fingers as I say, "Give it up"?

Her nostrils flare as she cradles the phone to her chest, so I change my target and grab for her instead of her phone. Once my hand is on her waist, I tug her closer, and she comes willingly, bumping up against my chest. Her hand falls against my side, and instead of pulling away, her fingers curl around my hip.

"Liv."

I feel the shiver that moves through her as I growl her name, but just as quickly she pushes free and says, "Lemme just hit send on this and then I'll be right with yo—*oof!*"

It's only after I've tackled her to the bed that I realize my tactical error.

I actually don't care if she sends the text. Plenty of people in town know my name so it's not *that* big a mystery. But I've landed on top of her, and all I can feel is how soft she is under me, how warm. All I can see are those liquid brown eyes heating as I press her into the mattress. All I can hear is the tiny catch of her breath when my dick slides against her stomach because yep, I'm hard enough to bust through drywall. I know it. She knows it. And I know she knows it because she wiggles a little bit, just enough to notch the vee of her legs against the head of my cock, forcing me to bite back a groan.

But Liv's not ready to stop messing with me. Her eyes spark as she lifts her hands over her head, holding the phone away from me.

I'm not ready to stop playing either, so I reach up and cage her wrists.

"What now?" I murmur, my breath hot against her cheek.

With a little moan, she drops her phone. I hear it thunk to the carpet, and then I don't hear anything because she's stretching up to brush her lips against mine. It's the briefest, lightest touch imaginable, but it's enough for me to know that she'll taste sweet, like angel sugar cookie and angel Liv.

When I move to kiss her back, she whispers "Hollis" and catches my lower lip between her teeth. As she does, her legs fall open, letting me sink farther into her. The fabric of her dress is thin—I've always thought the stuff she wears was too lightweight for winter—but I'm damn grateful right now because I can feel the heat of her pussy through our layers of clothes.

"Fuck," I growl against her mouth. "You and these dresses."

I keep her wrists pinned with one hand while I slowly start to pull on the sash at her waist with the other, watching intently so I can stop if she tells me to.

She doesn't tell me to stop.

When the tie comes undone and the front of the dress falls open, her eyes fall shut, and she arches her back in a clear invitation.

"Jesus, baby. Jesus." I let go of her wrists to drag my hands down her sides, then back up to rest just below her breasts. "Been wanting to unwrap you for ages."

She slides her leg up mine to hook around my upper thigh. It opens her up even more, and I grind into her until she's rocking against the hot friction of my erection.

"That's so nice, Hollis," she whispers. "That feels so nice."

She slides her hands under my hoodie, trailing her fingers along my spine until she reaches my shoulders and starts to push it off. That's when the tiniest flicker of alarm sparks to life in my brain.

Nice. Like naughty or nice.

Like Luke asked her before he got her off.

She doesn't know that I'm Luke.

Fuck. *Fucking fuck.* What the fuck am I *doing*?

I must tense up because her eyes slowly blink open, and she looks at me with a hazy, unfocused gaze. "W-what's happening?"

What's happening is that I got so wrapped up in the absolute rightness of Liv being in my house and meeting my family and lying in my bed that I forgot all the reasons I can't actually have any of that. So I steel myself to do the hardest thing I've ever done. I roll off her.

She pushes herself up on her elbows once I'm flat on my back on the mattress next to her. "Are you okay?"

No. "We can't do this."

"We can't? Why not?" Her words are baffled.

"We just can't." The second time I say it isn't any easier. What business does "can't" have in bed with us right now? I stare at the ceiling and try to convince myself to do the right thing. "I haven't been…"

"Haven't been what?"

"Honest with you," I say hoarsely. "About parts of my life."

I should've fucking told her. I should've told her that first night at the Crimson Lounge or the day she showed up at Verdant for an interview. And I definitely should've told her before I slipped my hand under her skirt. If I had, maybe we'd already be past it. Maybe we'd be here anyway, and I'd be able to kiss her and touch her and love her the way my entire being is crying out to do. But she literally just told me that she's embarrassed that I know about her crush on Santa, that she's worried about me laughing about it behind her back. And if I confess now, she's going to think I'm a complete sociopath who's been toying with her for weeks instead of an idiot who didn't realize until too late that he should've shared a relatively small secret before it got bigger and more impossible with every passing day.

But I didn't tell her, which means I don't deserve her. Not her soft eyes or her eager mouth or a single inch of the luscious body that I'm dying to take my time exploring in the sunlight. When I risk a glance at her, I feel even worse. She's sitting upright, confusion replacing arousal on her face.

"You've got to be kidding me." She crosses her arms over her chest. "Are motivational pep talks your kink or something?"

I laugh, but it's brief and then it's gone. "I guess so. When it comes to you, anyway."

"I cannot believe my nipples are hard and my panties are wet and I have to hype up the guy who just turned me down for sex," she mutters before grabbing my face and forcing me to look at her. "Okay, here goes. You're incredible. I want this."

And I want to believe her. So, so badly. But she doesn't have all the facts.

"You don't really know me." I almost choke on the bitterness of my tone.

"I think I know you well enough." She tilts her head and lets her dress fall open again, her gingerbread hair sliding over a bare shoulder. The come-on in her voice is hot as fuck, but I absolutely cannot keep touching her if I don't come clean about everything. Lying to her, not telling her who was really with her in that VIP room, letting her spill her fantasies about Luke to me and about me to Luke. Pissed won't cover it. I imagine her betrayal, her tears, her hurt, and it shreds something in my chest. There's no way to navigate this that doesn't cause her some kind of damage.

Unless. She's leaving town in two weeks. If I stop us right now and we go back to being work friends only, I can maybe, possibly justify not telling her. In that scenario, she'll leave Beaucoeur and forget all about her short-time buddy Hollis and her short-lived infatuation with Santa Luke. No harm done.

Well. Harm to me once she's gone from my life. But that's the price I'm paying for this clusterfuck.

Okay. I can do this. I have to do this.

"You're leaving," I say slowly. "And I think it's best that we just stay friends for the rest of your time here. If we move forward with this, I'd have to tell you things that would make you hate me, and I don't"—I have to swallow before I can get the rest out—"I don't know if I could live with that."

The words hang in the air.

"What could you possibly say to make me hate you?" She sounds incredulous. "Whatever stupid things you did or used to do or whatever it is that makes you think you're a bad guy, it's not who you are now. I don't have to *know* you to know that."

Her faith in me is a punch in the gut. I slide to the side of the bed and drop my head into my hands, willing my cock back down, wishing for a time machine, wondering about every decision in my fucking life that led to this moment where I'm burning up for the woman of my dreams but I can't have her because she's accidentally tangled up in my mess.

I can't be with her without being honest. And I can't be honest with her without changing her opinion of me. She's going to think I'm a user, a manipulator. Someone cruel who enjoyed hiding the truth from her. The last thing I want to do is make her feel like that. And yeah, I'm also selfish enough that I don't want her thinking those things about me. Since I met her, all I've wanted is for her to like me. Maybe even to love me. But that's off the table now because of the hole I dug for myself. I'll replace that Canadian motherfucker as the villain in her story, and she doesn't deserve another villain. She doesn't deserve any of the shit that telling her would bring.

The silence stretches so long that Liv clearly decides she's had enough. She stands, movements jerky as she reties her belt and walks to the other side of the bed to collect her phone.

"I don't know what your deal is," she says stiffly. "Maybe you're actually with one of the girls from Chicago, or maybe you really meant it that you don't date people at work. Maybe I really am too much like Darby to ever be your type. But I clearly misunderstood things, and I apologize for that."

A howl builds in my chest, but there's nothing I can say to stop her other than the truth. I'm just a guy who didn't realize until too late that he was keeping a huge secret from someone he was falling for, and it's gotten too big to share without it blowing back on both of us.

I watch helplessly as her face crumples when I don't contradict any of the untrue things she said, and I fumble for a way to make things okay again. To keep her in my life for as long as she's around.

"Can we just"—my voice cracks—"can we go back to how we were? Before. Just put this behind us. Like you did with Canada, right? Let's pretend this didn't happen and go back to being friends. Can we do that?" Because unlike a lover or a boyfriend, a friend you won't see again at the end of the month can keep his secrets without it being a betrayal.

Her lower lip trembles for a horrifying second before she straightens her spine and schools her face.

"Sure." The word emerges clipped. "We'll just go back to how things were. And don't worry, *Hollis*," she says, her voice acid. "Your secret's safe with me."

"My secret." I laugh without a trace of humor and listen to her footsteps moving down the hall. By the time I find the strength to follow her, she has her shoes and coat on, and her hand is on the doorknob.

"Liv, I—" My jaw works as I struggle to come up with the perfect words to fix what I fucked up. She turns to me expectantly, and for a terrifying second, a confession hovers on the tip of my tongue. The truth is right there, ready to flood out like poisoned honey.

But I can't. I can't do it. So I follow my own terrible fucking suggestion and try to channel the way I've been with her. My smirk. My snark. My confidence.

I cock my head and slant her a grin that physically pains me to produce. "Have fun with the girls tonight, Fielding."

The hope in her face flickers and dies, and I watch her revert to the cool, untouchable woman I met that very first night.

"Sure, Jonesy," she says. "I hope you and the guys have fun too." Then she pushes open the door and leaves.

SIXTEEN

Jonesy

"I'm sorry, you kicked her out of your bed?"

Wyatt punctuates his question with the *thwack* of his club against the golf ball.

"No," I correct him. "She left my bed when I told her we couldn't have sex."

"Aren't you the guy who let the older sister of the bride eat scrambled eggs off your stomach one time?"

This is from Gabe's brother-in-law, Sebastian. I met him three hours ago, and he's already giving me shit. What has my life become?

"Ha ha, so funny. Everyone stop and laugh at the loser who's completely fucked up his life." I'm sprawled on the lush grass of the Beaucoeur Country Club driving range watching as Wyatt hits another ball high into the night sky.

"The wind really caught that one," Gabe snickers.

"Let's see if you can get it higher." Wyatt bats at the cracked plastic candy cane dangling off the bucket hat he's wearing.

"Can and will." Gabe takes a swig from the bottle of Patrón, then swaps it with Wyatt for the driver and the hat, which Gabe settles carefully onto his head so he doesn't knock off any of the holly berry sprays that have been threatening to come loose for a few years now.

The designated golfer hat is an important part of Golfmas, our annual holiday celebration. Wyatt found the red-and-green plaid monstrosity at a dollar store forever ago, and we've been adding to it every year since, gluing on little Christmas knickknacks and the scraps of decorations that we scrounge from our parents' houses, that kind of thing. Some year it's going to get too heavy to actually wear, but this year is not that year.

We've been celebrating Golfmas since Gabe and I were sixteen and Wy was seventeen. That summer, we landed jobs at the country club golf course and had the farmer's tans to prove it. As the season wound down in December, our terrible boss Mr. Finchy called us into his office one by one. We were terrified we were being fired, but instead he gave us each our year-end bonuses and an invitation to come back the following season. It was more money than any of us had ever seen.

We celebrated by sneaking onto the driving range after hours with a tray of fried chicken, two fruitcakes, half a bottle of tequila, and some spiked eggnog—all left over from the club's Christmas party the night before—and had golf cart races and hit a crate of balls all over the range until we couldn't see straight and had to sleep it off in the equipment room. It was the best night of any of our lives up to that point, and since then, it's grown into a slightly more adult event.

We even have T-shirts. This year's is bright green and features a golfing Santa saying "Ho-ho-hole in one" under the idiotic logo Gabe designed for our fifth annual event. He swears he picked out this year's Santa theme before I ended up in a weird jealousy throuple with Liv and my Luke alter ego, but I'm not sure I believe him.

"Take that!" Gabe shouts, sending his ball sailing so high into the air that it arcs straight up and lands a few yards away.

"Impressive," Wyatt says before turning back to me. "So what are you going to do about Liv?"

"There's nothing I *can* do," I say. "I already hooked up with her as snake-hips Santa, which means I can't hook up with her as myself. And I can't explain why we can't hook up now without telling her we already hooked up. The end."

Hook up. My stomach curls at the dismissive phrase, but talking about sex with Liv is too big and too personal for me to parse while I'm on a golf course drinking tequila straight from the bottle.

"So you're just going to pretend nothing happened the next time you see her?" Sebastian asks skeptically. He and his girlfriend were in town to do Christmassy things with Darby this weekend, so he's experiencing Golfmas for the first time.

"I've been pretending nothing happened with Santa Luke, so why not keep it going?"

"Right, but she doesn't know you know that something happened with Santa Luke," Gabe says.

"And she definitely knows nothing happened with you." Wyatt, our designated driver tonight, adds after taking a sip from his thermos of green tea.

"Fuck." I tug on my hair in frustration. How did things get so complicated? "All I know is, I'm going to keep things light and friendly at work, and I'll keep doing that until she leaves town." It'll suck balls, but I'll do it.

"Or you could tell her," Gabe offers.

"Sure. Because she'll forgive me immediately and decide to stay in town so we can get married and have a million babies." For a second, I let myself imagine it. My dream scenario. Then I face reality. "Here's what's really going to happen if I tell her—she pepper-sprays me and then never speaks to me again, and when she leaves town, she'll always remember me as the worst asshole she ever met."

Gabe winces. "Okay, yeah, I see what you mean."

"She already got fucked over by her boss in Canada. I cannot be another guy who breaks her trust. So I'm gonna stay her funny little pal Jonesy who's too shallow and inconsequential for her to remember once she's out of here." The pain I should be feeling over that is dulled by the Patrón, which probably explains why I tip the bottle back again.

"Do you know the way to fix all your problems?" I look up to see Gabe holding out the club and designated golfer hat and haul myself to my feet, swaying a little. I've had significantly more tequila than chicken tonight.

"Time machine," I say. "I've already considered it." I tug on the designated golfer hat and line myself up in front of the tee. I can't keep wallowing in my own misery. Not on Golfmas. So I toss my head like a show pony, knowing it'll jingle the tiny sleigh bell pin that Sebastian brought as his price of admission to the group. Then I squint at the tee, like I have a chance in hell of figuring out sight lines and angles and wind speed, close my eyes, and give the ball a blind whack. When the guys start to trash-talk, I risk looking and see that it cut to the left and vanished into the bushes that separate the driving range from the rest of the course.

"Laugh all you want." I take another swig of tequila and prepare to go again. "But don't forget that I'm famous for another type of ball control at work." As I hoped, it makes them dissolve into guffaws.

The three of us took very different lessons away from our time at the golf course. Wyatt learned how to schmooze with rich men and is the only one of us who actually golfs now. Gabe learned how to care for plants and other living things thanks to his grounds crew assignment. And me? My tenure at the golf course was shorter than the other two, and I learned how easy it is to let your boss down and lose a job you love.

Pushing the thought aside, I draw the club back and bring it down as smoothly as I can. The ball goes skidding across the grass like I'd tried to skip a stone on water.

The guys crack up again, so I whirl on them. "Sure, you can all put a ball in a hole, but can you do a dozen body rolls in a row while women shove cash in your thong?" I start to gyrate as I speak, dropping it so low that my ass practically brushes the ground. My life's a mess, but at least I've still got moves.

Gabe scoffs. "Can I body roll?" He breaks into a smooth slide, spin, roll routine, his technique surprisingly good. "How do you think I got Darby to agree to marry me?"

"Dude, no! That's my sister!" Sebastian yells. But he's also drunk and laughing, and even though his attempt to mimic me and Gabe is halting and a little jerky, he commits to it, and I give him snaps for effort.

After watching the three of us, Wyatt—serious, stone-faced Wyatt—says, "Is that all there is to it?" and holds a nine iron over his head with both hands while he swivels his hips with such an intense look of concentration that I collapse in tequila-fueled hysterics.

"Gabe I can work with. The rest of you, back to the kiddie table," I wheeze. "Watch and learn, motherfuckers."

I gyrate my way over, dancing up on them like they're paying guests with fat stacks of cash. Well, I dance up on Gabe and Sebastian. Wyatt wards me off with a single arched eyebrow.

"Goddamn," Sebastian says when I'm done, his face flushed red from laughing. He reaches into his wallet and fishes out a twenty that he stuffs in the back pocket of my jeans. "Worth every penny."

"Why, thank you!" I pull it out, kiss it, and tuck it away again. "I'm gonna use this to take your mother out for a nice lobster dinner."

Sebastian squawks in outrage. "You leave Margaret St. Claire out of this!" He lunges toward me, intent on taking his twenty back. "Margaret St. Claire is a saint!"

Laughing, I dodge away, but his pursuit only makes it as far as the blanket we spread near the club's giant outdoor heaters. He stops to grab another piece of chicken, and I flop to the ground with a shiver. Even though it's December 15, it's in the fifties tonight thanks to a weird little global warming uptick in our usual temps—hello, climate zone 6a —but it's still cold enough that I'm glad I threw a coat on over my Golfmas tee.

"No, but seriously," Gabe says when he wanders over to sit next to me. "There's an easy answer to many of your problems."

"Hit me," I say.

"Quit your jobs and come work with me."

"Okay."

"I just think that it's past time for you—uhh, come again?"

"Okay," I repeat. "I'll quit my jobs and come be the H in HG Landscaping." I sit up so I can see his slack-jawed look of surprise up close. "You did say I could start on January 2, right? Or was that a one-time offer?"

"The offer is still very much on the table." A grin spreads across his face. "Are you for real right now?"

I nod, and he throws his head back in a victory whoop, grabbing my shoulders and shaking me so hard the bells jingle on the designated golfer hat that's still on my head.

"Fuck yes! Next step, global domination."

"Let me know if you need an MBA along for that ride," Wyatt says.

Sebastian raises his hand. "I'll pilot your private jet."

Eventually, we all end up on the grass, staring up at the winter sky. The stars are bright diamond points in the crisp night air, but the tequila we're passing around is doing its job keeping our insides warm.

"Not that I'm not grateful for your New Year's resolution, but what brought this on?" Gabe asks. "Liv?"

It's a good question, and I stall by grabbing the chicken bucket and digging through it until I find a drumstick. If I'm actually giving up dancing, it means I can have another goddamn piece of chicken. I'm not fucking around with that fruitcake though.

I take a bite as I consider how to answer.

"I'd say it's more like I'm changing for me." I speak around a mouthful of fried bird. "Don't get me wrong, I'm pretty sure I'm in love with her." I pause for their reactions, but nobody falls to the ground in shock. In fact, Gabe and

Wyatt exchange glances like maybe they've already discussed this possibility. "Wow, okay, life-changing announcements don't have the same weight these days," I grumble. "Anyway, Liv's spent the past month talking about what a decent guy I am. She's clearly wrong, but what the hell? I may as well see if I can be slightly less of a chaotic mess."

Wyatt scoffs, and I glance over in time to see the most big brotherly of eye rolls.

"Oh my God, Holly. Get *over* yourself. You were a good guy, you are a good guy, you've always been a good guy." He sits up carefully, like he's still favoring the incision site. "You watch out for the little sibs, you always show up to family dinners, and you told Lisa Pfeffinger that you wouldn't go to homecoming with her your junior year because you knew I wanted to ask her."

I blink. "You know about Lisa?"

"She took my virginity. We're still close." A smirk crosses his face before he's all business Wyatt again. "But we're talking about you. You and the way you're tying yourself in knots to protect Liv whether she wants it or not. You've believed some really weird stories about yourself your whole life, and it's fucking tedious how wrong they are."

"Harsh," I say mildly, but inside my brain's rioting. Wyatt doesn't think I'm a fuckup? Wyatt noticed how I helped him out in social situations during high school?

Gabe jumps in. "I do actually give a shit about the business, you know. I haven't been busting your ass nonstop about joining me just to be nice. I want to be business partners for life, dude."

He holds out his hand for a fist bump, so I rub my greasy

fingers on a napkin and give his knuckles a tap, a little too overcome to speak.

"I only know you as the guy with all the stripper stories, but these two are very convincing," Sebastian says as he gnaws on a hunk of fruitcake. Of course that goody-goody likes fruitcake.

Still, what Sebastian said sticks in my craw. "Right. Can't forget all the ridiculous stripper stories."

"Don't confuse ridiculous with unreliable," Wyatt says. "You're one. You're not the other."

"Ridiculous?" That doesn't sound good.

"Goofy," Wy amends.

"A free spirit," says Gabe.

"Funny as hell." That's from Sebastian.

"Uh. Thanks, guys."

But Wyatt's not done. "For what it's worth, I know for a fact that you don't want to fall in love with someone who expects you to be better. You want to fall in love with someone who *makes* you better by loving you back."

Gabe gives a low, descending whistle that ends with his hands exploding outward. "Wyatt Jones with the truth bomb."

He shrugs. "I'm just saying. Talk to her. Give her the benefit of the doubt that she cares about you enough to give *you* the benefit of the doubt."

My lifelong track record doesn't really lend itself to the benefit of the doubt, but I don't bring that up. I'm trying to stay positive here.

"Damn, Wy," Gabe says. "When did you get so wise?"

"Yeah, and when are you gonna tell us what happened with you and Reese?" I add, attempting to shift the spotlight on someone else's tragic love life for a bit.

"Never." Wyatt lies back down, links his hands over his

stomach, crosses one ankle over the other, and shuts his eyes.

I'll get it out of him, I pantomime to Gabe.

"And no, you're not going to magically get me to spill," he says without moving a muscle.

"That's some older brother witchcraft," I mutter. Wy cracks open one eye to glare at me, and I hop up and reach for the eggnog. "Time for the toasts!"

The two experienced Golfmas-ers groan, and Sebastian looks around in confusion. "What's happening?"

"I mean, do *you* want an eggs- and dairy-heavy drink right now?" I shove a plastic glass into his hand and pour some of the thick, rummy liquid into it, then do the same for the rest of us.

Sebastian goes a little green. "Now that you mention it—"

"You'll drink it and you'll like it," Wyatt orders, then holds his glass aloft. "To Mr. Finchy! You were a miserable prick of a boss, but you were our miserable prick of a boss."

We cheer, sip, and grimace.

"To Jerry, you ham-loving bastard!" I say, and we happily drink to the burnout nighttime security guard who gives us the run of the driving range one night a year for the low, low price of one sugar-cured ham that he'll cook for Christmas dinner, as well as our promise that we won't leave chicken bones on the greens.

It's Gabe's turn. "To our women! Past"—he nods at Wyatt—"present"—he nods at Sebastian—"and potential." He nods at me, and I slam the rest of my nog.

"Uh, here's to our women who are trying to reach us," Sebastian says with a glance at his phone screen. "Birdy says we should come by."

Wyatt twirls his keys as we gather all traces of our party

and shove it into the trunk of his Audi. Once we're all piled in, he asks, "Where are we headed?"

Gabe rattles off an address that I don't recognize. At my confused look, he slants me a shit-eating grin.

"You can thank me later, buddy."

SEVENTEEN

Liv

"Wait, so he kicked you out of his bedroom?" Darby's looking at me in utter confusion.

"No," I say, gesturing with my glass to emphasize my point and sloshing peppermint martini on my wrist as I do. I lean forward to slurp up the spilled drops. "We started making out and he got weird about honesty and, like, expectations, and then I left."

CJ's nose wrinkles. "He knows you're only here for a little bit longer, right? This is a fun hookup situation. Easy breezy, everybody wins."

"That's what I thought!" I toss my hands in the air. "But he was all, 'No, fair maiden, I cannot sully you with my beastly reputation.'"

"Really," Darby says. "Jonesy said all that."

"Close enough." I deflate onto the couch. "And then he told me to forget about it so we could go back to being friends."

And I'd wanted to smack him for it. I watched Hollis and his tortured vulnerability vanish, to be replaced by that forced Jonesy smirk that lodged itself deep in my chest.

"I begged him to sleep with me, and he turned me down." I stare into the bottom of my martini glass like there might be an explanation in there somewhere. "And that sucks because I *like* him. Like for real."

CJ pulls me into a hug. "I'm sorry, love. He's an asshole."

"He is," I say into her neck. Then, "He's not."

CJ sighs. "I know."

For a moment, I'm back at Hollis', inhaling the warm, sleepy smell of his sheets, feeling the hardness of his body, watching his eyes flare when I bit his lip. He's not an asshole, which is what makes this afternoon so confusing.

Darby's almost-sister-in-law Birdy raises her hand like we're in class. "Can we just go back to the hot stripper for a second?" She punctuates her question with a loud slurp of her drink.

I press the backs of my hands to my overheated cheeks at the memory. It took two and a half martinis for me to spill everything about the past week to CJ, Darby, and Birdy. And I do mean *ev-uh-re-thing*, starting with Hollis turning me down and working backward to the fact that I'm pretty sure making me come made Luke come.

"The thing with Luke," I say, "is that before he bailed, he was surprisingly sweet. Just kind of holding me and stroking my back and breathing hard against my neck. It was weirdly, I dunno, intimate."

Darby bites her lip before speaking. "That does sound like it was special."

"Which is wild, right? We're strangers."

I hop up when the oven timer goes off to swap the Christmas tree-shaped cranberry-brie pull-aparts with the wreath-shaped pigs-in-a-blanket pull-aparts. The big plans CJ, Darby, and I talked about a few weeks ago turned into an evening at CJ's house, drinking and gossiping and snacking our way through a charcuterie board while Gabe and Darby's brother Sebastian were off with the Jones brothers doing some kind of Christmas tradition that I don't fully understand. We've gotten to the part of the evening that requires heavy hors d'oeuvres to soak up the alcohol, so we did it up festive style.

"That smells amazing!" Birdy says, reaching for a doughy circle of brie when I set it on the coffee table in the living room, then hissing when it burns the tips of her fingers.

CJ hands her a fresh martini. "Here. This'll help."

Birdy smiles her thanks, then says, "I haven't met Jonesy yet. What's he like?"

"Total charming flirt," CJ says. "Hot as hell. Tons of fun."

The description makes me frown, and I glance over to see that Darby's expression is similar.

"I think he tends to get underestimated," she says.

"And he underestimates himself," I add. "Ho—uh, Jonesy has some wildly incorrect ideas about the person he is." Shit. Even though he's Hollis to me now, I did promise that I'd keep it to myself, so Jonesy it is in public.

Darby's eyes find mine. "You should talk to him."

"I tried," I say briskly, searching for a distraction. The brie should be cool enough to at least serve, so I grab one of CJ's sledding snowman plates and fork up a portion. "He basically shut down."

"Yum," Birdy says when I hand her the plate. "But

yuck. Maybe you should try again. God knows it took me and Seb a few tries to get the communication right."

I hand the next loaded plate to Darby, who nods encouragingly.

"What's the point?" I sigh. "The Minneapolis job is pretty much a done deal."

CJ stabs her fork into a brie ball. "Orrrrr you could keep racking up the freelance jobs from companies desperate to work with you outside of the limitations of big, stuffy firms, which you can do from my guest room until you find your own place here in town."

"Ohhh, I like that!" Darby says. "You should do that."

"How many inquiries are currently in your inbox, and are they enough to support you while you live with me for free?" CJ demands.

"Um. More than a few." Way more than a few actually. I've heard from a surprising number of former clients asking if I'm available to create campaigns for them next year. It's enough to seriously consider giving it a go as an independent ad director. I could probably even pay CJ rent. But it's a huge gamble, and despite recent behaviors—Hollis, Santa Luke, that sexy red bra—I really am committed to cutting back on risks.

"Then again, what do I know?" CJ says around a mouthful of bread and brie. "I'm just a badass corporate consultant and international assassin wrangler."

"I knew it!" I say, grateful to move off my employment woes.

Birdy snorts. "I hope all of that's true."

CJ shrugs enigmatically.

"Anyway," Darby says, "if you were sticking around, I do think Jonesy would open up to you more. Without betraying any confidences, I think he"—she considers before she speaks again—"he got in over his head with you and doesn't know how to get out of it."

"I think I'd rather have that conversation with Luke," I joke.

Birdy cough-laughs and almost spits out a cranberry.

"Kidding," I say quickly. "Luke was... *guh*. He's that person you get one night with that you think about when you're old." My mind wants to whisk me back to that little room, but no, that's not what we're talking about now. "With Jonesy, I'm all tangled up. Talking to him sounds terrifying because I don't want to get the 'let's stay friends' lecture again."

Darby hesitates before speaking again. "Guys have all kinds of sides they can show us if they're brave enough." She looks like she's about to say more, then she shrugs and reaches for her drink. "Give Jonesy a little grace. I don't think he's ever had a relationship he was truly scared to lose before."

I'm about to ask her to tell me more, tell me *everything*, about his past relationships and why ours might be different when her phone lights up with a text.

"Speaking of the guys, they're almost here," she says.

"The guys?" I repeat. "As in Hollis?"

"Who's...? Oh my God, Jonesy's first name is *Hollis*?" CJ shrieks.

I screw my eyes shut and try to sink into the couch. "Pretend I didn't say that."

Darby just laughs. "Don't worry. I know all his secrets."

"I don't!" CJ leaps to her feet. "You're telling me that ridiculously hot man is named *Hollis*?"

"And get this. His family calls him Holly," I say as I set my empty plate on the table, glancing down at what I'm wearing. I'm not Verdant dressy or Crimson Lounge fancy, but my jeans and sweater are cute enough for a guy I'm mad at, right?

"They're here!" Darby announces, and for some reason, this gets us all to run to the front window like little kids, crowding around the Christmas tree CJ and I decorated last weekend.

"God, my man is hot," Birdy sighs.

"He is!" CJ says. "He's totally..." Her voice trails off with a croak and she takes a step back from the window.

"You okay?" I ask.

"Wyatt Jones is walking up my driveway," she says in a funny, faraway voice. "Why the *fuck* is Wyatt Jones walking up my driveway?"

"Who, Hollis' brother?" My answer comes out like a question, and CJ spins to face me, her eyes wide.

"Jonesy's brother is *Wyatt Jones*?"

I've never seen my best friend this rattled, ever, but before I can drag any details out of her, the front door opens to reveal a grinning Gabe.

"Any sexy ladies in the house?"

Darby runs into his arms with a squeal, and Birdy does the same when Sebastian walks in behind him, sporting the same thick brown hair as his sister.

Behind him is Hollis, who enters the house cautiously, his eyes locking on me the second he's inside. I'm sure I'm about to say something profound and witty, something that'll make it be not weird and awful between us, but CJ beats me to the punch.

"No." She storms up to the man who just crossed the threshold. "Get out, Wyatt."

Hollis' brother stops dead in his tracks, his face blank for a moment before his lips pull into a sneer. "Charlotte Jane. What a surprise to see you in a house."

She crosses her arms over her chest. "Where else would I be?"

"I honestly never gave it much thought," he says in a bored voice. "Hiding in a Venus flytrap? Or at the center of a labyrinth?" He snaps his fingers. "No, I've got it. On a rock, luring unsuspecting sailors to their death."

He's smiling now, showing all his teeth, and CJ trembles in fury. "Get *out!*" she says again, this time putting her hands on his midsection and shoving. He winces and takes a step back, and Hollis springs into action, putting himself between CJ and his brother.

"As curious as I am about what's going on here," he says with his bright Jonesy smile, "can Wy stay if he promises to be on his best behavior? I swear he's housebroken."

"No!" CJ shouts as I say, "Of course he can."

I wrap my arm around my friend's waist and drag her away. "Why don't you go check on the pigs in a blanket?" I say brightly.

"Pigs in a blanket?" Gabe's head snaps up from where he's been whispering with Darby.

"Pigs in a blanket," Darby confirms as she herds everyone into the living room, including a mulishly silent CJ and a wary-looking Wyatt. It leaves me and Hollis alone in the front hallway.

"Hi," he says quietly, his warm brown eyes drinking me in.

"Hi." His cheeks are pink, maybe from alcohol or maybe from the night air. God, I wish it was from seeing me. You know, his *friend*.

He shrugs out of his coat, revealing the shirt underneath, and all other thoughts flee. "What on earth are you wearing?"

He plucks at the front of the eye-searingly green fabric. "Hot, right?"

"Santa," I say inanely as I take in the buff, golf club-wielding Saint Nick plastered across his torso. Flustered at the even tangential reminder of my encounter with Luke, I start to turn away, but Hollis stops me with a hand on my arm, then lets me go immediately, like my skin is lava.

"I want to apologize for earlier," he says, his expression as serious as I've ever seen it. "There were a million better ways I could've handled it, and instead, I said and did things that hurt your feelings. Christ, Liv, it's the last thing I'd ever want to do. But I did, and I'm so sorry."

He doesn't demand my forgiveness. He doesn't even ask for it. He just looks at me with those melting brown eyes, oozing sincerity and remorse. It doesn't change anything, obviously, but it's at least nice to hear the words.

"Yeah, well, I'm sorry too," I tell him.

"What? No." He shakes his head, the motion almost frantic. "You did nothing wrong."

"Oh, I'm aware," I say sharply. I left his place thinking I'd misread things between us, but going back over it in my mind, I know I didn't. He wanted me as much as I wanted him. "What I'm sorry about is letting you almost club me to death with all that baggage you carry around. Unless you're a Bitcoin entrepreneur or something truly heinous like that, I can't imagine what you've done in your life that's so terrible."

His face contorts, but he doesn't offer up an explanation, so I shrug like I'm unbothered.

"You were right. I'm leaving soon, so it's fine. It's... whatever. It's fine." It's not fine. I'm still hurt and confused and burning for him, but if he wants friends, I'll give him friends. I'll be the best goddamn friend in the world. "I appreciate the apology though."

He shoves his hands into his pockets and curls in on himself just the slightest bit. "I can't believe I'm really about to say this, but it's not you, it's me."

I roll my eyes at the cliché. "I mean, obviously. I'm great." I say it lightly, trying to make it a joke, but he pins me with his gaze.

"You really are, Liv. I need you to know that." His eyes are almost pleading, but for what? *He's* the one who made the choice for both of us, just like he's the one acting like he regrets it now.

He blinks and ends our staring contest. "Anyway, congrats. You're off the hook for shopping on Tuesday."

"Oh." In all the upheaval, I kind of forgot about it. "Um, okay. If that's what you want."

"Of course that's not what I want." His voice is a frustrated whip crack, and it's a beat before he continues in a calmer tone. "Sorry. I'll be fine on my own. Thank you again for the offer."

He has that intense look on his face again, the one that makes me think he has an internet's worth of words that he wants to unleash but doesn't know how. And that's when my anger starts to soften into pity.

Let's review what we know. Point one: Hollis clearly has self-esteem issues and a warped idea of the kind of person he is, possibly stemming from some capital *I* issues with his brother. Point two: Hollis has never had a serious relationship if Darby's comments are anything to go by. Point three: I strongly suspect that Hollis really does *like* me like me, to put it in grade-school parlance. And point four: Hollis knows I'm leaving town soon.

So what conclusions can we draw? A man with a shaky

sense of his own worth likes a girl but doesn't know how to be in a relationship, particularly one with a clear end date, so he got in his own way, fucked everything up, and regrets it.

This leads me to the fifth and possibly most important point: Despite everything, I still like him too.

I surrender to the temptation. "Hollis, would you like me to go shopping with you on Tuesday? I really was looking forward to helping you shop for the girls." Then I add, "As friends of course," just to make it clear that I respect his wishes and won't be throwing myself at him again.

"Really? Yes! Obviously, yes." His relieved, delighted smile makes my heart squeeze, and my friendly intentions waver as I fight the urge to shake him and then kiss him.

"If you two want any pigs, you'd better get in here!" Gabe shouts, rescuing me from my way-too-tender feelings.

Hollis grins at me one more time before calling back, "Save us some pigs!"

"And blankets!" I add.

Before we head to the living room, he stops me to whisper, "Do you have any idea what's up with Wyatt and CJ?"

Friends. I can do the friends thing. "None," I whisper back. "What the hell? I've never seen her so pissed."

"I've only ever seen Wy that pissed at me. But yeah, we need to get to the bottom of it." He whispers that last bit and then heads to the living room to join the rest of the group. I follow more slowly, pondering how quickly I was demoted from "I want to peel her out of that dress" to "I want to platonically solve mysteries with her."

Our friends are seated around the coffee table in the living room, working their way through the brie tree, the pig wreath, and the restocked charcuterie board. Birdy's on

Sebastian's lap in the overstuffed chair, and Gabe's hand-feeding Darby a blanketed pig on the couch. CJ and Wyatt ended up sitting across from each other, and she's glaring at him over the rim of her martini glass while he calmly covers a baguette slice in hot pepper jam.

CJ pulls her gaze away and pointedly smiles at Hollis as he settles next to his brother.

"Hi!" she says to him. "Birdy and Seb were just telling us that they're taking a first-anniversary road trip next week."

I reclaim my drink and sit down next to her as Wyatt says, "Liv, have you ever heard of the Christmas festival in Bermuda, Ohio?"

Hollis and I make brief eye contact, and I can see he's as amused as I am by the *who's the better listener* competition they have going on.

"Don't make us pawns in your little game," Hollis tells the two of them before turning to Birdy and Sebastian. "Tell us all about your trip."

The pair launch into a description of Niagara Falls hotels and rental cars, and Hollis slants a private smile my way as he layers salami and cheese onto a cracker. I hesitantly return it, grateful for his apology and how it helped clear the air while at the same time not wanting to stray outside of the new boundaries we've established for ourselves.

Once they're done outlining their full itinerary, Birdy lifts her wineglass and straightens the green Christmas bow nestled in her hair. "Here's to my man landing a ho-ho-hole in one in every hotel we stop in!"

Sebastian hauls her in for a kiss as the rest of us raise our glasses to whoop and holler.

My phone lights up in the middle of the celebration, and I glance at the text.

"Holy shit! A plea!" I look up to see everyone staring at me, so I hold out my phone like that explains everything. "Richie's prosecutor just texted. He accepted a guilty plea for his many crimes. Vindication!"

CJ's the first to screech in victory, and everybody else joins in, even Birdy and Sebastian, who don't know the story.

"Ten years!" My god, Canadian justice feels good. "It'll be entered tomorrow. Fingers crossed for no early release on account of good behavior."

"To bad behavior!" Hollis yells, and we all clink and drink.

"While we're toasting..." Gabe leans forward to look at Hollis, who gives a *what the hell shrug*. That was apparently the permission he was looking for because Gabe clears his throat and says, "I'm proud to announce that next year, HG Landscape will finally live up to its name."

Darby's gasp fills the room. "For real? Jonesy, you're finally joining the business!"

He flushes bright red, an almost bashful smile spreading across his face. "I gave Darryl my two weeks at work today."

She squeals and runs to hug him as Gabe lifts his glass. "To Jonesy!"

"To Jonesy!" we all scream back.

Well, they all scream it. I bite my lip and wish I didn't want so badly to be the one who got to hug him.

EIGHTEEN

Jonesy

I'm a mess of nerves as I pull up in front of Liv's on Tuesday morning.

She's giving me a second chance. Not at anything romantic, which is fine. That's the way it has to be. I'm thrilled that she's willing to spend any time with me, period. Our relationship, whatever that may look like now, is resting in my palm, as delicate as rose petals and as easily crushed.

Fuck, I don't want to crush it.

My hand's on the release to hop out of the truck and knock on her front door, but she beats me to it, stepping onto the porch and floating down the stairs with a sunny smile directed at me.

"Good morning!" She climbs into the cab before I can get around to open the door for her.

"Morning!" I exclaim. "Wow, it's cold. Can you believe the cold? I have the heater up on high so if you get hot, let me know. Or if you're cold, I can adjust it."

Oh my god, shut uppppp. I'm famously good at talking

to women, but Liv makes my tongue feel too big for my mouth, and my hands are clumsy as I gesture at the coffee in the cup holder at her knee.

"I got you your favorite."

"Scorched from the bottom of the pot at the gas station?" She picks it up and takes a long slurp. "Perrrrrrrfect."

I laugh and nudge a bakery bag in her direction. "Also this."

She hums in delight and breaks off a chunk of the red-and-green sprinkle-topped donut she finds inside. While she's chewing, she breaks off another section and offers it to me.

"I got that for you," I tell her.

"Yep. And I'm happy to share."

I know she is. She's everything good. As sweet as that bite of donut and as fun as the sprinkles on top.

My eyes drift to the temptation between her fingers. I'm still getting used to the idea that I don't have to keep my body in pristine Luke condition, and the longer she holds that donut bite out, the more I waver.

"Twist my arm," I finally say, letting her drop it into my palm.

I was wrong. As delicious as that sprinkle donut is, Liv's even sweeter... which is not what I should be thinking on this casual, friendly, no-big-deal shopping expedition.

After more soul-searching and self-reflection than I've ever done, I've accepted the fact that I'm damned if I do and damned if I don't. I can't change the fact that I didn't tell her I was Luke on day one, and with every passing day that I don't tell her, it just gets worse. That, in turn, makes it even harder to tell her, which makes continuing to *not* tell her an even bigger worse than the previous worse. I am, as the ancient Greek philosophers would say, fucked. My head hurts thinking about it.

Now if she was staying, maybe it'd be different. If there was a chance at a real relationship with her, maybe then it'd be worth the risk. But she's not. So we'll just be casual friends, and I won't lay a single grubby, lustful finger on her, no matter how much I dream about it.

The slight hitch in my plan is the question of whether casual friends go Christmas shopping together. I suspect they don't, but I didn't have the strength to say no at CJ's. She looked disappointed at not being part of it, and when she asked me directly, the words erupted out of me like a geyser.

Of course I want to shop with her. I want to *everything* with her. So now here we are, and above all else, I need to play it cool today.

That starts with a report on our joint investigation.

"I got nothing out of my brother about CJ," I say as I navigate us toward Beaucoeur's shopping center.

"Same. CJ completely shut me down when I tried to ask her about it yesterday." She takes another pull of her coffee. "It's bizarre. CJ and I tell each other everything."

If my truck swerves a tiny bit at her announcement, nobody'll ever know it but me. "Everything?"

Her absent nod sets my brain spinning. Does that mean CJ knows about Sunday at my house? Christ, does she know what Luke did to Liv in the VIP room? How I came in my fucking shorts like a teenager touching his first boob? I shift in my seat, urging my dick to stay calm. Unfortunately, neither of us has been able to forget how thrilling it was to finally have Liv in my arms, panting and pliant and completely gone.

"So what does your family do for Christmas?" Liv

glances at me as she licks a smear of donut icing off her thumb, and I can practically smell the smoke as my brain catches on fire.

"Uh." I force myself to think warm family thoughts. Warm. Family. Thoughts. "Mom and Phil take the kids to Mass on Christmas Eve. Wyatt and I usually skip." I cut my eyes over to her and see an amused grin. "Then Christmas morning is an orgy of gift opening that Wyatt and I never miss. The adults usually just sit back and ride the madness."

"That sounds nice," she says wistfully. "What about food?"

I relax a bit, getting into the conversation. She's good at getting people talking.

"Oh, we snack all day, usually in the living room with the fireplace going and Christmas movies on TV. Phil makes his fondue and Mom does Italian beef in the slow cooker, and there's cinnamon rolls and cheesy potatoes and cheddar popovers and all kinds of cookies." Christmas is a week from tomorrow, and my mouth's already watering. "It's all extremely cheese-based, now that I'm saying it out loud."

"It sounds like *heaven*."

I peek at her again and am rewarded with her blissed-out, eyes-rolled-back expression.

"I take it that's not how Christmas goes for you?"

She grimaces. "I'm an only child, and Christmas morning is always quiet at my parents' house. There's an orderly exchange of three gifts apiece, and then we have prime rib and yams and cranberry sauce at one p.m. on the dot."

I try not to let my dismay show and fail utterly. Thankfully, she just laughs it off. "See why yours sounds like so much fun?"

Come with me. I don't make the offer, but I want to so badly, my throat burns. Instead, I pivot. "Mom says the kids haven't stopped talking about how great you are."

"Really? Even Drea?"

God, I love her. She paid so much attention during the brief time she spent with my feral pack of siblings that she knows how rare it is for my spiky little sister to actually say a positive thing about an adult.

"Especially Drea. Out of everyone, I think she's had the worst time this year. She tries to be tough, but inside she's a little marshmallow." And Liv made her smile by teaching her how to draw a lion. A wave of emotions threatens to choke me when I remember the way she patiently walked Drea through shading techniques at my kitchen table. Thankfully, I'm about to pull into a parking spot and can change the subject. "We're here."

The bell over the door jingles merrily when we enter Lyrical and are assaulted by the smell of flowers and soap, incense and coffee, soil and paper. The store's a riot of *things*. Postcards, mixing bowls, socks, earrings, suncatchers, skirts, lotions, plants, and countless other gifts that somebody in your life is bound to love, all of them handmade and carefully picked by the owner. It's one of my favorite places in town.

"Remind me of our price range?" Liv's all business as she surveys the lay of the land.

I tell her, unabashedly proud of the way I busted my ass for that pile of cash. "Mom and Wy have grabbed a couple of small things, but I'm in charge of the centerpiece presents for everybody," I say. "I've already got the star projector for Kai's bedroom and a laser tag kit for Tristan. And LEGOs of course. So many LEGOs."

"And Sophia?" She trails her fingers over a collection of

necklaces hanging from a tiny tree made of actual tiny branches, holding one up so the light sparkles off its polished stones.

"She's getting a boatload of CuddlePuffs. I'm still tracking down the one she wants the most, but the rest are secured." I gesture helplessly around me. "It's Becks and Drea who've got me stumped."

She nods confidently. "I've got this, Holly."

Fuck, that stupid nickname sounds like music coming from her.

She's evaluating the artisan soaps when a beaming middle-aged woman comes bearing down on us.

"Hollis! What a surprise! It's so good to see you."

"Hi, Mrs. Washington." I bend down to give her a hug. Her tight black curls have more silver in them than I remember, but her dark skin's still unlined and glowing.

"How are you?" she asks when she releases me. "How's your mom doing? And Wyatt? I heard he had a tough recovery."

Two months ago, that question would've been enough to have me sprinting out of the store, but instead, I answer without an overload of angst. "They're both great. Wy's pretty much back to normal"—I don't mention his recent breakup—"and the doctors are thrilled at Mom's recovery."

She presses a hand to her ample bosom. "Praise the Lord." Then her eyes track to Liv, as focused as a matchmaking robot. "And who's this?"

"This is my friend, Liv Fielding," I say. "Liv, Mrs. Washington was our neighbor when Wyatt and I were kids."

"It's nice to meet you." Liv offers her hand. "Your store is incredible. I want to buy *everything*."

Mrs. Washington laughs. "Please do. We're having a good fourth quarter, but it can always be better."

Liv holds up the soap in her hand. "I'm helping Hollis pick out gifts for Becks and Drea, but I'm not sure if this is the right scent for either of them."

The older woman's nose wrinkles. "Definitely not. Let me think..." Her face brightens. "Follow me. I have just the thing."

I let the women go on without me, taking my time to study the big brass paperweights shaped like grasshoppers and frogs and pomegranates.

Liv's right. I kind of want one of everything Mrs. Washington's selling here.

I amble over to where the women are frowning at a display of chunky fingerless knit gloves.

"Which ones?" Liv holds up a pink pair with yarn-embroidered flowers and a black pair with peace signs on the wrists.

"For Becks? The pink," I say, and she nods in agreement. I scan the rest of the gloves with a frown. "Nothing's quite right for Drea though."

She turns to Mrs. Washington. "See? I told you he has a great eye."

"He always has," she agrees. "He helped me with some cleanup work around the house last summer and insisted on planting tulips. They bloomed this year and transformed my whole yard."

I force myself to accept her compliment with a little more grace than usual, but then she threatens to upend my entire existence when she digs through the pile of knitted winter wear and holds up the worst possible thing in the world.

"Hollis is so thoughtful. Wouldn't this be perfect for

him?" she jokes, brandishing a red hat topped with a white pom-pom... and an attached knitted Santa beard. "You need to keep your chin warm while you're doing your good deeds."

She holds it in front of my face, and I backpedal in horror.

"Nope!" I say too loudly. "Ha ha! No, um, no, thank you! It's cute, but no!"

Liv's looking at me like I've lost my mind, but Mrs. Washington just smiles even bigger. "You're so right, my dear. Santa's certainly not the reason for the season." She glances at Liv. "You've got a good one here. You two let me know when you're ready to check out."

After she's gone, I bury the Santa hat under the colorful pile of mittens.

"So we're not at a joking place about my Santa thing," she says. "Noted."

I'm sure as hell not, not when I'm still jealous as hell about the things she did with Santa. Who is also me. Jesus.

I've turned away, needing a moment to gather myself, when I see it.

"Oh. This. We're getting Drea this."

I pick up the craggy, tennis ball-sized black rock with a wide split across the top that reveals glittering purple crystals and turn it to Liv for her approval.

"A geode?" Her teeth flash against the corner of that pink lip as she takes a quick nibble in thought. "Yeah, I think it's perfect."

At the register, Liv runs her finger over a delicate gold link bracelet at the register. "For your mom?"

"She'd love it, but Wy and I already got her a fancy new embroidery machine, and she threatened our lives if we got her more than one thing this year."

As Liv returns the bracelet to its peg, Mrs. Washington asks, "How's your stepdad doing, Hollis?"

"Well, he's getting a new wrench set for Christmas," I say. "So Phil's about to be the happiest man in town."

"And how's his knee?"

"Still bothering him."

She clucks and slips a small white packet into the bag. "Tell him to try this soak for the bath. It'll help ease the ache." Then she leans across the counter to kiss my cheek and wishes us both a happy holiday.

"You too, Mrs. W. Tell your boys to keep studying hard. I expect them to be my bosses someday."

Liv hugs the bag to her chest when we're back in the car. "What a great store."

"Right? Her husband died a few years ago, and she opened this with the life insurance money. Says he'd love to see her supporting herself with the kind of pretty things he used to buy for her."

She glances over her shoulder as we pull away. "That's so sweet." She's blinking rapidly when she faces forward again.

"Hey, I didn't mean to make you cry." In fact, most of what I'm doing these days is expressly trying to keep her from crying.

"They're not bad tears." She sniffs, tosses her head, and gets back into personal shopper mode. "Okay, I think you need a little more for both of the older girls. Are you willing to go for a drive with me?"

"Oh my god, please," I say. "I'm completely at your mercy."

She giggles at the despair she hears in my voice, unaware that I'm speaking honestly on a number of levels.

"Teenage girls aren't so bad," she says as she takes over navigation duties. "I mean, I used to be one."

"Teenage Liv. The way I would've wanted to ask you out," I say with a dramatic sigh. Friends tease each other like this, right?

She wrinkles her nose. "Would've wanted to but wouldn't have?"

We're on the highway to the outlet mall outside of Chicago, where Liv swears the answers to all my problems are waiting.

"I'm guessing you dated the Wyatts, not the Hollises. Smart guys headed for college, not smart-asses who cut class."

She winces. "Guilty. But I didn't know what I was missing," she says with a sly glance in my direction.

My heart lurches at the suggestion that she means me, then immediately flattens when she changes the subject. "What did Mrs. Washington mean about Wyatt's recovery?"

My fingers tighten and release on the steering wheel. "He was the living donor for Mom's liver, and he had a few setbacks afterward."

"Holy shit. That's... wow." She's silent for a beat and shifts in her seat so she's facing me. "Let me guess. You wanted to do it but couldn't for some reason, and you turned it into a personal failing of yours, which is why things were weird that day he came to the restaurant."

"Jesus Christ," I mutter. "Am I that easy to read?"

She shrugs. "If you're paying attention."

And my jumping-jack heart's back in the game.

By the time we turn into the outlet mall parking lot, I've learned that Liv's a good singer who belts out Christmas carols on the radio, and I'm a guy who loves listening to Christmas carols when they're sung by Liv.

But that warm holiday glow doesn't mean I don't object when she directs us to our first stop.

"Not to be a guy about it, but please don't make me go in there."

She clucks her tongue and herds me into the fancy purse store. "Don't be such a stereotype." She moves with purpose toward a display of weird little croissant-shaped bags. "What color for Becks?" She gestures to the black, brown, teal, and yellow options. I cautiously poke the yellow one.

"Good choice. These are just starting to blow up on TikTok, and I knew we'd be able to score a good deal on one here. I think Becks'll lose her mind."

I hand over the cash without arguing, trusting Liv to be the girl-whisperer.

"Okay," she says as we walk out. "What about Wyatt?"

"I renewed his annual membership to the stick-up-the-ass club."

She turns a flat expression on me, and I sigh. "He was complaining that his ex got all the good kitchen stuff when she moved out, so I was thinking maybe something kitchen-y."

After a quick scan of the stores around us, she nods briskly and tows me across into a place that has more pots and pans than I knew existed in the world.

"Pick a color," she says when we reach the wall of Dutch ovens.

"Goddamn," I gasp when I pick one up. "It's a good thing he's cleared for weight-bearing activities. This is heavy enough to pop stitches."

"That's why they're magic," she says brightly. "Is that the color?"

I grabbed a pot at random, and now that I'm studying it, it actually reminds me of my brother. The jewel-tone blue seems flat at first, but when you look closely, you can see the subtle variations in color, the depth and richness of the pigments. "Yep," I say. "This is the one."

"Cool," she says, and like that, it's one more gift checked off the list.

Our last stop of the day is a few minutes away from the outlet mall.

"You genius," I say when we walk into the mega-art supply store. "I should've thought of this."

"You weren't a nerdy, art-loving high school girl. I was."

We take the most time here as Liv decides what supplies Drea can't live without, but in the end, she's assembled a kit that'll keep my prickly sister in self-expression heaven for a very long time.

Once we're loaded in the car and debating where to stop to eat, I admit to myself that I don't want this to be an easy-breezy friendship. I want to keep Liv in my life for a very long time too. I just wish I knew how.

NINETEEN

Liv

"Verdant after dark is wild."

June nods as she tops off my wine. "You wouldn't think an uptight weirdo like Darryl would throw such a good party, but..." She sweeps her arm in a wide arc over the bacchanalia that took over the restaurant after we closed today.

Samson and his kitchen team whipped up a Feast of Seven Fishes for the annual staff holiday party, and then they added all the other meats on top of that, along with three meals' worth of sides, and now they're stuffing their faces around the mega-table we created to accommodate everyone. Bass-heavy music has replaced the tinkly Christmas soundtrack we've been listening to for weeks, and the busboys are in a dance-off to the death with the dishwashers. The servers I've gotten to know so well are laughing and cheering them on, and every single one of us is drinking like we're all seven of the fishes we just devoured. Darryl's watching it all with tipsy joy on his fleshy, SPAM-colored face. He loves this party so much that he actually shuts the restaurant down the day afterward to let us all recover.

Then there's Hollis. My buddy, my pal. He's pounding shots with the sous chef. He's shaking his ass with the busboys. He's nudging Marcus and Ariel toward the mistletoe, as if they need an excuse to make out. He's telling stories and cracking jokes and hugging anyone who wishes him well on his new career.

He's also starting to lose his cool as our coworkers express their ongoing shock that he's leaving Verdant. They might not see it, but I do. The skin around his eyes is tight, and his smiles are frighteningly toothy. He's keeping it together but barely.

After a particularly rough round of, "Aww, man, I thought we'd be working together forever!" from Rob the busser, I can't just sit by and watch it happen anymore. Even better, rescuing Jonesy lets me set my master plan for the night into motion.

"You know," I say as I approach, "when I started work here, Jonesy told me he was the best silverware roller around."

He spins to face me, and I watch as the tension on his face morphs into surprise, then understanding and finally gratitude.

"And as I recall, that was because you said *you* were the fastest roller around." He runs his tongue along the inside of his lower lip as he tilts his head and looks me up and down. "You thinking what I'm thinking?"

A chorus of *Ooohhhs* and rises from the rooms, and before I know it, June's organized the field of battle—a four-top with a stack of napkins and a tub of clean silverware on each side.

Before we take our places, Hollis sidles up to me. "Thank you. I was about to snap."

"Yeah, I noticed. They're kind of obnoxious about how much they're going to miss you." I don't point out that it's another piece of evidence against his whole irresponsible and unreliable bullshit. Self-esteem conversations remind me of his mysterious reasons for not wanting more from our relationship, and I don't particularly want to touch that burner again if I don't have to.

"Let's go, Fielding." He holds up his fist for me to bump, and I do, dying a little at such a bro-y exchange with the guy I have actual feelings for.

He moves to the far end of the table, hopping in place, stretching his neck from side to side, and grabbing his left arm to pull across his chest like he's limbering up to run a marathon. I, meanwhile, calmly step out of my high heels.

Hollis' brows shoot up. "Interesting," he drawls. "Very interesting." As he speaks, he circles around me like a boxer trying to psych out his competitor.

"What are you playing for?" Ariel calls, which intensifies the shouts and catcalls from the audience.

Hollis gives me another once-over before inclining his head in my direction. "I'll let the lady choose."

I hide my smile over how well my plan's coming together.

In a cool voice, I say, "Winner's choice of favor, to be determined."

Hollis lifts his brows and turns to the crowd with an *are you not entertained?* gesture.

"Okay!" Darryl calls, brandishing his phone with the timer pulled up on the screen. "You have five minutes. The most properly completed silverware rolls at the end of this time is the winner. On your marks... get set... *go!*"

Hollis attacks the bin, his fingers seeking out a knife, fork, and spoon in the jumble to swaddle in a napkin that he secures with a self-adhesive paper band. I, meanwhile, grab a handful of silverware from my own bin and start dividing them into piles, one per utensil type.

"What are you doing, Liv?" Ariel calls. "He's smoking you!"

"He thinks he is," I say, glancing at the rolled bundles he has in his pile. "Darryl, time?"

"Three minutes, fifty seconds left!" he calls.

Hollis sneaks a peek at my progress, and confusion colors his face. "You're not even making it hard for me, Livvie-Liv!"

My heart clenches to hear that nickname from him. He hasn't called me that since before our almost-hookup.

"Yeah, man!" Rob calls. "Kick her ass!"

June's irritated sigh echoes my own. "You got this, Liv!" she yells in what's quickly becoming a boys-versus-girls competition.

I'm not about to let my ladies down.

"Actually," I say with another glance at Hollis' finished rolls and my own sorted piles, "I believe I do, in fact, got this." And then I dive in, easily plucking a knife, fork, and spoon from their individual pile, neatly twisting the napkin around them, and slapping on the band. While Hollis scrabbles around his tub for the three pieces he needs, I'm able to cut through my stacks like a hot knife through butter, and with twenty seconds to go, our piles are roughly the same size.

"Five... four... three... two... *one!*" the group chants together, and Hollis and I both lift our hands in the air like contestants on *Top Chef*.

"Samson! If you'd do the honors," Darryl calls, and the

scowling, tattooed chef swaggers forward, making a show of inspecting each roll in our piles and dramatically tossing out the ones where the knife protrudes too far or the paper band is sloppily stuck together. If I may say so, I have far fewer disqualified rolls.

"Final count!" he calls. "Jonesy managed sixty-nine proper silverware rolls."

"Nice!" Rob shouts.

"And Liv had seventy-three!"

I scream in triumph as the female employees surround me in victory. Hollis makes a show of coming around the table to congratulate me.

"The champion!" he shouts, lifting our linked hands over his head. "Long may she reign!"

I quickly drop his hand, not wanting to give anyone the wrong idea about us, including myself, but when I try to walk away, Marcus calls, "What's your favor, Liv?"

"Yeah! Claim your prize!" one of the dishwashers shouts.

I shouldn't. I absolutely should not. But other than striking a blow for all womankind, one thought spurred me on to victory. It's the thing I shouldn't want, shouldn't ask for. Yet I shoot Marcus and Ariel a quick look before I say, "I request a *Dirty Dancing* lift."

And then I hold my breath. This is the closest I've come to even hinting that I want more from Hollis than he's willing to give me. What can I say? It's four days until Christmas, and I'm weak. I've been endlessly, relentlessly chipper to avoid even a hint of dissatisfaction about keeping him at arm's length, and I'm exhausted by it. So I'm asking for what I want under the cover of a stupid party game, and now I'm waiting to see if I've screwed everything up again.

When I finally get brave enough to look at him, he's

pacing toward me, a slow, pleased smile moving across his face. "I would've done that without the need to humiliate me in front of our friends and coworkers," he murmurs when he's close enough.

I tilt my head. "Would you have, though?"

His expression goes blank as he gets my meaning. Sure, he's lifted half the people in this room based on the stories that I've heard, but it would've been different with me, and we both know it. So yeah, I played him a little bit to get what I wanted. But in my defense, I want this *so much*. It's silly, but I've been thinking about it for weeks, and this might be my last chance.

As we've been staring at each other, June worked her magic again, clearing a runway and getting somebody to switch the music to the *Dirty Dancing* soundtrack. And then I'm standing at one end of the restaurant while Hollis stands at the other. He changed into jeans and a V-neck sweater for the party, and he looks so fucking good waiting for me to run to him that I forget how to breathe for a second. Then he grins, points, and beckons me forward.

I do. My last thought before I run full speed down the length of the restaurant, ignoring the laughter and shouts from the people forming human walls on either side of us, is *thank god I put black tights on under my dress this morning*.

I launch myself at him, trusting that he'll catch me, hoist me, and keep me in the air without injuring either one of us. No practice, no trial run, no conversations about timing or technique. I just fling my whole body at him, trusting him to keep me safe.

And he fucking does.

"*Aaaiiiiieeeeee!*" I shriek as he catches me and lifts me over his head as if I weigh nothing, spinning us both in a circle so all I see is a sparkling, twinkly blur of red and green and white and gold thanks to the decorations we hung. My dress has a full skirt, and I'm sure it's fallen onto his head and might even be covering his eyes, but his strong, steady grip on my hips doesn't waver. I've never felt so supported, quite literally, in my life, and when he does finally set me down, he lowers me slowly, letting my front slide over his so I can feel every inch of his body against mine as I descend. By the time I'm back on the ground and my skirt's settled around my legs with a swish, my head is full of him. So's my heart. I want to kiss him so badly, and it clearly shows on my face because his eyes go molten.

I take a step back, needing the space to say what I'm about to say.

"Hollis," I whisper, heart in my throat. "What if I stayed in town longer? Put off Minneapolis and took some freelance work to see if I could make a go of it on my own?"

Again, I watch emotions cycle across his face. Shock, joy, fear, hope.

"That would be..." He hasn't let go of me yet, and his fingers tighten around my waist. "That would be incredible." Then his expression shifts. "Can we go somewhere private? To talk more about this?"

I nod, excitement racing through my veins. Maybe what he needed was to know that I could stick around. Is this what was stopping him last week?

"I've bought gifts for June's kids, but I left them in the car. Let me run out and grab those, and then I'm ready to go."

He nods, looking thrilled and a little nervous. "Cool. I'll say goodbye to everyone and meet you in the back."

I nod and float away, then realize before I'm halfway through the kitchen that my purse with the car keys is stashed in the hostess stand, not my locker. I turn to head back and end up peering through the window that separates the kitchen from the dining room as Hollis hops on the bar to grab a liquor bottle from the top shelf.

"Got it," he announces. He goes to jump down, but one of the line cooks shouts, "Do the thing, Jonesy!"

Hollis laughs and says, "Sure, sure. One last time." And rather than simply jumping down, he lifts himself into a one-armed handstand that he holds for a long moment before he twists up and off the bar to land lightly on the ground.

For a split second, I'm frozen behind the door in the kitchen, a confused smile plastered to my face.

He's Santa.

My friend Jonesy is snake-hips Santa. He's been snake-hips Santa the whole time I've known him.

I take a step backward, then another. I keep going until the dining room isn't visible through the kitchen window anymore.

This whole time, he's been... he's been *him.* He's been the same guy.

He let me talk to him about Santa Luke. He *asked me questions* about Santa Luke. And Santa Luke asked me questions about Hollis. He let me tell him things I never would have shared if I'd known. If he'd told me.

He lied over and over.

My breaths start coming too quickly as my vision turns black at the edges.

"You okay, kiddo?

I look up to see Darryl peering at me in concern and realize I've walked all the way to the break room on autopilot. I shake my head, unable to form words.

I always thought Lois Lane was the thickest woman in the world. How'd such a smart journalist not realize Clark

Kent was Superman? How could she be so goddamn blind?

Easy, as it turns out. So fucking easy. And now that I know, it's so obvious.

I should've known from day one. He smirked when we brought up the club. He's always been strong and graceful. Oh shit, his jobs. *Plural.* Gabe and Darby knew. That's why she was so weird last weekend when I was telling her about what I did with Santa Luke.

What I did with Hollis.

I moan, and my hand flies to my mouth. Darryl grabs my upper arm to steady me.

"Do you need some water? Was the salmon bad? I thought it smelled off—"

"No, I..." I shake my head. "I'm just feeling a little queasy. I think I need to sit down."

I let him guide me to a chair. "What can I get you?" he asks.

He's so earnest and concerned that moisture gathers at the corners of my eyes. "I left my purse in the hostess stand. Could you..."

He's out the door before I finish my sentence, and he's back almost as quickly. All I've managed to do is stand and stare at my locker.

"Here." He thrusts my bag at me, then takes a step back, presumably afraid I'm about to puke bad salmon on his shoes.

"I'm... I'm going to be taking an out-of-state job soon, and I should really start focusing on that." My voice sounds like it's coming from underwater. "I know this isn't two weeks' notice, but..."

I brush at the tears that dare to make an appearance on my cheeks as Darryl's expression shifts to proud-papa mode.

"First Jonesy, and now you. My best people, off chasing their dreams." He pats me awkwardly on the shoulder. "If today needs to be your last day, just let me know where to mail your final check."

His face lights up when I say, "You're a really good boss, Darryl." What a sweet, dopey man. I yank my coat out of my locker, mumble "Merry Christmas," and race to the exit.

I'm almost to the safety of CJ's car when I hear my name being shouted.

"Liv! Hey, Liv! Wait!"

I walk faster, hoping I can fling myself inside the car and drive away, but he's too fast.

"Liv." His hand rests on the driver's side window next to my cheek. "Are you okay?"

God, I love his hands. The strength in the wrist, the map of veins, the golden-brown glint of hair. And those fingers. Those long, strong fingers.

Fingers that were inside of me.

My eyes snap up to his, and I search his face for some explanation, some sign that he got off on keeping me in the dark.

"What's wrong?"

You. You're what's wrong. You let me go on and on about my Santa fantasy. You let me embarrass myself in front of your friends. You were only willing to kiss me when you were using a fake name.

He shifts his weight from foot to foot when I don't answer. "Darryl said you put in your notice? And you're taking the Minneapolis job?" His tongue darts out to wet his lips, and he scrubs his hands down the front of his jeans. "Does that mean you're not interested in... in the freelance thing?"

The urge to scream rises so fast that I have to clench my

teeth together to hold it in. Because how fucking dare he? I was thinking about making plans around him while he was probably wondering why the hell I was too much of a Lois Lane to figure out his secret identity.

I suck in a breath to hurl my questions at him. Why he lied. If he's been laughing about how gullible I am. How he's been able to go on like normal when he actually knows what I sound like when I come.

But what's the point? No explanation he can possibly give is going to make this better. I was halfway in love with him, but it turns out that he's just another untrustworthy guy. Why bother trying to make it make sense?

He's still waiting for an answer, his eyes burning with concern that I no longer believe is real.

"Things changed, Jonesy." I swallow back a sob. "I'm going home. I don't feel well."

He frowns. "Do you want me to drive you?"

I shake my head, too exhausted to answer.

"Okay. Is CJ at least there to take care of you once you're home?"

She's with her parents at their extended family Christmas in Madison, but he doesn't need to know that. "I'll be fine. I just want to sleep."

His forehead creases. "At least text me when you get there."

"It's a ten-minute drive." The concerned act is starting to grate, and my tone is sharp. If he cared so much, he would've told me.

That first time, I barely knew him. That's excusable. But after working with him, laughing with him, feeling my pulse jump at the sound of his voice, I can't believe I didn't recognize him in the VIP room. He kissed me. Put his hands all over me and growled dirty things in my ear. I was surprised that I got off so quickly with Luke. I don't usually with a new guy. But in retrospect, maybe it's not so strange. All this time, did my body know? My heart? Meanwhile, my brain refused to make that connection because it was such a ludicrous thing to even think.

God. I can't stand here looking at him for one second longer. Putting my hand on his chest, I give him a shove so I have room to open the car door. He lets me move him without complaint.

"Goodbye, Jonesy." I shut the door and shut him out.

As I drive off, a realization hits me. He tried to tell me. Those odd stop-and-start conversations. Santa Luke trying to talk me out of our hookup in the VIP room. He tried to tell me, but he sure as fuck didn't try hard enough, and I sure as fuck didn't want to hear it. I had a complete blind spot for the fact that Hollis was Luke Lawless.

Oh god. It rhymes.

I am so very fucking stupid.

<h1 style="text-align:center">TWENTY</h1>

Jonesy

"Is it true, old man? You're quitting the biz?"

I look up from where I've been staring at my phone, willing Liv to text me back, to see Landon and Ben grinning at me.

"You heard right." I brace myself for chop-busting and shit-giving, but instead, they tumble all over themselves like puppies to shake my hand.

"We just, we learned so much from you," Ben says, pumping my arm up and down.

Landon elbows him aside to say, "Witch hazel and coconut oil saved my bikini line."

"Uh, you're welcome," I say, rather than pointing out that I'm not *that* much older than them, and I flip off a laughing Deke behind Landon's back when the younger guy pulls me into a hug that leaves smears of body oil on my chest and arms.

Landon wanders off to hit a vape with some of the other

guys, but Ben hangs back. "Hey, man, no hard feelings for taking your spot, right?"

He gestures down at the Santa gear he's wearing, and I wave him off. When I'd asked off for tonight, Nick and I agreed to let Ben step into the holiday numbers as Santa. Then Liv went home sick and I ended up with nothing better to do than show up here after all, but I'm not going to be a diva about my place in the show.

"Take it with my blessing, kid."

He shoots me a double thumbs-up and ambles off to join his buddy in the corner of the dressing room. Once it's just me again, Deke sidles over.

"I need you to know that you made me the man I am today, Jonesy," he says with mock seriousness, dropping his massive hands on my shoulders. "You showed me how to pleasure a woman and how to stuff a sock in my pants so I can succeed in this business. *Thank you.*"

"Fuck off," I say with a laugh. "You know neither of us needs a sock."

"Obviously." He spins to the mirror and starts to position his polar bear ears around the mass of curly hair in a bun on top of his head. "It was nice of you not to kick the kid's ass and take your role back."

I wave it off and go back to staring at my phone. I don't care about being Santa, but I am pleased to use this unexpected free night as my final Luke Lawless performance. Let Ben be Santa. I'll trot out a few of my greatest hits and just have fucking fun one last time.

I only wish I didn't have a little voice in my head telling me that something's seriously off with Liv.

"Staring at it won't make her text you back."

"I know!" I growl and shove my phone into my backpack. She'd texted that she'd made it to CJ's and was headed to bed, and that's it. No response to how she's feeling and if she needs anything I can pick up for her. She did look a little off when I caught her in the parking lot as she was trying to leave. Darryl said her stomach was bothering her, then wandered off muttering about the salmon, but not before he casually dropped the news that she was leaving Verdant even sooner than I was because of her Minnesota job. That's when *my* stomach started bothering *me*.

"I just wish I knew what happened," I tell Deke for the fourteenth time. "She said she might stay in town."

"Could be a million things," the most patient man on earth replies. "A family thing, a money thing. Maybe Illinois kicked her out too."

That pulls a small smile from me, but it vanishes quickly. Why would she just quit the restaurant like that?

"Good news is, you don't have to wear the Santa beard tonight." Deke shimmies into his snow-white thong, turning to adjust the straps over his meaty ass in the mirror.

"That is the upside of never seeing her again," I say gloomily. I'm also planning to go without the sunglasses for my final outing. Then another thought strikes me. Liv might not be the only person I never see again after tonight. "Hey, we'll still be bros, right?"

Deke scoffs. "'Course. If we're not hanging out on Saturdays anymore, you'll have to start coming to my book club."

"Okay then," I say as Eugenio shouts the five-minute warning. "Go get 'em, Diesel."

Pounding bass drifts up from the second floor as the show gets underway. It's weird not to be out there for these opening numbers, but at the same time, I don't feel like I'm missing out. It's good that I'm moving on, Liv or no Liv.

I have a good half hour before the holiday numbers end

and we pivot to the secular parts of the show, so I do what I used to do back in the day when I needed to pump myself up. I get suited up—tight gray dress pants, tight white button-down, a loosely tied red tie—and sit on the floor, leaning against the wall, one ankle crossed over the other, AirPods in, playlist cranked, eyes shut. A few of the newer guys at the club are also in the dressing room, warming up, but after all these years, I'm good at tuning everyone else out to mentally walk through my upcoming performance, the moves I'll make, and how they'll make someone in the audience feel. Normally, it's an anonymous someone I picture, but tonight it's Liv. She's all I picture these days, all the time.

And she never got to see me dance for real. Santa's fun, but what I do as Luke is a little different. I wonder if she'd have liked him better than ol' snake-hips.

I wonder if she'd have liked him better than me.

Well. It's moot. He's retiring, and she's leaving.

Nick pops his head into the dressing room followed by yet another enormous mutt. "You guys ready?"

The other dancers chatter as they head out, sliding into their firefighter jackets and military flack vests. I'm the last to my feet, and I check for a text from Liv as I pull out my earbuds and stash them away. Nothing.

When I look up, Nick's smoothing a hand over his short, white beard. "We'll miss you around here."

"I'll miss you all too," I say, bending to accept doggy kisses from Dash. Doing this job wasn't always easy, but I really did love it and the people along with it.

Nick walks to the tiny window that looks out over the front parking lot, which glows a slightly demonic red thanks to the neon sign. "I've been thinking. The club could use some curb appeal. We might want to freshen up the land-scaping this spring."

I press my lips together at the surge of emotions this pulls out of me. "Thank you. That... it means a lot."

"Speaking of," he says. "What happened with you and Olivia?"

All I can do is shake my head and scratch Dash's favorite spot behind her left ear. "I decided not to tell her. She's leaving town."

His mouth curls into a frown. "Did it occur to you that she might stay if you were honest with her?"

"Or she might leave faster."

"That's the risk you take, son."

I jam my fingers into my hair and pull, feeling more lost than I've been since last year when I learned that my mom was really, really sick and there was nothing I could do to help. "Is it worth it?"

"For love?" Nick whistles, and Dash zips to his side. "Of course it is."

I wish I could tell him that this isn't love. That guys like me don't fall in love for real, and they definitely don't do it in a matter of weeks with women who see things in you that don't exist. But none of that's true. I fell in love for real, it happened fast, and I may never get over it.

Even though I don't say any of this out loud, Nick recognizes the despair on my face.

"Well," he says. "No choice is forever. You may get another chance." He starts to leave, then turns back as if something just occurred to him. "By the way, did I hear that you were looking for a black cat CuddlePuff for your sister?"

"How did you..."

He taps the side of his nose. "People talk. Stop by my

office before you leave tonight. I've got one set aside for you."

The electric groove of my opening number fills the room, and a thrill races up my spine when I hear an excited murmur sweep the crowd. Some of them know me, know my song, and are excited to see me. If this is my final performance, it's not a bad way to go out.

I prowl out onto the stage to the slow beat, each step deliberate. The trick to this, to keeping it sexy instead of campy, is to focus in, not out. I'm moving for me and for the woman I'm picturing instead of playing to the full crowd like Santa does.

I slowly pull out the knot on my tie and slide it out from under my collar, letting it slide through my fingers in a caress before it slithers between my fingers to the floor. My feet are bare, and I walk to the plain metal chair set in the center of the stage, wrapping my heel around one of the legs and spinning it so it's at an angle. I sprawl on it, stretching out my legs, tensing my thigh muscles so they strain against the fabric of my pants. And then I go for the money shot—the cuff roll.

Undo the button at my wrist. Take my time cuffing the sleeve until my forearm comes into view. Move the whole time, just little shifts of my shoulders, my neck, my chin. An outward turn of my wrist as I start on the other sleeve. A quick bite of my lower lip, like the slide of the material over my skin is a turn-on. All of it slow, steady, a deliberate tease.

I make it clear that I'm undressing for a specific person, and I make sure everybody in the crowd wishes they were in my bedroom, watching me undress, or in my office after hours, ready to violate some company policies. Whatever the fantasy, I'm giving it, sweeping my tongue across my lower lip as I pop the top button of my shirt free in time to the heavy thump of the music.

I stand, my hips moving. My pelvis. Another button flies open, and I let my eyes fall shut like I'm picturing what I'll do to my partner once I'm naked. As the song's tempo picks up, I start to move faster, letting my body flow like water across the stage, adding a spin that drops me to the floor on my knees as I tug my now fully unbuttoned shirt free of my waistband. I take my time pulling it off, leaning back so my body's at a sharp forty-five-degree angle from the floor, letting my head fall back like I'm fully giving in to the need. As I do, I hear the shrieks from the crowd, but I don't let it penetrate the intimacy of the performance I'm giving.

I leap to my feet and move faster now, letting the music pull me along as I undo the snap on my pants and start to lower the zipper before flipping face down on the stage with a kick, catching myself on my hands at the last second. As I surge across the floor in a way that I know damn well reads as in-and-out thrusting that drives the crowd crazy, I let the pants slide lower and lower until the top of my thong's visible. The trick is to kick back up to my feet without tripping over the extra material at the ankles, and thank fuck I manage it. Then I tear them all the way off, and the bubble of my isolated mood is no match for the screams that ensue.

The music switches to my second song, and the faster tempo lets me jump into actual dancing. Without the Santa disguise, I can use my eyes, my mouth, my entire body to dance for *her*. For Liv, even though she's not here to see it. If Luke's her fantasy, then getting to be myself like this for her would be mine.

I'm breathing hard and covered in sweat by the end of my set, which only sells my performance more, and I'm racing with endorphins when I head backstage to towel off and reset for the final set with the volunteer audience members.

Ben's bouncing on his toes when I get backstage. "Being Santa fucking sucks," he says in a disgusted voice.

I barely hold back a laugh. "The beard life isn't for everyone."

He follows at my heels as I head upstairs. "Switch with me? Please? Nick wants Santa in the final song tonight, but I can't wear this hat for a second longer." He yanks it off his head and throws it to the ground like it's personally offended him.

God, this kid. "Let me see if my stuff's still in my bag." Pawing through my backpack, I find my red booty shorts, hat, and beard. "Good enough for me."

"Thanks, dude!" He bounds away to change into some kind of non-Santa outfit, and he, Deke, and I quickly add a fresh layer of oil to our chest and abs. The three of us and Tony, a dancer who's up for the night from St. Louis, are doing the final number with four women pulled from the audience to join us onstage.

I meet Deke's eyes in the mirror and hold up my hand for a knuckle bump. "One last time," I say, and he knocks his fist into mine, repeating, "One last time."

When we head onstage, the four volunteers are sitting back-to-back in chairs set in a tight circle in the center of the stage. Tony and Ben walk directly to the woman they want to dance for. Since it doesn't matter to me, I take the blonde in the tight black dress who's vibrating in excitement to be onstage, leaving Deke with the leggy redhead since that's generally his type.

Eugenio comes out to stand in front of the curtain at the back of the stage and shouts into the mic, "The moment you've been waiting for is here! Please welcome our special guests to the stage—and try not to be too jealous as they get the undivided attention of four of our hottest dancers."

The women in the circle scream in excitement. Well, all but one. The woman Ben's chosen is in jeans and a T-shirt, her red bra clearly visible through the thin white fabric. Her face is tipped down, and her hair's tucked away under a ball cap. She's dressed down compared to most of the other crowd and doesn't seem all that enthused to be here.

"Allow me to introduce you to our volunteers!" Eugenio booms. "Ladies, give a little wave as you're introduced. Tonight we're joined by Amariah!" Tony's chosen woman screams and shimmies forward, her breasts dangerously close to flopping out of her low-cut shirt.

"The redhead to my right is Reagan!" Eugenio says, and Deke steps forward to pick her up, chair and all, and swings her in a circle, making her hair whip around them both. I'd bet money that they'll see each other again after tonight based on the way my friend's grinning at her.

"Next, we have Amy. She's a birthday girl, and she's getting a dance from Luke Lawless in his final outing at the Crimson Lounge!"

I saunter forward all cocky and chuck her under the chin, murmuring, "Happy birthday, gorgeous."

"And finally," Eugenio says, "we're joined onstage by the lovely Liv!"

I've been smiling down at Amy, but my head whips up as Ben steps forward to claim his partner, the stripper Spidey sense I've developed over the years clanging.

I know. I know exactly what I'm going to see when she lifts her head. And sure enough, the ground beneath my feet falls away as the prettiest pair of brown eyes I've ever seen skip right over Ben to lock on me.

"Well, hey there, Liv," Ben croons as he approaches her. "I'm gonna show you a real good time tonight."

I'm in motion before he can touch her. "The fuck you are," I growl, shoving him aside, then dragging him in front of the confused Amy.

"What the hell, dude?" he hisses at me, but my answering snarl has him backing off immediately. "Okay, man," he mutters before spinning to Amy, his stage smile back in place. "Good news," he tells her. "I'm the birthday specialist. Let me help you celebrate."

I'm barely aware of Amy's excited scream as I turn in slow motion to face her. Liv. Onstage. Staring me down with fury in her eyes. She's a Roman candle, a thousand pounds of dynamite ready to explode, but her voice is steady when she speaks.

"Hi, Luke. I'm a *huge* fan." She holds up a stack of cash. "How much for a dance?"

TWENTY-ONE

Liv

"Liv, I... I..."

God, I almost feel sorry for him. Then I remember what brought me here, and that wave of sympathy crashes into the stone wall I built around my heart as I drove away from the restaurant.

"Shhh." I reach up and press my finger to his lips, halting his stuttering. His eyes are wild as he takes me in. "You look different without your sunglasses." The music's so loud that it's hard to think, let alone have a conversation, but I'm pretty fucking motivated.

"Can we go someplace private?" Those sad brown eyes plead with me, his breath coming in short bursts. If I didn't know better, I'd think he was close to a panic attack.

"Why, so we can have a repeat of the VIP room? I don't think so." I narrow my eyes and lean back in my chair, crossing my legs. "It's not so funny when this"—I wave my finger back and forth between the two of us—"goes the other way, is it?"

"Nothing about this has ever been funny," he says hoarsely.

I'm dimly aware that the other dancers are going through the motions with their partners, teasing and grinding and tossing them around. In theory that's what we're here to do too. The crowd wants a show, so I guess I'd better give them one.

Digging in my pocket and holding up a ten-dollar bill, I ask, "Is this enough to get you to lose the beard?"

He shakes his head. "Liv, please—"

"Take off the beard, Hollis," I snap, crumpling the bill and tossing it at his chest. It bounces off and lands on the ground. "Let me see you. I think it's past time."

He complies slowly, pulling it off and the hat too for good measure.

Now that every last bit of his disguise is gone, I can see his face up close, this face that's become so precious to me. I can see the devastation in his expression, the hopelessness in his eyes. A crack threatens to form in that hard stone wall, but I won't let it. I refuse.

"Livvie." He drops to his knees at my feet and rests his hands on my thighs. "You have to believe that I never wanted this."

"I don't have to believe anything." But I don't slap his hands away, which lets him keep making those gentle back-and-forth motions with his thumbs along the seams of my jeans.

He pushes my knees apart, wedging himself between them so he can scoot closer to me. His hands travel up to my waist, and his fingers tighten as he tugs me so my core presses against his bare stomach. We both shudder at the contact.

"I tried to tell you. I really did." He plucks my sun-faded Diamondbacks hat off my head, tossing it to the side.

"You should've tried harder." I want to sound harsh and untouchable, but he has his fingers buried in my hair, working them through the strands until he finds the clip I used to hold it all back. He pulls that out too and lets it spill around my shoulders.

He surges up to bury his face in the mass of it hanging against my neck. "God, I love when you wear it curly," he murmurs. Then he stands in one smooth motion and lifts me up with him. I have no choice but to wrap my arms around his neck and my legs around his waist. He curls one arm under my butt to hold me up. With the other, he cups the back of my head.

"I should've tried harder," he agrees. "I should've just *done* it." He tugs on the hair at my nape, tilting my head back so far that I'm looking at the audience upside down. I'm dizzy from the position, from doing this so publicly. From the strength of his arm holding me up and the solid press of his torso as he molds himself against the arc of my body.

"I didn't think I'd ever see you again after the first night you came here," he says. The music thunders around us, just the way it did that night, but everything's different now. Everything's upended. "And then when you turned up at Verdant, I didn't think there was any reason for me to say anything. I had no idea you'd give a second thought to one of the dancers you saw onstage that weekend."

The world shifts again as he lifts me upright and spins to sit down on the chair, positioning me so I'm straddling his lap, my knees bracketing his hips.

"I gave you second thoughts and third thoughts." I don't know why I'm confessing this. Maybe it's his fingers on my ankles, leaving little cracks in that stone wall and threatening to crumble my resolve. "There were some nights when I gave you all my thoughts."

His head falls back on a groan, and I lean forward to press my lips against his Adam's apple. God, what am I doing? I came here to confront him, not lick his neck. After I left the restaurant, I realized I couldn't just sit at home with my fury and my unanswered questions. My whole body threatened to vibrate into oblivion if I didn't find him and force him to confront his lies. And I had a pretty good idea where he'd be.

As I slumped at a table in the very back of the room, I was the one hiding my face while his was on full display. Watching him perform as his full Luke-self had twisted my anger into an inferno of lust and rage and desire. It's what drove me to volunteer for the onstage show, causing Nick to raise his brows when he noticed my hand in the air and to ask me a quiet, "Are you sure?" I had been... until I was sitting in the chair alongside the other volunteers waiting for the dancers to join us onstage and I started to reconsider my impulsive decision.

And now I'm grinding on his lap in front of one hundred and fifty strangers, wanting answers. Wanting vengeance. Wanting him. That last need is why my mouth is still touching his throat when he speaks again, which means I can feel his words against my lips almost as well as I feel them in my bones, my sinews, my heart.

"After we became friends, I didn't know how to tell you." The urgency in his voice as he attempts to explain tries to chip away more of my protective wall. So does his gentleness as he lifts my right arm and runs his lips from my wrist to my elbow before wrapping it around his neck. "I never dreamed you'd actually feel about me the way I feel about you."

His eyes flash with vulnerability as he repeats the action with my left arm, kissing his way along my sensitive skin and settling my hand on top of the one that's already gripping his hair.

"You're so smart. Talented. Professional," he says. "What would you want with me? What could I possibly give you?"

His fingers dig into my ass and he hauls me against him, all gentleness gone. He's hard, and now I'm the one who loses the battle against the sensation. The tension I've been holding in my body melts away, and he wraps one hand around the back of my head, tipping me toward the audience so my hair brushes against his knees. With his other hand, he traces a line down my cheek, my neck, over my sternum. His fingers catch in the neckline of my shirt, and he pulls, dragging it down so the top of my bra is exposed.

His gaze drops to the tops of my breasts, visible between the satin ribbons and the edge of the red lace cups.

"Fuck, baby. Is this what you were wearing when we were together in the VIP room?" He bends forward to run his tongue over the exposed skin, rocking me against his erection as he does. My breath escapes in a hot exhale.

"I wondered," he growls. "It kept me up that night wondering what you'd look like if I'd been able to see you. All of you."

He wraps a possessive hand around my jaw, his grip rough, but he presses the softest, sweetest kiss to the very corner of my mouth. "The most beautiful girl I've ever seen."

I'm about to give in to the temptation of his mouth, but the memory of where we are and why I'm here bobs to the surface like a tiny cork in the middle of a stormy ocean. I break his hold and slide off his lap, desperate to hang on to the betrayal I felt. The betrayal I feel.

"You lied to me." I'm breathing hard, my chest rising and falling, and he looks up at me helplessly.

"I didn't know how to tell you without losing you. Everything"—he lifts his hand to encompass the stage, the room, me and him—"got out of hand. I'm so sorry. I'll never stop being sorry, Liv."

At his raw tone, my stupid, traitorous heart knocks against the other side of that increasingly shaky wall. I wanted to see him too, that night in the VIP room, and I have the perfect view now as he's sprawled in the chair, the ridges of his abs glistening, his cock pressing against the material of his shorts.

My body betrays me by swaying forward so I can run a finger along the slabs of muscles marching up and down his stomach. "Would you have eventually?" I ask. "Told me?"

Every place I touch, there's an answering twitch of the muscles just underneath the surface, like I have the power to summon electricity through his skin.

"Yes," he says through gritted teeth. "If you were staying in town, yes. I was going to tell you tonight."

"And if I wasn't going to stay?"

When he doesn't answer, I dig my nails into the muscles wrapping around his rib cage. He gives a little groan. But it's not pain I see pulling at his mouth and making him shift under me. It's pleasure at those sharp points of contact.

"You never should've touched me," I hiss. "And you never should've let me touch you." I trail my hands down his abs, my fingertips gliding over his slippery skin. I'm not sure if I'm doing it to punish him or to please myself, and when I reach the edge of his shorts, my fingers are a whisper away from either side of his straining cock. His hips buck upward as he gives a helpless grunt.

"I know. It's why I—ah fuck, baby!—it's why I stopped us in my bedroom," he pants.

I step back. "But you didn't stop us in there." My arm swings in the direction of the VIP rooms.

"No." His chest heaves as he gulps in air. "I didn't."

"Why?" I crawl onto his lap, straddling him and leaning forward to catch his lower lip between my teeth. I bite down and pull away before he can turn it into a kiss.

"Because I didn't know how to tell yo—"

"No. Not that excuse again. Why didn't you stop us?"

His eyes burn into mine as he fists my hair and holds me in place.

"Because I wanted to," he finally says. "And I didn't think I could have you any other way."

There it is. The truth.

"Did you consider *asking* me?"

"And did you consider how I'd feel knowing you wanted him to get you off, not me?"

We're both breathing hard now, staring at each other as he lifts a thumb to the center of his lip where my teeth left a mark. I dimly become aware that we're surrounded by a shouting, cheering crowd, as well as several of his coworkers, and that we may have just put on more of a show than either of us intended.

"There you have it, friends!" the deep-voiced announcer says into the microphone. "Put your hands together for Luke Lawless and the lovely Liv! I'm not entirely sure, but after that performance, I think they're either legally married in Montana or legally divorced in certain parts of Utah."

I scramble off his lap as the audience laughs and

applauds, aware as I do that Hollis has an extremely visible erection. Good. He deserves to be left unsatisfied.

Reaching into my back pocket, I grab the cash I stuffed in there before leaving the house and fling it at him. It flutters around him, ones and tens, fives and twenties, drifting to the ground at his feet.

"All those times when you asked me whether I'm naughty or nice?" My lip curls into a sneer as I look down at him. "I should've been the one asking you. Because you, Jonesy, are definitely not nice."

Then I turn and walk off the stage. This time when I tell myself I'm not coming back, I mean it.

TWENTY-TWO

Jonesy

I have no idea what kind of reception I'm going to get when I pull up outside Liv's place around midnight. I definitely don't expect her to open the front door and watch me walk up the sidewalk.

She doesn't greet me or even wait for me to make it onto the porch. She just turns and goes back inside, leaving the door open so the light from inside spills into the night.

I enter cautiously and find her curled in a corner of the couch, an untouched glass of wine on the table in front of her. She's in leggings and a frayed, faded sweatshirt with streaks of yellow paint on it, her hair in a lopsided braid and fuzzy socks on her feet. It's the sloppiest, least pulled together I've ever seen her.

She's perfect.

"Do you want something to drink?" Her tone is flat, and she directs her question to a spot just over my left shoulder.

"Water. I'll get it."

She nods and says nothing as I hang up my coat and

move around CJ's kitchen, finding a glass, filling it, draining it in a few long swallows, and filling it again. I rushed here as soon as humanly possible, stopping only to towel off the sweat and body oil, throw on the first pieces of clothing my fingers touched, and grab the CuddlePuff from Nick's office. Then I basically ran every red light to make it to her house.

And now here I am, exhausted, dehydrated, and terrified about what I've lost. The only thing keeping my heart pumping in my chest is the knowledge that she was expecting me, and she let me in. I take a seat on the couch opposite her, and for a long moment, we just stare at each other. The only sound in the house is the hum of the refrigerator.

"You left this." I set her D-backs hat on the coffee table next to her wineglass. All the cash she chucked at me is stuffed inside.

She wraps her arms more tightly around her midsection and makes no move to grab it. "Thanks."

"So I take it you're not really sick."

Her mouth curves into the barest hint of a smile. "Nope."

"Well, that's good." I have no idea if CJ's here and am almost scared to ask. I assume if she was, she'd have run me through with a katana by now. "When did you find out?"

"The staff party."

Ah. "The handstand?"

"The handstand."

"That's what I get for showing off."

She rearranges her legs, shifting so the left one's curled under the right. "Well? Do you want to make your excuses now?"

Obviously. I burn with the need to explain and apologize and beg her forgiveness. But she heard the main gist of my arguments onstage and probably had enough time on the drive back from the club to think through them.

I tell her something different instead.

"Women sometimes treat me differently after they find out about the stripping." I have her attention, that's for sure. She wasn't expecting this. "When I'm onstage, I get that I'm an object. I love it. That's the point. But when I'm in someone's bed..."

I wet my lips, bracing myself to share something I've never really talked about before, not even with Deke or Gabe.

"It's kind of shitty to know that you're going to be somebody's outrageous story as soon as she showers off your night together. *Did I ever tell you about that time I fucked a stripper? Best sex of my life.* It's happened to me before, and it sucks. And the thought of you treating me differently if you knew... it killed me."

My gaze flicks to her, and I see a flash of guilt cross her face before her lips tighten. "That's no excuse for not telling me."

"Of course it's not. The only excuse I have for that is my own ignorance and trying to spare you from pain. And neither of those are good enough reasons to not tell you either."

"No. They're not." Then her gaze drops to her lap. "I told CJ and Darby and Birdy what we did." She glances back up. "Me and Luke, not me and you."

"Yeah. I figured."

"I told them you were a magical one-time fling that I'd think about when I'm an old woman."

Even though I expected it, her confession settles like a dull pain in my chest.

"I also told Luke that he's nothing but wild times and glitter and that you, Hollis, were the person I actually wanted in my life."

"I remember," I say evenly. "It made me feel amazing and disposable at the same time."

Her face twists in dismay before she hardens up again. "And whose fault is that?"

I raise my hands in surrender. "Mine. All mine."

"I told you things in confidence. And we..." She glances away again, pink creeping into her cheeks.

"We...?"

"That wasn't how I wanted it to be with us the first time."

"In the VIP room?"

She nods, still not meeting my eyes.

"Was it so bad?" Of all the conversations I don't want to have tonight, her telling me that I showed her a mediocre time in the VIP room is pretty damn high on the list.

"Come on, you know it wasn't." She's still blushing, but she's rolling her eyes too. "I didn't know I was having my first kiss with *you*, though."

"Does that matter?"

"Yes, it fucking matters," she snaps. "I thought about kissing you all the time, and when it happened, I—"

"You thought about it?" My heart jitters, and I press my sweaty palms against my jeans.

"So many times."

"So why didn't you?"

"Because you're Jonesy!" Thank god, her calm mask is starting to slip. The more she sounds like herself, the better I feel. "You flirt with Mrs. Wickenwarg and you hang out with hot Chicago blondes and you do the *Dirty Dancing* lift with Marcus." She flings her hands into the air. "I thought you were like that with everybody! I had no idea you were interested in *me*."

"Baby, for weeks now I've been telling anyone who'll listen how much I love you."

Oh. Shit. Well, that's out there now.

Her eyes widen. "You... you don't."

"Yeah, Liv, I do."

She surges to her feet, glances wildly around the living room like she's trying to find an answer or an exit, then sits down again and reaches for her wineglass. But a second later she sets it back on its coaster without taking a drink.

"Is that why you were scared to tell me you're Luke?"

"A big part of it, yeah."

"Is that also why in the VIP room, you..." Her eyes drop to my lap, and I laugh as she delicately nibbles on her thumbnail.

"Yeah, Livvie-Liv." I shift, the memory alone making my cock perk up. "You know your fantasies about Luke? Well, my fantasy's hearing you scream my name when you come. You can't blame a guy for having to walk-of-shame it back to the dressing room after that." I shoot her a crooked smile. "A visible wet spot's kind of a party foul in the stripper handbook."

"Ha!" The laugh escapes her, but she falls forward and hides her face in her hands immediately afterward. "I usually don't come so fast." Her words are muffled. "It's like I knew it was you somehow. Like my blood and cells and mitochondria said, 'It's *him*.'"

Shit. Add that to the list of fantasies I didn't even know I had.

"Question." She lifts her head to peer at me. "Why don't you smell like you at the club?"

I blink. "I have a smell?"

She gives me an exasperated, affectionate look. "Come on, you have to know it's the best smell in the world. Warm skin and shampoo and *boy-I-like*."

Holy shit, she thinks I have the best smell in the world. Also...

"*Boy-I-like?*"

"It's a smell, okay?" she says defensively.

I set my elation aside to consider a question I've never really thought about. "I shower in the dressing room with whatever soap and shampoo's lying around, usually when I get there because I work out immediately beforehand to get a pump, and then always afterward. When I'm at home, I use my own stuff." I shrug. "No big mystery."

"God, it must be easy being a man."

"I did find that patriarchal privilege and the sexual double standards significantly mitigated the toll of my profession."

She stares at me like I've sprouted antlers.

"Landon—uh, Kelvin—took a women and gender studies course last semester at Rayman. We talked about it a lot in the dressing room."

Her pretty pink lips fall open. I'm sure she's picturing the discussions happening as we were oiling up in our thongs, and honestly, she's not wrong.

She shakes her head and refocuses. "Well, the different showers thing makes me feel a little better. It's one less clue for Lois Lane to have missed."

"Lois Lane?"

The lightness that was starting to creep into her tone vanishes. "You know, the stupidest journalist in the world."

"No." I'm off the couch and around the table as soon as I realize what she's implying, and I put my life in my hands by sitting down on the couch next to her. I keep a respectful distance, but at least we're in the same square footage.

"Do you feel bad that you didn't figure it out? I worked so hard to keep you from realizing it was me." Her gaze narrows, and I quickly add, "Which I know is manipulative and controlling and deceitful. I was an idiot who was terrified of losing you, and I knew that every day I didn't tell you was just making things worse. Please don't kick me out of your house yet. I have at least six more hours of apologizing planned."

"Six?"

"Sixteen. Six hundred. Whatever it takes."

She exhales and sags against the back of the couch, silent as she stares straight ahead, lost in thought.

"Okay," she eventually says. "I can maybe—*maybe*—understand why it wasn't easy for you to come right out and say 'Hey, I'm snake hips. We cool?' when it first came up." Her eyes cut to me. "It still doesn't make it okay, but I understand how it all happened."

I slip off the couch and kneel in front of her. I did this onstage too, pleading for her understanding. This time's different. It's private, and I don't let myself touch her. I just gaze up at her and speak from my heart, which batters itself against the messy emotional coils wrapped around it.

"I'm sorry about everything. I made assumptions about how you'd react; I didn't respect your right to make your own decisions, and I didn't stop things when you asked for the private dance. But I swear, I never intended to lie to you or mislead you. I just sort of... fell into it. And I never laughed at you, never made fun of you. Not once. I tried to do the things that would hurt you the least. I tried to stay just friends with you so when you left town, you'd just forget about me instead of remembering me as the guy who tricked you for so long."

"Wait." She sits up. "You thought I was going to forget you if I left Beaucoeur?" At my miserable nod, she slips off the couch and kneels to face me, her voice incredulous. "You seriously thought that?"

My mouth opens. "Um. Yes. Why would you rememb—"

She kisses me, grabbing my shirt and pulling me forward for a fast, slightly awkward press of her lips to mine. It's the best kiss I've ever had.

"I love you too, you know."

My stomach goes into free fall at her words, and I can't pull together a single response. Not even a croak. That's how enormous and earth-shaking those six words are.

A grin spreads across her face as I stare at her in wonderment. "Wow. Is this what it takes to leave Hollis Jones speechless? I should have told you I love you ages ag—"

This time I'm the one launching myself at her, flattening her to the carpet so I can feel her whole body with my whole body. "Yes. You should've told me you loved me ages ago." Our lips are a fraction of an inch apart, and I whisper, "Is this okay?"

A line appears between her brows as her lips tilt into a small frown. "I'm still mad at you."

My heart drops, and I start to push myself up. Then she slides her hand into my hair and tugs me back down.

"But I also love you." Her grip tightens on the strands, and she glares up at me. "Don't do anything like this again."

"God, no. Even if I had it in me to put us through this again, in what universe would we have a situation even half as complicated or stupid?"

The pressure on my hair eases as she laughs. "Hey, Hollis? Shut up."

And she kisses me. Liv kisses Hollis.

It's slow and sweet and hot, and there aren't any secrets weighing me down as I slide my tongue against hers, which means I can savor her little whimpers, the heat of her mouth, the softness of her body against mine. Her hands are in my hair, sliding over my biceps, tracing my spine, reaching down to cup my ass and press me tighter against her. Like she has to ask twice.

When we come up for air what seems like hours later, her lips are pink and swollen. *I* did that to her, and I'm never going to take that for granted.

"Baby," I tell her, "I'm gonna be so honest with you from now on, you're gonna beg me to stop oversharing."

A laugh escapes her, and she sounds so much like my Livvie that it shakes loose the final shard of fear that was lodged in my heart. I think we're actually going to be okay.

Maybe more than okay, if the way she's moistening her lips and peeking up at me through her lashes is any clue.

"So is CJ home?" My voice drops. "Because I'm telling you right now, I want to get naked soon and I want you to get naked soon too, and I'd like to know if we're going to have an audience for that."

She gives me a long look. "You do know CJ's seen you practically naked multiple times."

I press a hand to my chest, all outraged modesty. "Yes, but I'm retired now."

"Also, you're mine now," she says, her eyes flaring.

I groan and drop my forehead to hers. "Say it again."

She scoots forward and climbs into my lap, twining her arms around my neck and pressing as close to me as she physically can. "You're mine," she breathes.

I press my forehead against hers and shut my eyes, trying to live in this moment for as long as possible. She knows everything, and she's still in my arms, saying things to me that affect my heart as much as they affect my dick. No man alive is luckier than I am.

I crush her against me. "I love you so much." Now that I've actually said it to her, I'm never going to stop.

"Marcus and Ariel are going to be so jealous," she says from her half-smushed position against my chest.

"And so very not surprised that I'm in love with the angel who sat in my section and talked about committing international crimes."

She pushes away from me with a gasp of outrage. "Excuse me, that was CJ. I'm extremely law-abiding."

"Of course you are." I stand, lifting her with me as I do and adjusting my hold so she's more secure.

Her head lolls to the side, and her eyes flutter shut. "Do you know how hot it is when you do that?" she murmurs.

"Is it?" I ask in delight. "In that case, I'll start carrying you everywhere."

"Deal. Let's start with you carrying me to the bedroom." She wriggles into a more comfortable position in my arms as I move down the hall. "Oh, and to answer your question, CJ's out of town until tomorrow doing Christmas with her family. We can be as naked as we want."

"Excellent."

"Not that it matters," she says. "CJ's more of a Diesel girl."

My steps falter, then I pick up the pace again. "We'll be revisiting *that* later."

Much later. Because right now, I have plans for us.

TWENTY-THREE

Liv

My new kink is Hollis picking me up and walking me places. That's normal, right?

"Mmmm," I purr as he walks us to the bedroom. "Are you available to carry me everywhere I need to go until the end of time?"

"That depends." He smiles down at me. "Are you okay with your personal transportation having an extremely visible erection until the end of time?"

"I mean, that's kind of like a stick shift, right?"

He laughs and lowers me to the ground. I start to protest until I realize I'm in a better position to investigate the erection he promised. And that's when I notice what he's wearing.

"Are those breakaway pants?"

"Probably. I got dressed fast." He glances down. "I actually think they're Landon's. Oops." He unzips his hoodie to reveal a tank top.

I make a strangled noise. "Is that... rippable?"

He looks down again. "From my stash." He points to a tiny slit in the neckline. "You get it started so it tears easier onstage."

I'm pretty sure my pupils dilate like a cartoon cat's as I picture it, and a Luke grin slides across his face.

"See something you like?" He runs a hand over the muscles of his chest and catches his thumb in the waistband of the black pants.

"You know I do," I say, but I scoot back on the mattress just a little when he takes a loose-limbed step in my direction. I shake my head. "So um, I'm trying not to objectify you, but you're making it really, really hard."

"I've got something really hard for yo—" He stops walking. "Oh, you're serious."

His Luke smile vanishes, and he's Hollis again, coming to sit next to me on the side of the bed.

I ball my fists in my lap. "I don't know how to do this without making you feel like glitter wild fun guy."

He uncurls my fingers and presses a kiss to my palm. "I actually thought about this on the drive here. I'm kind of the best of both worlds."

I squint at him. "How so?"

"You like me."

"I love you."

"That's right, you love me." There's that heart-stopping smile again. "And you're hot for Santa Luke."

Gulp. "I am."

He spreads his arms wide. "Best of both worlds, baby. Two for the price of one. All your fantasies right here."

I think back to a conversation I had with CJ weeks ago. "The perfect face, the perfect body, the perfect personality."

"Personality?" He sounds surprised, and I roll my eyes.

"We have to work on your self-esteem." Then I consider what he's suggesting. If he's okay with it, I guess I am too. More than okay, actually.

So here goes. I glance up at him through my lashes, fiddling with the end of my hair and coyly biting my lip. "Do you think maybe if you and your amazing personality have sex with me, it might help with those self-esteem issues?"

I watch all the lights go out upstairs as all the blood travels downstairs.

"I'm willing to try," he rasps.

"Okay, good." This time my lip bite is thoughtful. "So I really liked watching Luke dance. Do you think Hollis could do a little of that for me right now?"

He inhales hard. "Yes. But you've got to do something for me while I do it." When I lift my brows in question, he says, "Get naked and touch yourself."

My eyes widen as heat prickles all over my body. I've never done anything like that before. He notices the indecision on my face and leans forward to kiss me. It's gentle and loving. It's Hollis. "It's okay," he whispers. "That's my fantasy, but if you don't want to do it, it's okay."

He stands and messes with the lights, turning off the one overhead and turning on the bedside lamps. I realize he's giving me time to think about what I want to do.

His fantasy is me, naked and appreciating him. I can give him that. Without a word, I kick off my pants and pull my sweatshirt over my head. I'm still wearing the red bra from Fantasia, and when he turns around, his eyes flutter shut.

"Fuck," he says, short and sharp. "Leave that on for now. Lose the panties."

I obey, and he watches with hooded eyes, his body

starting to move like he's hearing his performance music. Then he rolls his hips and slips his pants a little lower on his waist, and it's all the encouragement I need. I run a finger down my slit and gasp.

"Tell me." His voice is a command.

"I'm so wet," I moan. "And you haven't even touched me yet."

He's cocky as he strides forward and puts his hands on either side of my body. "Do it again."

Our gazes lock as I run my finger through my wetness and use it to circle my clit. His hand snaps out to grab mine, lifting it to his lips and sucking my fingers into his mouth.

"The sweetest thing I've ever tasted," he murmurs. "Keep going. Gentle strokes. Eyes on me."

And then he's Luke, seducing his audience of one. But he's also Hollis, love in his eyes. I stroke myself for both of them.

"Watch," he growls, grabbing his shirt at the notch in the neckline.

"Yes," I say with a gasp. "Do it."

He rips that shirt from top to bottom, and I moan. "Get over here."

He walks to the edge of the bed where I'm dripping for him, and I slide my free hand under the torn edge of his shirt. "I imagined doing this the first time I saw you." I flick a fingernail over his nipple and run my nails over his ribs.

"Use both hands." His eyes are pinned on me as I lift my slick fingers away from my aching body and slide them up his chest, leaving a trail of my arousal. "Fuck, Liv. Yes. Mark me. I'm yours."

I hook my fingers into his waistband and tug him closer for a kiss. It starts gentle and turns fierce immediately. He grabs my hair, doing that head positioning thing I love, holding me in place so his tongue can dive into my mouth and claim me. Stroke my desire even higher.

"Fucking touch yourself," he growls against my lips.

I disobey. I touch him instead, and he jolts at the feeling.

"Naughty," he groans, yanking at his pants. They are, in fact, breakaway, and when he shrugs out of his tattered tank top, he's standing in front of me in nothing but those tiny red shorts.

"Hey, we match." I point to my bra, and he freezes, then bursts into laughter. He's one hundred percent Hollis as he crushes me to his chest.

"God, I love you. Take off the bra. Lie down. I'm gonna eat you like I'm starving."

I obey, dizzy from the mix of affection and command in his voice. It's a combination I'm starting to realize is what you get when your two fantasy men collide in one body.

He kneels in front of me, catching my gaze before he lowers his mouth to my pussy. I practically arch off the bed.

"Easy." He laughs and presses a hand on my stomach, pushing me into the mattress. "Let me work, woman."

He gentles his tongue and licks me up and down, groaning as he tastes me. The hand that's holding me down travels up to my breast, and his fingers catch my nipple.

"What does your body say?" he breathes against my mound. "Does it still recognize me?"

"It does." My head thrashes against the comforter. "It knows you're the person I love and it wants your tongue and it wants your fingers and *oh my god, fuck!*" I cry when he pumps them into me.

"Tell me how bad you need to come, Livvie." He looks up at me as his fingers slide in and out, curling up to stroke a spot inside of me that I didn't know existed until right now. "Tell me how bad you want me to make you come," he says before he ducks his head to suck my clit into his mouth.

"S-so much," I pant. "I need... I need..." My fingers scrabble on the comforter, looking for something to anchor me. They find it in his hand.

His fingers lace through mine as he goes to work licking me in rhythm with the press of his fingers. I slide my other hand into his hair so I can grind myself against him, shamelessly working my pussy on his face until his nose is bumping my pubic bone. "Yes that, good, *so good*, yes, Hollis," I babble as the pleasure gathers, shivers down my spine, and breaks me open. I briefly leave my body and meet God.

After who knows how long, God decides she's had enough and sends me back to earth, and I lift myself up on one trembling arm to see Hollis smiling down at me as I recover.

"Close." He runs his hand over my stomach and up between my breasts to rest on the hollow of my throat. "But my fantasy was for you to come *screaming* my name, not whispering it."

"Ha." I laugh weakly. "Guess you'd better try harder next time."

I can practically see flames igniting in his eyes. "Guess I'd better," he growls. "Condoms?"

I gesture at the nightstand. CJ made a show of stocking them during her "you should have a fling" campaign. Joke's on her. I think I skipped right over fling and landed in a relationship.

Hollis flips back into show mode and slowly, slooooooowly slides his shorts down his hips, over that ass I've been dreaming about biting, and along the thick muscles of his thighs. And that's when I see his cock for the first time.

I swallow thickly before I can speak.

"I knew it," I murmur. He's long, thick, and cut with the slightest curve to the left. "Perfect."

He gives himself a lazy stroke, watching me watch him, and when he rubs his thumb over the slit of the head, we both gasp.

"Think you can use that to make me scream?" I ask.

He frees a condom from its packet and rolls it down that gorgeous length. "I think you're gonna love how hard I try." He grabs himself and runs the tip up and down my seam, stopping at the top to tap it against my clit.

Yeah, this man is going to have no problem making me scream.

"Eyes here." He taps my clit again, and I shift my focus to his hand on his cock and then his cock as it slides into me. "Oh fuck. You're so tight. You're so..." He throws his head back and groans as he sinks all the way inside me. Then his hips shift back, and he plunges into me again, harder this time. And again, harder.

Then he does the thing. He gathers me in his arms and lifts me up in one fluid motion. But unlike before, he's buried inside me, so every shift of his body sends pleasure rocketing through me. He settles me against his groin and makes sure my legs are securely wrapped around his waist, then grabs the nape of my neck to work me on his cock. Every motion sends fireworks pinwheeling through me. I have no idea what kind of core strength it takes to lift me and hold me in place as he pounds into me while also thumbing my clit and keeping himself upright.

Don't ask me the physics. The only thing I can tell you for sure is that as I'm staring into his sweaty, smiling face, he does some kind of Luke rotation with his hips while pressing on my clit, and I throw my head back and shriek, "Hollis, fuck, fucking... *Hollis!*"

His groan's almost as loud as mine. "Jesus, your pussy's squeezing me, baby. It's so tight. I... I..."

My orgasm's retreating as he swings us around and lays me on the bed, again without breaking our physical connection. But now that we're stretched out, his body covering mine, everything slows. The slide and retreat of his hips turns liquid and deliberate, and he dips his head to lazily suck my nipple into his mouth.

"So pretty," he murmurs against my breast. "So fucking pretty."

I slide my knees up along the sides of his body so he can drive even deeper, and he sinks into me with a soft little sigh. His gaze dances over my face, sliding from my eyes to the corner of my mouth, the curve of my neck, my earlobe, back to my mouth. With a groan, he captures my lips, and this kiss is as gentle as his movements when he rocks into me.

"Love you so much, Livvie," he murmurs between kisses, between thrusts. He slides his arms up to bury his fingers in my hair, resting his weight on his elbows. The position brings us so close that I can feel every hitch in his breathing, and I can tell when it falls out of rhythm.

"I want you to come," I whisper. "Come for me. Come inside me, baby."

His breath catches in his throat, and his lips capture mine again, his tongue licking into my mouth. Soon enough, his motions turn jerky and uncontrolled, and he tilts my chin up.

"Gonna come, baby," he pants in my ear. "Gonna come, and it's all for you. Gonna... ah, god, love you, love you, Liv, fuckkkk." He buries his face in my shoulder as his body shakes and eventually falls still.

Sooner than I'd like, he rolls off me to deal with the condom. I barely have time to miss him before he's back and scooping me against his chest, pulling a blanket over us.

"That was incredible," he says sleepily, his eyes drifting shut. "Sex with someone you love. Who knew?"

I huff a laugh and burrow into his side. "Hey, remind me tomorrow. I want to tell you about the time I slept with a stripper. Best sex of my life." But I press my lips over his heart as I say it, kissing my love into his skin, and his chest moves under me in laughter.

"He sounds amazing. Can't wait to hear all about it." His voice gets fainter, and the last thing he says before he drops off is, "Love you, Livvie."

We're drinking coffee in bed the next morning when Hollis asks, "When do you leave for Indiana?"

I grimace. "Apparently a stomach bug's taking down my extended family one by one, including my mom. Christmas will be rescheduled once everybody's keeping fluids down."

"Bummer." He taps his thumb against his mug, his hair adorably mussed from all the sex we had and all the sleeping we did afterward. "What'll you do instead?"

"Tag along with CJ, I guess."

"Or."

When he hesitates, I say, "Orrrr?" I'm pretty sure I know what he's gearing up to ask, and I want it so much that it physically pains me.

"Or you could come to my family's." He's trying to sound casual. He's failing. "They'd love to have you there."

"Oh *they* would, would they?"

He wraps his fingers around the ponytail that's barely containing my own post-sex hair. "*I* would." He drops a sweet, coffee-flavored kiss on my mouth and murmurs, "Come home with me."

"Okay." I can't contain my smile as I snuggle into him, tracing my finger over and over in the shape of a heart on his chest. "Hey, what were you going to ask for if you'd won the silverware challenge?"

"Marry me."

I pause mid-heart. "Come again?"

"I was going to ask you to marry me."

I laugh, but his face is serious.

"Wait, for real?"

He shrugs. "Is it any crazier than asking for the *Dirty Dancing* lift?"

"Yes!"

"I coulda dropped you on your head, Livvie. Marriage is way safer than that."

I open my mouth to argue. Marriage is the most risky, unpredictable thing in the world, especially for two people who've known each other for less time than the shelf life of organic milk. It's ludicrous, and I'm sure the tiny voice in my head shouting *say yes!* is just post-sex endorphins and a general feel-good holiday glow. I tell it to shush as I say with a laugh, "Sure. Marriage is way safer than the *Dirty Dancing* lift."

"You scoff, but it's a standing offer," he tells me. "Just say the word. Any time, any day. I'll marry you right then and there."

"Just say the word?" I ask, amused.

"It's a standing offer. Just say the word." Then he kisses

me until we both forget everything except "here" and "yes" and "more" and "now."

A few hours later, CJ comes home to find me on Hollis' lap on the couch.

"Well, this is new," she says as she unwinds her scarf. "What'd I miss?"

He and I share a look.

"So much," I say. "I'll fill you in. But first, I'd like to introduce you to Luke Lawless."

TWENTY-FOUR

Jonesy

"Could you knock it off, please?" Wyatt says as he crumbles a wad of candy cane wrapping paper and tosses it toward the trash bag spread open in the corner of the living room.

I turn my perma-grin his way. "I have no idea what you mean."

"You are the smuggest, smiliest son of a bitch I've ever seen," he grumbles.

"Can't stop, won't stop."

My attempts at playing it cool at Mom and Phil's house on Christmas morning have epically failed, and the person responsible for that is sitting cross-legged in the middle of the wrapping paper wreckage with my sister, cooing over art supplies.

Mom joins us on the couch. "Have you ever seen Drea this..."

"Friendly?" I suggest as Wyatt says, "Non-rabid?"

"This girl of yours, Hollis." Mom wraps an arm around my shoulders and shakes me gently. "She's wonderful."

"She really is." Oh look, the grin's back.

"Tell me, does she have a friend for your brother?"

"Mommmmm," Wyatt yowls as I snicker.

"She does, actually," I take great delight in saying. "CJ and Wyatt know each other well, as it turns out."

"Perfect! I already like her better than that Reese."

Wyatt gives a gusty sigh, making it clear that no one in history has ever been more tested than he is right now. "I dated 'that Reese' for six years."

"I know, dear." Mom leans forward and pats his knee, the gold bracelet on her wrist catching the lights of the tree. It's the one that Liv spotted at Lyrical last week. She apparently went back and bought it so she'd have a gift for my mom this morning. She also added to the pile of presents under the tree with wrapped packages for the sibs, Phil, and even the sulky baby sitting next to me.

Mom gets up to stop a Tristan/Kai fight that's threatening to erupt over LEGOs, and I say to Wy, "That's a nice rice cooker Liv got you. Maybe the way to CJ's heart is through her stoma—god, okay, I'm sorry!" I twist away with a laugh as he slugs me on the arm.

"No fighting on Christmas," Liv orders, gesturing for us to slide apart so she can sit in between us like a referee.

I slide my arm around her once she's settled in, and the feeling of her melting into my side is like nothing I've ever experienced. It's love and gratitude and pride that I'm the person she's chosen. *Me.* I have to swallow past the lump in my throat over how good life is.

"Did I hear that you want to court CJ with rice dishes?" Liv asks Wyatt. "Because I think that's a great idea."

Wyatt hits her with his grumpiest glare. "I'd wear one of

Holly's show thongs in the Beaucoeur holiday lights parade before I'd share a meal with that queen of the harpies."

He stands and stomps off to join Sophie where she's perched atop CuddlePuff mountain, her skinny arms strangling the black cat that Nick miracled up for me.

"I guess we're not going to double-date," I say as Becks approaches us holding one of the wrapped boxes Liv arrived with. Its tag is addressed to the two oldest girls.

"Can we open this now, Liv?" Becks asks. At her nod, she rips into the paper while Drea watches from a wary distance.

"When did you do all this?" I ask quietly.

"Over the past week." She says it like it's no big deal even though she's already been a bigger part of Christmas morning for the sibs than "that Reese" was in her half a decade with Wy.

Becks pulls off the last of the wrapping paper to reveal a foam cooler the size of a microwave.

"Did you get Mom another liver?" Wyatt asks. "Because I think she's all set."

The first belly laugh is from Mom herself, and the rest of us are quick to join in. Then Becks' squeals drown out everything else.

"Oh my god!" Her entire body quivers in excitement as she holds up a bright-orange tub of ice cream. "How did you do this? They don't even make the chai spice flavor any more!"

"They do if you spearheaded a massively successful viral marketing campaign for them and you call in a last-minute holiday favor," Liv says.

Becks shrieks and throws herself into Liv's arms. "Thank you, thank you, thank you, thank you! This is the best gift *ever*!"

Liv closes her eyes as she hugs her back. "I'm so glad, sweetheart."

Drea, meanwhile, holds up the green container of pistachio horchata. "Cool. Thanks," she says in her typical deadpan fashion. Then she does a double take and reaches back into the cooler. "The art too?" She holds up a small watercolor painting of the ice cream that's in her other hand.

"It's the actual one we used in the ad," Liv says, and now Drea's hugging her too, and since fucking when does all this joy at Christmas make me want to cry?

While Liv and Becks explore the other flavors in the cooler, Drea wraps her arms around me in a stranglehold, pressing the uncomfortably cold ice cream container against my neck.

"I love her so much," she whispers.

"I know the feeling," I whisper back.

L iv looks at me like I'm short a few swans a-swimming when I pull to a stop in front of a dark, looming warehouse on our way home from Mom and Phil's.

"We're here!" I say brightly. I asked her if we could hold off on our gift exchange until later tonight, and she agreed, although she's clearly doubting her judgment now.

"This is even scarier than the basement at Verdant," she says as I let us in with Deke's key and lead her to the freight elevator that'll take us to the third floor.

"But not as scary as the haunted section, right?"

"Nothing's scarier than that cold spot." She shudders as the ancient metal elevator rattles to a stop, and I grab her hand and pull her out of the car. My gift for her is under my arm, and she's carrying the flat square package that she wrapped for me.

I flip on the lights to reveal the third floor. It's a completely open space with chipped, weathered brick walls and a soaring ceiling that's all metal ducts and support beams. In one corner, just like Deke and I arranged, sits a vintage metal desk and chair as well as a retro-cool gold velvet couch. A faded oriental rug defines the space, clearly carving out a work area on the wide-beamed floor that's scarred and stained after a century of existence.

"What is this place?" Liv's eyes are wide as she walks to the couch and sets the present down so she can check out the view of downtown Beaucoeur from one of the massive windows.

"I'll explain," I say, holding up her gift. She claps her hands and happily snuggles into a gold cushion, making gimme motions with her fingers. I sit down next to her, but I don't hand it over yet.

"Okay." I take a deep breath. Here goes. "Derek—you know him as Diesel—works for a demolition and salvage company."

"Hold up." She lifts a hand like a traffic cop. "Diesel's name is *Derek?*"

"And he's dying to meet you," I say. "Anyway, this is his company's warehouse, and this floor is for rent. Lots of space, lots of sunlight. And I know you like to use, like, found and reclaimed objects in your ad campaigns. His boss said that as a tenant, you'd be able to use the materials they salvage for cheap. In your campaigns."

She looks around in confusion, so I rush on. "But there's no lease or anything yet. I wanted to let you know that it's an option if you were still thinking about maybe sticking around town and wanted a place where you could shoot your ads. Even the furniture is negotiable if you don't like it."

She glances down at the couch, running her hand back and forth over the gold velvet nap so the color changes from dark to light. This isn't going well, I don't think. But it's not like I can stop now.

I set the gift in her lap. "Then there's this."

She looks at me curiously as she slides her finger under the tape and folds back the paper to reveal the item I had Mrs. Washington hunt down for me from a local leather worker.

"It's a travel bag," I say as she stares down at it. "Like a portfolio, but also good for art supplies and things." She flips it open to reveal all the different-sized compartments inside. "I figured if you take the Minneapolis job, you might come back to Beaucoeur sometimes, and this would let you bring your work with you. Or if you do the freelance thing here and have to travel for shoots, this would be handy."

She slides her hand into the wide pocket that could hold sketchbooks or small finished paintings like the ice cream water colors. Her continued silence makes me babble even more.

"And maybe you end up moving away and never coming back." I swallow hard. "If that's the case, I'll just be happy knowing you're out there in the world carrying something I bought for you."

Her fingertip traces the embossed LF that I asked the artisan to add.

"I didn't know if you'd want an L for Liv or an O for Olivia," I say nervously. "I picked the name I call you. I hope that's okay. So. Um. Merry Christmas."

Finally, mercifully, I stop talking, and she strokes the tan surface of the bag one more time before she sets it next to her on the couch. Then she turns and reaches for my fingers.

"I'm not leaving town. And even if I did—which again, I'm definitely not—I wouldn't forget you. I could never forget you, okay?"

In the four days since we gave the Crimson Lounge crowd the show of their lives, we've had sex and wrapped gifts and cooked dinners and watched movies and kissed for hours on the couch until CJ threatened to throw a bucket of cold water on us, but we haven't talked about Liv's plans after the New Year. I was fine being in denial a little longer if she was still planning on leaving, so I just... haven't asked.

I do now. "You're really staying?"

"Of course. I thought that was obvious." She strokes her thumbs over the backs of my hands. "I'm staying here and I want to be part of your life because I love you."

Ridiculous, unreliable me. That's who she's choosing. I'm about to give it my best to kiss all the breath from her lungs when she stands to grab the gift she carried in.

"Here. Maybe this'll convince you."

I'm a lot less careful with the shiny green paper than she was, and I rip it open to reveal...

"Lions!" I turn to her in delight, then immediately focus on the painting again.

It's a scaled-down version of *The Lion Fucks Tonight.* Except it's better.

Of course it's better. It's a Liv Fielding original.

She took every flaw she pointed out in the mural at the restaurant, and she fixed them. She exaggerated the flat proportions, making it bold and in-your-face and intriguingly off-kilter. When I look even closer, the lions themselves have familiar faces.

"Is this *us?*" I hold the canvas even closer, and sure

enough, the lion in front has Liv's round brown eyes and curving cheeks, while the lion in back sports a mane that mimics my hair at its wildest and a smirk I see in the mirror every morning.

I look at her open-mouthed. "Oh my god, I love it. How long…"

"Since the night we decorated," she says a little shyly. "At first I told myself it was to keep my skills sharp, but then it became about making something you'd love."

"Livvie," I murmur, carefully leaning the painting against the side of the couch so I can pull her into my arms and rest my chin on her head.

Her lips seek out my throat. "Holly." Her tongue's next, sweeping up my neck to my jawline. "Do you want to do things to me on this couch that make it so we're basically obligated to sign that lease?"

My shirt's off before she's even done talking.

"Yes. Let's do something naughty."

EPILOGUE

A year later

Liv

It's Christmas night, and Hollis and I are exhausted.

"Are they always so energetic?" he groans as we collapse onto our bed.

"Who, your Mom and Phil?" I ask. "I hope so for their sake."

He rolls on top of me, doing his best impression of a weighted blanket. "I meant the sibs, woman!"

I wrap my arms and legs around him, doing *my* best impression of an octopus. In the year since he quit the restaurant and stopped dancing, he's developed an amazing tan from landscaping with Gabe and a tiny bit more squish around his middle from cutting back on his diet and exercise routines. He says he's never been happier. I say the feeling's mutual, and not just because my freelance work's officially become Liv Fielding Creative, the in-demand boutique ad agency.

"Four hours in the car tomorrow," he says with a groan. "What time do you want to get started, and did you remember to buy snacks for the road?"

Now that we've done the holiday thing with his family, we're headed to my parents' for Christmas part two. And yes, going straight to bed and getting an early start would be the wisest course of action.

But I have a plan to put in motion.

"I'm not sure," I say, sounding as nonchalant as possible. "I left my phone on the side table in the living room. Could you grab it so I can check what time they said?"

"Sure." He presses a flurry of kisses to my face and then rolls off me and heads down the hall as I start counting. *Five... four... three...*

"Livvie? Could you come in here, please?" His voice sounds strangled, and I grin as I leap off the bed.

I force myself to walk calmly into the living room. "Yes, Hollis?"

He's staring at the lion painting that's the centerpiece of our gallery wall of art and photos and found objects that we've collected over the past year.

"Does this..." He turns to face me and gestures at the painting. "Does this mean what I think it does?"

"You don't like the hat?" I ask innocently.

While he was outside fussing with the Christmas lights on our porch that never want to stay lit, I quickly attached a cut-out Santa hat on the Hollis Lion's mane.

"That's"—he swallows hard—"that's not what I'm talking about."

"Oh, you mean the other one?" I glance past him at the newly added speech bubble that I placed next to the Liv Lion's mouth.

"Yes. Does it mean what I think it means?"

"Maybe," I say. "You know how art's open to inter-pretation."

"'The word,'" he says quietly. "She's saying 'the word.'"

"She is."

He steps closer. "As in the word 'yes'?"

My smile escapes my attempts at staying calm and collected. "Yes."

"Yes to the standing offer?" He's smiling too, and it's gorgeous. He's so impossibly gorgeous.

"Yes to the standing offer." I slide my arms around his waist.

"You're going to marry me." He says it like he's testing the sentence, saying it out loud to see if it holds up.

"Yes," I say. "I'm going to marry you and Luke and snake-hips Santa and the hot waiter and the good son and the amazing brother and the incredible boyfriend. I'm going to marry all of you."

He slides his hands in my hair and kisses me until I'm dizzy, then picks me up and starts toward the bedroom. But he only makes it a few steps before he spins back and tilts me so I can grab my phone.

"Text your folks. Tell them we're getting a late start tomorrow."

"Oh?" I smile up at him. "Why's that?"

"Because our engagement celebration's going to take all night."

Wyatt and CJ hate each other.
Next Christmas, they'll fall in love.
Sign up for Sara's newsletter so you don't miss out!
https://sarawhitney.com/mistletoe/

ACKNOWLEDGMENTS

Any author can procrastinate to the point of self-sabotage, but not every author has friends who'll make sure it never goes quite that far.

Skye Malone and Jordan Bloom, you saved this book. Brenda Rothert, Liz Alden, and Megan Remmel, you carried it over the finish line. Tanya Melendez, you put the eggnog in my coffee. (Not a euphemism; this is literal.) A tip of the designated golfer's hat to all of you.

ALSO BY SARA WHITNEY

Cinnamon Roll Alphas

Tempting Heat

Tempting Taste

Tempting Talk

Tempting Lies

Tempting Fate

Hot Under The Mistletoe

My Fake Bad Boyfriend

My Holiday Hookup Road Trip

My Not-So-Secret Santa

My Wicked Winter War

Standalone Novellas

Game On

Ghosted

Bold Vibes Only

PRAISE FOR SARA WHITNEY

Tempting Heat

"Perfectly written, hits all the beats... It was a real pleasure to read." *Jen Prokop, the Fated Mates podcast*

Tempting Taste

"Sara Whitney pulled together the most fun you'll have in a bakery with this one! Hello to my new book boyfriend." *Christina Hovland, author of the Mile High Matched series*

Tempting Lies

"The right blend of sass and steam. Sara Whitney's smooth, upbeat prose is a delight to read. I devoured it fast. Too fast." *Elle Greco, author of the LA Rock Star Romance series"*

Tempting Fate

"It balanced sweet, spicy, emotional and hilarious so incredibly well." *Sarah, Book Obsession Confessions*

My Holiday Hookup Road Trip

"Steamy and funny and just a damn good time." *Beth, B and her Books*

My Fake Bad Boyfriend

"This story had me laughing out loud from start to finish, and I completely adored it... One of my favorites of 2021." *Laurie, Laurie Reads Romance*

ABOUT THE AUTHOR

Sara Whitney worked as a journalist and film critic before she earned her Ph.D. and entered academia. She divides her time between professoring, authoring, and entertainment journalism, and she almost certainly has an opinion about your favorite TV show. Sara writes her sexy, sunny romance novels in Illinois, where she's surrounded by books, cats, half-full coffee cups, and practically empty bags of Swedish Fish.

Keep up with the latest news (and snag a copy of enemies-to-lovers romp *Game On* for free!) by subscribing to Sara's mailing list at **www.SaraWhitney.com/VIP** or use your phone's camera to scan the code below: